AUNT BESSIE ZEROES IN

AN ISLE OF MAN COZY MYSTERY

DIANA XARISSA

❈ Created with Vellum

For everyone who has taken this entire journey with Bessie and me.

AUTHOR'S NOTE

It doesn't seem at all possible, but this is the last book in the Isle of Man Cozy Mystery series. When I started with Aunt Bessie Assumes, I wondered how far I'd get in the alphabet before I'd stop writing, and now I've reached Z. Thank you to all of the readers who've enjoyed all of the books in the series. I've loved writing them.

This isn't the end of Bessie and her friends, though. At the end of the book, I've included a sneak peek from the first book in the new series that will be launching next year. Bessie and many of her friends will be back, working through cold cases together. I think Bessie has found quite enough dead bodies for now, but I won't promise that there won't be one or two popping up in the new series as it develops.

As ever, this is a work of fiction and all characters have been created by the author. Any resemblance that any character may bear to any real person, living or dead, is entirely coincidental. The Isle of Man is a wonderful place, and the historical sites mentioned within this story are real locations on the island. The author has created all of the events that take place within those locations, though. Businesses mentioned in the story are all fictional and have been located where convenient for the story rather than where any actual businesses may exist on the island. Any resemblance that they may bear to any real businesses, on the island or elsewhere, is also coincidental.

As the book is set on the Isle of Man, I use British English throughout the story. There is a short glossary at the back of the book for readers outside the UK who might not be familiar with some of the words or terms used. I do apologize for any Americanisms that have snuck into the text. The longer I live in the US, the greater the likelihood of these errors occurring. I welcome you to get in touch to let me know about any mistakes. I do try to correct them whenever possible.

All of my contact information is available on the "About the Author" page at the back of the book. I'd love to hear from you. I hope you enjoy this last adventure in this series.

CHAPTER 1

"*B*essie? It's Elizabeth Quayle. How are you?"

Bessie smiled as the bright and bubbly voice came down the receiver. "I'm very well, thank you," she replied. Elizabeth was in her mid-twenties, the youngest child of Bessie's friends, George and Mary Quayle.

"Oh, good. We were just talking about you, you see," Elizabeth continued.

"We?" Bessie repeated.

"Oh, me and Andy. Or Andy and I, if that's the correct way to say it," Elizabeth laughed.

The young woman had been seeing Andy Caine for some months. As far as Bessie knew, they were very happy together. "You were talking about me?" she questioned.

"Yes, because you know everything about Laxey."

"I'm sure that's not true," Bessie protested. She'd moved to Laxey shortly after her eighteenth birthday, desperate to get away from her parents whom she'd blamed for the death of the man she'd loved, Matthew Saunders. That had been a great many years ago, and Bessie was still living in the same little cottage on the beach that she'd purchased with the small inheritance that she'd received when

Matthew had died. She'd had two extensions added to the cottage, but it was still quite small. It was large enough to suit Bessie, though, who had always lived alone. If pressed, she might admit to being somewhat nosy, and in a small village like Laxey, that meant that she missed very little of what happened within the village, but she couldn't claim to know everything by any means.

"Andy is buying a house, you see, and he can remember some story about it, but he knew you'd know what really happened," Elizabeth continued.

"Which house?" Bessie asked. Andy had unexpectedly inherited a rather large fortune a few years earlier. He'd used some of the money to put himself through culinary school. Now he was back on the island, looking for a good location to open his first restaurant. Bessie had known that he was also house-hunting, but she hadn't realised that he'd found somewhere that he wanted to purchase.

"The estate agent told him that it was the old Looney mansion, but couldn't tell him anything more than that."

"The Looney mansion? Andy is buying the Looney mansion?"

"You sound appalled," Elizabeth said.

"John Rockwell looked at that house when he was looking for a property in Laxey. That was well over a year ago. It was in a terrible state then. I can't imagine what it must be like now. It needs a great deal of work."

"It does, but Andy can afford it," Elizabeth giggled.

Bessie frowned. "I'd hate to see him waste a lot of money on a property, especially when he wants to open a restaurant, too."

"We're actually buying the house together. Daddy is lending me the money for my share," Elizabeth confided. "I fell in love with the place when we visited the first time and I simply had to have it."

George Quayle was a very successful businessman who was now meant to be mostly retired. He tended to spoil his only daughter, but this seemed especially indulgent, even for him. "Is he, now?" Bessie said after an awkward pause.

"Not all of the money, just some of it. I've saved up quite a bit from my business, actually. It's been so much more successful than I ever thought it would be."

Elizabeth had started a party and special event planning company that was proving very popular on the small island. No doubt it helped that George had many wealthy friends, all of whom seemed to entertain regularly. Having Elizabeth plan a party for you was now seen as something of a status symbol in certain social circles on the island. While Elizabeth was enjoying her success, Bessie had been surprised and delighted to learn that Elizabeth also spent a good deal of her time helping some of the island's charities with their special events, without charging for her services. Similarly, Andy often provided catering for Elizabeth's events, charging charitable organisations for supplies but not for his time and effort.

"So you and Andy are buying a house together?" Bessie questioned.

Elizabeth laughed again. "It isn't quite as it sounds, though. We aren't planning to live together, not yet, anyway. The house is in a terrible state, so even if we did want to live together, there are months or maybe even years of work ahead."

"Yes, that was my thought when I saw the place last year."

"But the house itself is lovely. We're going to take our time and restore everything back to the way it was when the house was new. We'll be putting in a new kitchen, of course, but one that's totally in keeping with the age of the property. Since I spend all of my time planning things anyway, I'm going to keep on top of the builders and contractors. Andy wants to do some of the work himself, though. He thinks he can do quite a lot, but we'll have to see how that goes. Once the house is finished, we'll decide what we want to do with it. We might sell it for a huge profit or one or both of us might move in. We'll see."

"So you've already purchased the property?"

"Not exactly. We've made an offer, but it's contingent on an inspection and a few other things. We're going back around the house this afternoon. I was wondering if you'd like to come along? I'm sure you know the history of the property. Andy and I really want to hear the whole story."

"I do know the history of the house," Bessie agreed. "And I'd love a chance to take a good look around the entire building. John and I never got past the foyer, because it was so clearly not suitable for him."

"Excellent. I'll collect you in half an hour," Elizabeth said happily. She put the phone down before Bessie could reply.

"Half an hour?" Bessie echoed as she got to her feet. "That doesn't give me much time."

After a long walk on a very rainy beach that morning, Bessie had come back to her cottage, Treoghe Bwaane, and curled up in her favourite chair with a book. Now she looked down at what she was wearing and sighed. When she'd changed out of her wet things, she'd put on her most comfortable clothes. They were fine for a day at home, reading and relaxing, but not entirely suitable for going out with Elizabeth and Andy.

She climbed the stairs to her bedroom and changed into something more appropriate for her new plans. Elizabeth was often impulsive, and it was entirely possible that, after the house tour, she'd suggest going out for lunch or shopping or something. Bessie wanted to be prepared.

Having never learned to drive herself, she frequently found herself relying on her friends to get her around the island. In her younger days, she'd used buses to get from Laxey to wherever she needed to go, but once a friend of hers had started a car service, she'd come to appreciate being able to ring for a taxi whenever she needed one. That friend had given her a generous discount when he'd first started his business. When he'd sold the company to a large Douglas operation, they'd continued to offer Bessie special pricing. Now, thanks to clever investments by her advocate, Bessie didn't need to worry about the cost of the occasional taxi, but she was still frugal with her money. Books were her primary indulgence and, if pressed, she would have admitted to buying far too many of them, especially as the island had good libraries.

Someone knocked on her door as she walked back down the stairs.

"Bessie, hello," Andy said, pulling her into a hug.

Bessie happily embraced the young man. As she'd never had children of her own, Bessie had acted as something of an honorary aunt to the boys and girls in Laxey. Many of them had discovered that "running away" to Bessie's was a useful way to get away from parents who didn't understand them. Over the years, Bessie had had more guests than she could count, but Andy had been one who had visited rather more frequently than most. He'd had a very difficult relationship with the man he'd thought was his father, and his mother had been too busy working multiple jobs to keep a roof over their heads to intervene. Andy had sometimes spent weeks or even months in Bessie's spare room, and he credited her for his love of cooking and baking, things he'd first learned to do while staying with Bessie.

"How are you?" Bessie asked him as he let her go.

"I'm doing really well," he replied with a huge grin. "Mum is finally letting me spend a bit of money on her, which is great. I'm having proper central heating put into her cottage and putting on a new roof. That should help keep Mum a bit warmer next winter, anyway."

Bessie nodded. Andy's mother, Anne, had lived in the same tiny cottage for her entire life. Money had always been very tight and Bessie knew that the cottage probably needed a lot more than just heating and a new roof to make it comfortable again.

"After those two jobs are done, we'll see what else I can get her to let me do," Andy added. "She doesn't really want me spending my money on her, but there's nothing else I'd rather spend it on, of course."

"I'm sure she'll come around gradually," Bessie said.

"I'm hoping, once we've completely redone the Looney place, that Mum might agree to move in there. She's always loved that house. She worked there many years ago, cooking and cleaning, but only for a few months. Apparently Mrs. Looney didn't take to her."

"Valerie had a reputation for being difficult to work for," Bessie replied. "She had exacting standards, which were difficult to maintain in a small house with seven children living in it."

"Seven children?" Andy gasped. "But don't say any more. Elizabeth will be furious if you tell me everything when she's not here."

"Where is she?"

"She had a few errands to run, so she's going to meet us at the house. We were going to come together to get you and go to the house, but then one of her clients rang and she had to dash off to deal with a crisis."

"Oh, dear. That doesn't sound good."

Andy chuckled. "It's a party planning crisis, so it isn't anything too serious. It's for a wedding that isn't even happening for another six months, but the bride-to-be just got some samples for table linens and they aren't the colours she wanted. Elizabeth had to rush over with a pile of catalogues so that they could try to find the exact shade of blue that the bride wants."

"Elizabeth is far more understanding about these things than I would be," Bessie said.

Andy nodded. "I'm not sure how she does it, really. I can't imagine spending hours of my time discussing shades of blue or the perfect flowers for a bouquet, but Elizabeth seems to enjoy it all."

"You do spend hours perfecting a recipe, though," Bessie pointed out.

"That's different. If nothing else, I get to eat all of the mistakes."

They both laughed, and then Bessie locked up her cottage and followed Andy to his car. It looked brand new and Bessie smiled as he helped her climb into the passenger seat.

"This is a nice car," she remarked as he climbed in beside her.

"I decided to treat myself. I gave my mother my old car, since it was only five years old and she'd been driving hers for twenty-odd years."

"That was good of you."

Andy sighed. "I can afford it and a lot more, if only Mum would let me spoil her a bit."

"She isn't used to the idea of you having money."

"I'm not used to the idea of me having money. The nice thing about being away at school was that I could simply ignore the money and focus on my studies. Now that I'm back, Doncan wants to meet regularly to talk about my investments and that sort of thing. I don't know anything about investments."

"I'm sure Doncan can help you understand everything," Bessie said. Doncan Quayle was her advocate as well, following on from his father, and Bessie knew that he would be a smart advisor for young Andy.

"He's trying, but I find it all a bit overwhelming. I worried constantly while I was away that I was spending too much of the money on school, but it turns out that while I wasn't here, the money was making more money for me all by itself. Of course, buying this house is going to use up some of the money, and I'm still looking for a building for my restaurant, too, but every time I talk to Doncan it seems as if there's more money than I can spend."

"Surely that's a good problem to have."

"I'm not really complaining," Andy said quickly. "I'm just over-whelmed, that's all. Elizabeth is used to having money, so it doesn't worry her, but I'm terrified that we're going to get in over our heads on this house. I can afford the house itself, but it's going to cost a fortune to make it habitable again."

While they'd been talking, Andy had been driving slowly through the streets of Laxey. Now he pulled to a stop in front of the Looney house. Bessie looked up at it and shivered. It was clearly abandoned, with wooden boards covering some of the windows and a "For Sale" sign hanging crookedly next to the door.

"It's solidly built," Andy said, sounding as if he didn't believe his own words.

"It was a gorgeous house when it was new," Bessie told him. She opened her mouth to continue, but Andy held up a hand.

"Save the rest for when Elizabeth gets here," he said. "I don't want to you to have to repeat yourself."

"I'm surprised your mother didn't tell you the whole story," Bessie replied.

"Mum couldn't really remember much. As I said, she only worked there for a short while and it didn't go well. She told me she was too busy in those days to pay much attention to the local gossip."

7

Bessie nodded. "That's probably true. Your mother was always working at least two jobs back then."

Bessie had never had to work. The small amount of money that had been left over from her inheritance from Matthew after she'd purchased her cottage had been wisely invested following her advocate's advice. Those investments had managed to generate enough income for Bessie to keep food on her table and a roof over her head. Over the years, her financial situation had improved considerably. Not working had given Bessie plenty of time for gossiping with her friends and acquaintances over the years.

"Is the estate agent meeting you here?" Bessie asked.

Andy shook his head. "Elizabeth managed to convince the man to give her the keys," he replied. "We're having another look today and then, if we still want to go ahead, we're having an inspection done tomorrow. I've never bought a house before, and neither has Elizabeth, but her mother has been helping us with all of the details."

Bessie smiled. No doubt Mary would be a huge asset to the young couple on their venture. "I've only ever bought one house, and my advocate handled everything for me."

"Let's get out and walk around," Andy suggested. "I want a better look at the gardens at the back."

There was a fence around the property. Andy opened the gate and they walked through it before Andy shut it behind them.

"I feel as if we're trespassing," Bessie whispered as they walked down the path along the side of the house.

"We have permission to be here," Andy assured her.

"Does she?" Bessie asked, nodding towards a woman who was perched on the edge of a badly broken bench behind the house.

Andy frowned. "I've no idea," he said.

The woman was looking at the phone in her hand. Either their voices or their movement alerted her to their presence. She jumped up, colour rushing into her cheeks.

"I'm awfully sorry if I'm not meant to be here," she said quickly. "The gate wasn't locked, and I was ever so curious about the house."

She appeared to be around forty, with light brown hair and green eyes. Bessie thought she looked as if she'd recently been crying.

Andy raised an eyebrow. "I believe the house is private property," he said.

"Yes, of course, but I'm one of the owners. I mean, I suppose I am." The woman stopped and shook her head. "I'm sorry. I'm sure I'm not making any sense at all. This has all been very difficult for me."

"Why don't you start at the beginning," Bessie suggested.

The woman hesitated and then nodded. "Yes, that would probably be best. I should have rung the estate agent and arranged for a proper tour or something, shouldn't I? Coming was something of an impulse. My brothers always tell me that I'm too impulsive. I probably get that from my mother, but I don't know for sure."

Andy looked at Bessie, who shrugged. The woman wasn't making any sense to her.

"I'm Elizabeth Cubbon," she said. "Everyone calls me Bessie."

"Oh, hello," the other woman said with a bright smile. "I'm Susan, Susan Davison."

Bessie recognised the name immediately. "Your father was Gary Davison?"

Susan nodded. "That's right. Did you know my father?"

"Not well. I did meet him once or twice, but he wasn't on the island for long," Bessie told her.

"But why was he on the island at all?" Susan asked. "And how did he come to own a house here?"

Bessie stared at her for a minute. "He never told you about the house?"

"He never told us anything about anything," Susan said bitterly. "We didn't even know that he'd ever been to the Isle of Man, let alone lived here long enough to buy a house here."

Feeling shocked, Bessie took a deep breath, wondering where to even begin.

Susan stared at her and then sighed. "It's not going to be a very happy story, is it?" she demanded. "Something awful happened here, didn't it? I could feel the negative energy as soon as I walked through the gate."

"I don't believe anything awful happened here," Bessie replied slowly. A cold breeze made her shiver.

"Maybe we should go into the house for this conversation," Andy suggested. "I think Elizabeth is here."

The trio walked back around to the front of the property. Elizabeth was just climbing out of her cute little red sports car.

"Bessie, hello," she called. "Have you brought along a friend?"

Bessie shook her head. "This is Susan Davison. Her father owned the house."

Elizabeth frowned. "I thought it was the Looney house."

"It was," Bessie replied. "Let's go inside and I'll tell you all the story."

Elizabeth dug keys out of her handbag and led the others up to the front door. Bessie braced herself for the smell and the dust, both of which seemed considerably worse than they had been a year or more earlier when she'd last been there.

The foursome walked into the small, dark sitting room. There was a small couch along one wall with two metal folding chairs in front of it.

"Have a seat," Elizabeth said, sounding doubtful.

Bessie sat on one of the chairs, reasoning that it would be uncomfortable but also dry and free from mould. Susan took the second chair. After a moment, Elizabeth patted the couch and then shrugged.

"How bad can it be?" she asked as she tentatively sat on its edge. Andy joined her, carefully perching on as little of the couch as possible.

Bessie looked around and then sighed. "It really was a beautiful house when it was first built."

"The estate agent told us that it was built in the forties," Elizabeth said.

"That's right. Sam Looney did most of the construction work himself. He built it for his wife, Valerie, and their growing family. In those days people didn't worry about giving each child his or her own bedroom, which was a good thing in this case, as Sam only built the house with four bedrooms and he and Valerie had seven children."

"Seven?" Elizabeth gasped. "I can't even imagine."

"Large families were far more common in those days," Bessie told her. "They may have had even more if Sam hadn't passed away suddenly about ten years after the house was built."

"Poor Valerie," Andy said.

Bessie nodded. "She was some years younger than Sam had been. Only a few months later, she remarried. Her new husband was from across. I'm not sure where Valerie met him, actually. One day Valerie was in mourning for Sam and the next she and Gary Davison were engaged."

"Gary Davison," Susan echoed. "She married my father?"

Bessie nodded. "Valerie fell pregnant again almost immediately. This time she had a difficult pregnancy and the baby girl, when she arrived, had some serious health problems. There were all sorts of whispers about Valerie after the baby arrived. I suspect she had some sort of postnatal depression, but such things weren't often recognised in those days."

"So what happened to her?" Susan asked.

"About a year after she and Gary married, they went on holiday across with the baby," Bessie said, trying to find a way to tell the story that wouldn't upset anyone.

"And?" Elizabeth demanded.

"They were touring a ruined castle and, at some point, Valerie slipped and fell to her death," Bessie replied.

Susan drew a deep breath. "Where was the castle?" she asked, sounding badly shaken.

"Somewhere in the Lake District, I believe," Bessie replied. "I don't remember the details now."

Susan nodded. "What happened next?"

"Gary produced a will that was dated just a few days before Valerie's accident. In that will, she left everything she had to Gary. Her previous will, drawn up just after her second marriage, had left everything in trust for her children, but the second will invalidated the earlier one," Bessie explained.

"What about the children?" Elizabeth demanded.

"Sam's parents took them all in and did their best to raise them the way that their father would have wanted," Bessie explained. "The estate was battled over for years, until Sam's parents gave up because they couldn't afford to fight any longer. Gary inherited the house, but as far as I know, he never came back to the island after Valerie's death. It was rented out for a few years, but I was told Gary refused to spend any money on maintaining it, so after a while he was unable to find anyone who wanted to live here. The house simply sat empty after that. As you can see, it's suffered from a lot of water damage and other issues." Bessie waved a hand at the water-stained walls and carpeting.

"What a shame," Elizabeth said.

"He never told us any of this," Susan said tightly. "I didn't even know that he'd been married before he married my mother."

"What happened to the baby?" Andy asked. "Did Sam's parents take her in, too?"

"No, Gary kept the baby with him. When I said that he never came back to the island, that's exactly what I mean. After Valerie died, he simply stayed in the UK with the baby. The other children hadn't gone on the holiday with them and, as far as I know, Gary never saw any of them again," Bessie replied.

"I have an older sister?" Susan asked.

"I believe she passed away not long after her mother," Bessie said gently. "Gary remarried within a few months, but I'm not sure if that was before or after the baby died."

Susan shook her head. "How could he keep all of this a secret?"

"You didn't know about any of it?" Andy asked.

"When Dad died, we were shocked to learn that he had a house on the Isle of Man. None of us knew anything about the island and we certainly never suspected that our father had once lived here. I thought maybe he'd inherited it from a distant relative or something. This has all come as something of a shock to me," she told him.

"Your mother must have known," Elizabeth suggested.

Susan shrugged and then looked at the ground. "There are three of us. I have two older brothers, Ned and Neil. Ned is the oldest. He's six years older than I am. Neil arrived three years later, and I came along three years after that. Our mother died less than a year after my birth."

"I'm sorry," Bessie said softly when Susan stopped to take a deep breath.

She looked at Bessie. "She and my father were on holiday in Greece, just the two of them. They went to look around some ruins somewhere and had a disagreement about something. He left her there to go back to the hotel. Another tourist found her an hour later. It appeared that she'd climbed up to the top of a ruined staircase and then lost her balance. The fall broke her neck."

Elizabeth gasped. Bessie could only stare at Susan.

"The police never connected the two deaths?" Andy asked.

Susan shrugged. "I'm sure my father never told the Greek police about his first wife. He never told his own children about her, after all." She took a deep breath. "He killed them both. It's the only thing that makes sense."

"That's not necessarily true," Bessie said. "Accidents happen every day."

"Dad always refused to talk about what had happened to Mum," Susan said in a low voice. "He never married again, but he was involved with one woman after another. A few of them met with unfortunate accidents as well."

"Really?" Andy asked.

Susan nodded. "One fell getting into the bath, hit her head, and drowned. Another lost control of her car on the motorway and smashed into a barrier wall. I'm sure there were others as well. Dad sent us all to boarding school as soon as we were old enough. I never really knew what was happening in his life, except for a few weeks here and there when we were on breaks."

"I think maybe you should talk to the police," Bessie said as gently as she could.

Susan looked stunned. "My father was a serial killer," she said in disbelief. "I came over here to find out how he happened to own a house on an island I didn't think he'd ever visited. This was not what I was expecting to learn."

"I have a friend with the local force. Why don't you talk to him?" Bessie suggested. "I'm sure he'll be able to help you start finding out more."

Susan nodded slowly. "I can't quite get my head around all of this. If my father did murder Valerie Looney, then he shouldn't have inherited anything from her. This house should belong to her children, not my brothers and me."

"That's something to discuss with your advocate," Bessie suggested.

Susan shrugged. "Whatever, I don't want any part of this house. I'm going to ring my brothers and tell them the whole story. I'm sure they'll feel the same way." She glanced around the room and then sighed. "It can't be worth very much anyway, can it?"

"I have the particulars here," Elizabeth said, digging a sheet of paper out of her handbag. "There's the asking price."

Susan studied the sheet for a moment and then sighed. "That's more than I was expecting, but I won't feel right getting any money from the sale of this house. My father didn't have any right to it, not if he killed his wife."

"I think that's going to be impossible to prove after all these years," Bessie said.

"I'm going to see what the police have to say," Susan replied. "If they think it's all at likely that my father killed anyone, I'm going to refuse every bit of my inheritance. I'm sure I'll be able to persuade Ned and Neil to return this house to the rightful owners."

"Assuming the rightful owners can be found," Andy said.

Everyone looked at Bessie, who shrugged.

"Sam's parents took the children and moved to Birmingham in the late sixties. Sam's brother was living there and he was willing to help with the children," she told them.

Susan got to her feet. "I'm going back to my hotel. I need to ring my brothers."

Bessie got the woman's mobile number and also noted where she was staying. "I'm going to have someone from the island's constabulary contact you," she told her. "They'll help you work out who might be able to give you more information."

Susan mumbled her thanks as she walked to the door. Andy followed her, letting her out of the house.

"That was awful," Elizabeth said as Andy walked back into the room.

CHAPTER 2

"*D*o you really think that her father killed Valerie Looney?" Andy asked Bessie.

"Everyone thought so when Valerie died," Bessie replied. "Actually, opinion was divided between those who thought he'd killed her and those who thought that he'd driven her to kill herself. There were rumours that he was cheating on her, but I didn't want to tell Susan that part of the story."

"And you don't know how he and Valerie met?" Elizabeth asked.

Bessie thought for a minute and then shook her head. "I've no idea. At the time, it seemed as if he'd simply appeared out of nowhere. He and Valerie certainly had a whirlwind romance."

"Was it possible that they were involved before her husband died?" Andy asked.

Bessie frowned. "I don't believe so, but it was a long time ago. I suppose anything is possible."

"I can't believe that he murdered his second wife the same way he'd killed his first," Elizabeth said.

"What makes you so sure that Valerie Looney was the first?" Andy asked. "Maybe he'd already killed half a dozen other women."

Elizabeth frowned. "What a horrible thought."

"That's quite enough speculation," Bessie said sharply. The entire exchange with Susan had upset her, and she wasn't looking forward to telling John the story.

"Sorry," Andy said.

Bessie nodded and then dug out her mobile phone. "I'd better ring John."

Andy and Elizabeth sat together, holding hands, while Bessie spoke to the police inspector.

She and John had met over a dead body more than two years previously. In those subsequent years, John had gone through a difficult divorce from his wife, Sue. Following their separation, Sue had left the island and taken their two children with her. After her remarriage, the children had come to stay with John while Sue and her new husband took an extended honeymoon. Bessie was concerned that the story she was now sharing with John might feel a bit too close to home for John, as Sue had passed away on that honeymoon, but Bessie knew that John was too much of a professional to let that interfere with an investigation.

"I remember some of the story from when we looked at that house," John said when she was done. "I actually made a mental note to look into Valerie Looney's death, but life got in the way and I never followed up. I will now."

"Will you talk to Susan yourself?" Bessie asked.

"I may send Pete to talk to her, seeing as how she's in Douglas," John replied.

"I trust Pete to be gentle with her," Bessie said. "She's understandably upset."

"Of course. Pete or I will handle it," John assured her.

Bessie put her phone away and then smiled at the couple on the couch. "Shall we have a look around, then?"

"If Susan decides she doesn't want the house, what will happen?" Elizabeth asked.

"I've no idea," Bessie told her. "If she and her brothers all agree to sign the property over to the Looney children, well, I suppose someone will have to try to track down the children. I can't imagine any of them would actually want the property, but I suppose anything is possible."

"Meanwhile, it could drag through the courts for years and years," Elizabeth sighed. "We were hoping to get the paperwork all signed in the next month or so."

"Let's not worry too much for now," Andy suggested. "Maybe Susan's brothers will insist on keeping their inheritance."

"That seems likely, really," Bessie said.

Elizabeth nodded, but she didn't look convinced. A loud knocking noise startled them all.

"Maybe Susan has more questions for you," Andy said to Bessie as the three of them walked to the front of house.

When he opened the door, however, there was a man standing there.

"Ah, hello," he said. "I saw the cars and thought maybe someone was here. I couldn't resist the urge to knock. I, well, when I heard that the house was on the market, I had to come. I just had to."

Bessie studied the man, who looked to be in his fifties. He was short and bald, with a rounded tummy and an engaging smile. As he turned his gaze towards Bessie, she caught her breath.

"You have to be one of the Looney children," she said. "You look just like your father."

The man shrugged. "I'm Harold Looney," he replied.

Elizabeth gasped. "We were just talking about you," she blurted out.

"Me?" Harold asked, clearly surprised.

"Not you specifically, but the whole family," Elizabeth explained. "Bessie was just telling us the story about the house. There was this woman, you see..."

Bessie held up a hand. "But what brings you here?" she asked Harold, giving Elizabeth a warning look. She wasn't certain why, but she didn't want Harold to know that Susan Davison was also on the island.

Harold glanced from Elizabeth to Bessie and back again. "I don't really keep up with island news these days, but once in a while, when I'm in Liverpool for work, I pick up a copy of the island's newspaper. They stock it in a few shops near the docks, and sometimes I feel a bit nostalgic. Anyway, about a month ago I saw the house listed with one of the estate agencies. I tried to put it out of my mind, but, well, I couldn't stop thinking about it. I was only eleven when we moved to Birmingham, but I still remember this house. It was my first home and where we were happiest, with Mum and Dad, before Dad passed so unexpectedly."

"So you decided to come and see the house for yourself," Andy said. "Come in."

"The listing said that the house was in need of modernisation, which I reckoned meant that it had been left empty for many years. I thought maybe it would still look the way I remembered it from my childhood," he explained as he followed them into the sitting room.

"The house has actually been very badly neglected," Bessie told him.

He glanced behind her into the small foyer and nodded. "It looks as if it's been empty since the day Gary Davison threw us out."

"He threw you out?" Elizabeth demanded.

Harold shrugged. "That was how it felt to me, anyway. I was ten, and this was the only home I'd ever known. It was bad enough that my father had died and then Mum had remarried almost immediately. Suddenly, Mum was dead, too, and Mum's second husband owned our home, the home that our father had built himself."

"How awful," Elizabeth said.

"It was pretty terrible. There were seven of us, and we'd been pretty cramped in this house, but then we moved in with our paternal grandparents. They had a bungalow with two bedrooms. The girls all shared the second bedroom and the boys slept in the sitting room. We were there for more than a year before our grandparents moved us all to Birmingham."

"To a larger house, I hope," Elizabeth said.

"We all moved in with our uncle, our father's younger brother. He and his wife didn't have any children, and I'm not sure they were very excited about suddenly having seven of us to look after, but they never complained, at least not in front of us."

"We should sit down," Bessie suggested. She waited until everyone was settled before she spoke again. "Where are you all now?" she asked.

Harold sighed. "My grandparents both passed away in the seventies. Uncle Stuart died when I was fifteen. His wife, Aunt Beverly, passed away in the early eighties. My brothers and sisters and I are scattered all over the world, the ones who are still around, that is. Peter, the oldest, died a few years ago, and Sarah, the baby, died in a car crash last year."

"Do the others know that you're here?" Bessie asked.

He shook his head. "I don't talk to them very often. After everything we went through as children, we aren't really close now. I was closest to Sarah. If she were still alive, she'd have come with me. She always talked about wanting to move back to the island, but she never actually managed it."

"None of you ever came back?" Andy wondered.

"I don't think so. As I said, we aren't especially close, but I think if any of my brothers or sisters had decided to come back here, he or she would have told the rest of us. We used to talk about it all the time when we were younger. We used to talk about coming back here and buying this house back from Gary Davison so that we could live here again. In our memories, it was a huge mansion with dozens of rooms." He chuckled. "When I think back, all the boys were in one room and all of the girls were in another. Looking at it now, it's not a very large house at all, is it?"

"No, but it was your home and Gary Davison had no right making you leave it," Elizabeth said angrily.

"Mum left it to him," Harold countered. "I'm sure she thought he'd look after all of us when she wrote that new will, but he was never much of a stepfather. He didn't really care for children and he didn't try to hide that once he and Mum were married. They used to have terrible fights about it, actually."

"I'm surprised she wrote a new will, then," Bessie said.

"Once they'd had Heather, Mum wanted to believe that Gary had changed. He did seem devoted to Heather, I will admit. I'm sure Mum thought that Gary would do the right thing, otherwise she never would have changed her will."

"There were rumours at the time that the will was a forgery," Bessie said softly.

Harold shook his head. "We heard the rumours, but I never believed them. Mum was devoted to Gary. I always thought that she cared about him more than she had loved our father. Dad was around ten years older than Mum, and I think she married him because it was expected of her rather than because she was in love with him. Gary, though, she was madly in love with. Even at nine or ten, I could see how much she cared for him."

"But she wrote a new will after they married, leaving everything to her children," Elizabeth protested.

Harold grinned. "You really have heard the entire story," he said. "Mum did write a new will right after the wedding. My grandparents always said that she did it to test Gary, to make sure that he wasn't marrying her for her money. It wasn't as if she had much money, but she did have the house. Anyway, everything changed after Heather arrived. I'm not sure what was actually wrong with Heather, but she wasn't well. Mum was miserable with worry. They didn't just go across for a holiday. They went to see some sort of specialist for Heather."

"I didn't know that," Bessie said.

"I don't think Mum told anyone other than family. She didn't want people to know about Heather. She blamed herself for Heather's problems."

"The poor woman," Elizabeth said.

"We all went to stay with our grandparents, our father's parents, while she and Gary took the baby across. Mum rang every night with updates, but from what I was able to overhear, the doctors in the UK didn't think they were going to be able to help. Although my grandparents never believed that Mum rewrote her will herself, it

21

made sense to me. She wanted to make sure that Gary had the money he needed to take care of Heather. The doctors seemed to think that she was going to need a lot of expensive care as she got older."

"I can't believe she didn't leave anything to her other children, though," Elizabeth argued.

"As I said, I believe she thought Gary would take care of all of us. She was blind to the fact that he didn't actually like children, at least another man's children. He did seem to care for Heather, at least."

"Are you planning on making an offer on the house, then?" Elizabeth asked.

Harold looked around the room and then shook his head. "It's in a terrible state, isn't it? I didn't realise that Gary had let it get so bad. I don't have the time or the money to make it habitable again, even if I wanted to move back to the island, which I don't. Coming back to the island and buying the house was a childhood fantasy, but in reality, I'm very happy where I am."

"Do you think any of your brothers or sisters would want to buy it?" was Elizabeth's next question.

"I doubt it. I don't think any of them are even aware that it's for sale. None of them have mentioned it to me, anyway, although I've not mentioned it to them, either." He sighed. "We truly aren't close. I send them all Christmas cards and, when I remember, birthday cards, but that's just about the extent of our contact. None of us could wait to get out of the house when we turned eighteen, and in some ways, I think we all wanted to put everything that had happened up to that point behind us, even if that meant more or less cutting our ties with one another."

Elizabeth nodded. "We're really hoping to buy the house," she told Harold. "We've had our offer accepted, but we still have to have the inspection."

Harold glanced around again. "It's going to find a lot of issues," he said. "There's no doubt about that."

"We're hoping the structure is sound, anyway," Elizabeth said.

"Would you mind terribly if I had a look around?" Harold asked.

"It seems as if nothing much has changed since we moved out all those years ago."

"We came over to have a better look around ourselves," Andy replied. "When we came through with the estate agent, we never even went upstairs."

"And you made an offer anyway?" Harold asked.

Andy shrugged. "The location is great and the price is right. The current owners are being realistic about the amount of work the house needs. Whatever is upstairs can't be any worse than what's down here."

Bessie bit her tongue rather than disagree with Andy. In her opinion, though, there could well be some very nasty surprises waiting for them on the first floor.

"This was the sitting room, of course," Harold said, getting to his feet. "It felt a lot larger when I was a child. My brothers and sisters and I used to play games in here, chasing one another or rolling a ball around the room. I can't imagine now how seven of us could have fit in the space."

Bessie looked around the room as she stood up. It felt quite crowded with just the four of them there. It was impossible for her to imagine how it might have felt with seven children running around throughout the space.

"The kitchen is just back here," Harold said, leading them all through a doorway.

There were water stains on the walls and ceiling. The space was small, and Bessie noticed several gaps along the wall where appliances must have stood.

"Someone has taken out the cooker and the refrigerator," Harold said, gesturing towards the empty spaces. "Everything else is exactly the same, though."

The countertops were cracked and stained, and several of the cupboard doors were broken or hanging crookedly from their hinges. An old toaster with a frayed cord was shoved into a corner.

Elizabeth stepped forward and opened a cupboard. The pile of plates inside it surprised Bessie.

Harold stepped forward and took the top plate off the pile. It was covered in a thick layer of dust. He wiped it with his hand and then sighed. "I was hoping these might be my mother's old plates, but they aren't. Gary probably had everything valuable packed up and sent to him in the UK before he rented out the house."

"Those plates certainly don't look valuable," Bessie said as she studied the plate in Harold's hand.

"The door here opens into the back garden," Harold said, waving towards the door in one corner of the room.

Andy crossed to it and tried the knob. He frowned when it turned under his hand. "It doesn't seem to have been locked," he said as he pulled the door open.

As Harold had said, the door provided access to the garden at the back of the property. Bessie followed the others into the garden where they had found Susan some time earlier.

She took a few deep breaths, trying to clear the dust from her nose. "It looks as if it's going to rain," she said.

"I hope not," Andy replied. "There's enough water damage to the house already. Our first priority, if we do buy the house, will be to replace the roof to stop more water from getting in."

They looked around the small garden for a moment, before returning to the house as a light rain began to fall.

"Make sure you lock that door," Elizabeth told Andy.

He nodded and slid the deadbolt into place. "It may have been unlocked for years," he remarked.

"I suppose we're lucky no one has been squatting here," Elizabeth said.

"Even squatters have some standards," Harold said with a shake of his head. "The dining room is next." He led them through the kitchen and into what must have been a lovely room at one time.

A large wooden table that was stained and warped stood in the middle of the room, centered over a threadbare rectangle of carpet. Only two of the six chairs that surrounded the table looked capable of being used, and Bessie wasn't sure she'd trust either of them, really.

The large cabinet in the corner had once had glass doors, but only a few broken shards of glass remained.

"My mother loved that cabinet," Harold said, taking a step closer to it. "The table and chairs weren't hers, but that cabinet was. She kept a few special plates and things in it, a commemorative plate from a royal wedding, a fancy vase that my father had given her for some special occasion, things like that."

From where Bessie was standing, the cabinet looked empty. Harold took another step closer and then carefully opened one of the doors. As he did so, a large piece of glass slipped out of the frame and crashed to the ground.

"Sorry about that," he said, grimacing. He ran a hand along one of the shelves. "I always used to beg my mother to open the cabinet and let me use one of the fancy mugs or glasses that she kept in it. She never did, though. I'm sure I would have broken anything she'd let me use. I was always quite accident-prone when I was a child." His voice was low, as if he were almost talking to himself rather than the others.

"If we do buy the house and all of its contents, you're welcome to take the cabinet," Elizabeth said.

Harold looked surprised. "Really? I'd love to have it. I'm sure I could find a place that could restore it." He patted the shelf and then slowly removed his hand. "I'm sorry. I'm not usually this sentimental, but after everything we'd seen so far, I wasn't expecting to see any furniture that had been Mum's."

"It's fine," Elizabeth told him. "As I said, you're welcome to the cabinet."

Harold nodded. "I truly appreciate that. I can get it valued and pay you what it's worth, if you'd like. I can't imagine it's worth much in its current condition, though."

"No need," Elizabeth replied. "It's lovely, but my mother has several storage units full of furniture. She's hoping we'll use some of it to furnish this house once it's habitable again. We'll probably get rid of just about everything that's in the house now."

Bessie wasn't surprised. Every bit of furniture that she'd seen so far had been badly damaged. From what she could tell, none of it had been expensive or well made, either, with the possible exception of the cabinet that still seemed to be mesmerising Harold. While it was probably the nicest piece she'd seen in the house, it wasn't anywhere near as valuable as the sorts of furniture that Bessie knew Mary had in storage.

"We had a larger table," Harold said, slowly turning away from the cabinet. "It barely fit in the room. We had ten chairs around it, too, although they didn't all match. One of them was really too small to use at the table, but we used it when we had to, as we didn't have any choice. Sarah always used to complain because Mum made her use that chair whenever we had an extra person at meals."

"Because she was the youngest?" Elizabeth asked.

"Exactly. She had to sit in the baby chair and she never got anything new bought for her. It was different when Heather came along, though. Mum and Gary bought her a whole wardrobe of baby clothes. Sarah was only maybe four at time. I'm not sure she really noticed, but the rest of us did."

"Gary must have been excited about having a baby of his own," Bessie suggested.

Harold shrugged. "I suppose so. Mum was usually more practical than that, though. She had the seven of us to provide for, after all."

"Where does that door go?" Elizabeth asked after an awkward silence.

"To my father's office," Harold told her. "We weren't allowed to go in there, or even to knock on the door when our father was working. He always kept the door shut and locked, too. I remember feeling rather desperate as a child to see what was behind that door. After he died, my mother kept the door locked. Eventually, she let Gary use the room, but we still weren't allowed inside."

"I wonder what's back there now," Bessie said as she crossed to the small door. She tried the knob, but it didn't turn. "It seems to be locked," she said.

Harold sighed. "Even after all these years, I'm still not going to get to see what's back there."

Elizabeth laughed. "I think I have the key," she announced.

Harold's eyes lit up as Elizabeth dug the keys out of her bag. A moment later, she'd unlocked the door and pulled it open. "Ta-da," she announced as she stepped back to let Harold take a look.

"Well, that's disappointing," he said a moment later.

Bessie looked into the room and frowned. It was almost entirely empty. A single folding chair sat in one corner and a large floor lamp with a broken bulb sat in another.

"Maybe your father just used to go in there to hide from the seven of you," Andy suggested teasingly.

Harold laughed. "You could be right. Maybe there was never any furniture in here. Maybe it was just his hiding place."

"Should I lock it again?" Elizabeth asked after she shut the door.

"I can't imagine why it matters," Andy replied. "Leave it unlocked."

Elizabeth nodded and dropped the keys back into her bag. Then she looked expectantly at Harold. "Where next?"

"Upstairs, I suppose. There are three bedrooms up there. The loo was just down the corridor here, near the stairs."

Bessie looked at the small water closet in one room and the sink and tub in the other. It was a fairly typical design at the time the house was built, but now she couldn't imagine why anyone thought it was convenient. Her own cottage had had a similar arrangement when she'd purchased it, but that had been replaced when she extended the property for the first time.

"No plumbing on the first floor?" Elizabeth asked.

"Oh, no. We all shared that one loo," Harold replied with a shake of his head. "I live alone now and have two loos, but back then there were nine of us sharing this one and we never thought to complain. Of course, I knew a few people who still didn't have indoor plumbing, so I suppose we didn't think we had anything about which to complain."

Bessie nodded. "It's amazing how quickly standards for such things have changed."

"Modern houses have separate en suite facilities for the master bedrooms in addition to family loos," Elizabeth said. "Nearly every bedroom at Thie yn Traie has its own en suite bathroom."

Thie yn Traie was the large mansion situated on the cliff that over-looked Laxey Beach. George and Mary had purchased the mansion some time back, and Bessie knew that Elizabeth had her own wing in the huge home.

"Things have definitely changed," Harold chuckled. "But let's see what sort of state the bedrooms are in, shall we?"

The foursome filed down the corridor and up the narrow staircase.

"This staircase will probably have to be replaced," Andy said as they climbed. "I'm pretty certain it's too small and too steep."

"I'm sure my father wanted it to take up as little space as possible so that he could make the bedrooms as large as he could. My parents already had two children when they started building the house and the third arrived before it was finished."

"I wonder why he didn't add more bedrooms," Bessie said.

"He would have had to make the entire house larger in order to do that," Harold replied. "No doubt money was a major factor. He did most of the work himself, not because he wanted to, but because he couldn't afford to hire someone else to do it. I think this was the largest house he could afford to build."

Upstairs a short corridor had four doors along its length, two on each side. They were all shut.

"This was the girls' room," Harold said, opening the first door on the left.

Bessie looked into the small space, noting that the ceilings were low and that the room felt cramped and tiny. There were two bed frames pushed against the walls but no mattresses on them.

"Do you think anyone would mind if I opened the curtains?" Elizabeth asked. She crossed to the wall and pushed the curtains to one side. The tiny, dirty, and cracked window did little to let light into the room.

"At least the rain isn't coming in," Andy said with a sigh after he'd inspected the window.

"Why are we buying this house again?" Elizabeth whispered loudly to him.

He shrugged. "We should have looked up here before we made our offer. I was expecting the bedrooms to be larger."

"They would feel a lot larger if you raised the roof," Bessie said. "I'm not sure it could be done, but if you're having a new roof fitted anyway, you should find out."

Andy nodded. "I can barely stand up in here."

"How many people shared this room?" Elizabeth asked as she slowly turned around in the space.

"There were four boys and three girls," Harold told her. "The girls all shared this room, and we had the room across the hall." He turned and opened the door on the opposite side of the corridor.

Bessie followed. "I think it might be a tiny bit larger," she said doubtfully.

"It is," Harold assured her. "We measured it one day when one of the girls was complaining about how little space she had. We measured both rooms and then divided by the number of occupants. The girls had a slightly smaller room, but there were only three of them, so they each had a tiny bit more space than we did."

Bessie was starting to feel slightly claustrophobic in the small, dark, empty room. She walked back into the corridor before she replied.

"Of course, once Heather came along, the numbers were even," she said.

Harold nodded. "But Heather was still sleeping in a cot in Mum's room. With her health issues, she may never have been moved into the other bedroom."

"There are two more doors," Elizabeth said. "I thought there were only three bedrooms?"

"This room was just used for storage," Harold told her, gesturing towards the next door. "None of the bedrooms had enough space for wardrobes, so this room was filled with wardrobes and other pieces of furniture where everyone could keep his or her clothes and things. It probably wasn't the best use of the space, but it's a very tiny room, really."

29

He opened the door and stuck his head inside. "There's still one lonely wardrobe in here, but it isn't one that I recognise."

Bessie looked into the room and shook her head. The wardrobe on the back wall seemed to take up nearly a quarter of the room. If they'd had two or three of them in there, space for anything else would have been practically nonexistent.

Elizabeth opened the wardrobe, sneezing at the cloud of dust the action raised. "It's empty," she announced.

She checked one of the drawers and then shrugged. "Also empty. If we do buy the house, we'll be certain to check it more thoroughly before we get rid of it, of course."

"Just one more bedroom to see," Harold said tightly. "I have fond memories of coming down the corridor in the early morning and crawling into bed with Mum and Dad. Dad used to complain because usually at least two or three of us would come in at the same time, but Mum always ignored him and welcomed us all. That changed once Gary moved in, of course. He refused to let us into the bed with him and Mum. Now that I'm older, I suppose I can see his point. We weren't his children, after all, but at the time it was painful."

He reached for the doorknob and then frowned. "Locked," he said.

Elizabeth pulled out the keys again. She tried three different keys in the lock before she found the right one. "And we're in," she giggled as she finally pushed the door open.

Bessie looked into the room and was surprised to see that a large bed took up nearly all of the space. The room was dark, and it took her eyes a moment to adjust to the low light levels. Harold's eyes seemed to adjust more quickly.

"What's that on the bed?" he demanded.

"I think we need to ring the police," Bessie said.

"The police?" Andy echoed. He was still standing in the corridor with Elizabeth. The couple had let Bessie and Harold into the room first. Now the pair crowded into the room behind them.

"It's a squatter," Harold said loudly. "You were right to be worried." He crossed to the bed and put his hand on the large shape. "Hey, wake up. You don't belong here."

"I think we need the police," Bessie repeated herself.

Harold made a noise and then stepped back from the bed. As he did so, the body on the bed rolled onto its back. Bessie gasped when she saw the knife that was sticking out of the man's chest.

"Ring John Rockwell again," Andy said tightly as Elizabeth screamed.

CHAPTER 3

Of course, Bessie's mobile was at the very bottom of her handbag. When she finally dug it out, she dialled the number for the station's front desk. It was a number she rang often, as her closest friend, Doona Moore, was one of the receptionists who answered the calls. She'd just rung John's mobile number, but she hated to use it twice in the same morning. Bessie regretted her decision when the call was answered, though.

"Laxey Neighbourhood Policing, this is Suzannah. How can I help you?"

Suzannah was one of Bessie's least favourite people. She could never get Bessie's name right and she usually refused to connect Bessie with John. Gritting her teeth, Bessie was as polite as she could be. "It's Elizabeth Cubbon. I need to speak to John Rockwell, please."

"I'm sorry, Mrs. Cubbly, but Inspector Rockwell isn't here at the moment. Can I take a message or would you rather speak to someone else?" was the not unexpected reply.

"I'm really not in the mood for games today," Bessie replied tightly. "Please put me through to John."

"But he truly isn't here, Mrs. Custard. I can connect you to Constable Watterson."

"Do that, then," Bessie said.

"This is Constable Watterson. How can I help you?"

Bessie felt herself relax a bit when she heard the familiar voice. She'd known Hugh since he'd been a small child playing on Laxey Beach near her cottage. He'd spent many nights during his teen years in her spare bedroom, escaping parents who didn't approve of his desire to join the police. While Hugh was now in his twenties, to Bessie he still seemed incredibly young. He and his pretty blonde wife had recently had a baby of their own, though.

"Hugh, it's Bessie. I really wanted to speak to John, but I'm sure you'll know what to do."

"John's out dealing with a break-in at one of the shops near the Laxey Wheel. You have his mobile number, though, don't you?"

"Yes, of course, but I'd already rung him once this morning. The thing is, we've stumbled across a body, you see."

"A body," Hugh echoed. He sighed. "I'm not even surprised."

Bessie shook her head. It wasn't surprising anymore, sadly. In the past two years she'd found far too many bodies and been involved in more murder investigations than she wanted to count. "It's still rather awful," Bessie told him.

"Of course it is," Hugh replied. "Where are you?"

"At the old Looney mansion. Andy and Elizabeth are thinking about buying it."

"Were thinking about buying it," Elizabeth said flatly. "This has changed my mind, though."

"I'll send the closest car and let John know," Hugh said. Bessie heard him talking into another phone for a minute before he came back to her. "Where is the body?"

"In one of the bedrooms on the first floor," Bessie replied.

"You and Elizabeth and Andy should wait on the ground floor, then," Hugh suggested. "I hope no one has touched anything."

"Harold tried to wake the man. When he touched his shoulder, the body rolled towards us a bit."

"Who is Harold?"

"Ah, right, Harold is Harold Looney. He's one of the Looney chil-

33

dren who used to live in the house before his mother's death. He's just visiting the island, and when he saw the cars outside the property, he knocked and asked if he could have a look around," Bessie explained.

Hugh sighed. "You should all wait on the ground floor," he said. "I'm going to head there now. I should be there in five minutes, but the closest constable should be there considerably sooner. John is on his way as well."

"Just one more thing," Bessie said in a low voice. "I think I know the identity of the dead man."

"Who is it?"

"I think it's Grant Robertson," Bessie whispered.

Hugh whistled and then sighed again. "Get everyone well away from the body," he said. "I'm sure I don't have to tell you what a huge complication that is."

"No, you don't," Bessie agreed before Hugh ended the call.

She dropped her phone into her handbag and then looked at the others. "We need to wait in the sitting room," she said. "The police are on their way."

Harold took another look at the body on the bed and shuddered. Bessie waited until he and Elizabeth and Andy had left the room before she followed them. Elizabeth kept close to Andy, holding his hand while they walked and then pulling him into a hug as soon as they reached the sitting room.

"What could have happened to the poor man?" Harold asked. "I mean, it looked as if he'd been stabbed, but who would want to kill a random squatter? Do they fight over properties? I'm afraid I don't know anything about such things, not in the UK or on the island."

"He wasn't a squatter," Elizabeth said dully. "He was a wanted criminal, one who very nearly ruined my father's life."

Bessie frowned. She'd been hoping that the girl hadn't recognised the dead man.

A loud knocking startled them all. Bessie jumped and then shook her head at her foolishness. She'd been expecting the police, after all.

The uniformed constable at the door wasn't one that Bessie knew. She let him inside and told him where to find the body.

"I'm not going to go up there," he told her. "I'm just here to keep an eye on the suspe, er, witnesses, until an inspector gets here."

"We're waiting in the sitting room," Bessie told him, leading the constable the short distance to where the others were all standing around awkwardly.

"I'm afraid I'm going to have to ask you not to speak to one another," the constable said. "We'll need to get witness statements from everyone as soon as an inspector arrives."

"I'm a witness?" Harold asked. "I'm not sure what I'm a witness to, exactly. I don't know who the dead man is or why he was in the house. This is my first visit to the island in over thirty years. Anyway, the man has probably been dead for weeks or even months. I haven't been here anywhere near that long."

"You're a witness to the discovery of the body," the constable told him.

Harold shrugged. "I suppose I can't argue with that. It's all rather fascinating, really. I've never seen anyone who'd been murdered before. I suppose that must be true for all of us, though, aside from the constable?" He glanced around the room, looking at Bessie and the others.

Bessie wasn't quite sure how to reply, so she was grateful when the constable held up a hand.

"As I said, you really can't speak to one another right now," he said. "Inspector Rockwell will be here soon."

Another knock made Bessie jump again. The constable headed for the door and was back only a moment later with Hugh on his heels.

"Are you okay?" the new arrival asked Bessie.

She nodded at the young man, who looked tired and badly in need of a haircut. "How's Grace?" she asked.

He grinned. "She's doing well. We went out for dinner last night and managed to get through an entire meal before she insisted on rushing home to the baby. We were out for nearly an entire hour."

Bessie chuckled. "I suppose that's an accomplishment."

"It was the longest she's been away from Aalish since her arrival. Her mother and father kept Aalish at their house while we went out. I very nearly managed to get her to order a pudding, which might have taken us past the hour mark, but in the end she decided against it."

"My wife was that same way with the first baby," Harold said. "By the time the second one came along, I think she'd have let any random stranger on the street take her for an hour or two, just for a break."

Hugh shrugged. "I'm not sure I'll ever be ready for a second one."

Bessie introduced Hugh to Harold. Hugh took careful notes in the small notebook he'd pulled out of his pocket.

"Bessie, can you show me the body, please," he said after he'd finished writing down Harold's name and contact details.

Making a face, Bessie headed for the stairs.

"I can show him, if you'd rather not see it again," Andy offered.

Bessie looked back at the young man and gave him a grateful smile. "Thank you, but you stay with Elizabeth," she replied.

The girl took a shaky breath and then released her grip on Andy. "It's okay. I'm fine, really."

Bessie just shook her head and led Hugh out of the room. He stopped her at the top of the stairs.

"I'm sure I can find the body on my own," he said. "I just wanted a minute alone with you. Are you sure you're okay?"

"I'm fine. Finding bodies is almost a habit now, after all," Bessie said with a touch of bitterness.

Hugh pulled her into a hug and squeezed her tightly. "I'm sorry," he said softly.

"It's not your fault," she said as she stepped back from the embrace. "At least I hope it isn't your fault."

"How certain are you of the identification you made?" he asked.

"I'm pretty sure it's Grant. Elizabeth recognised him as well. He appears to have lost a lot of weight and changed his hair colour and style, but I'm still pretty sure we've found Grant Robertson."

"Why would he have come back to the island?"

"That's a good question," Bessie replied. "He had to know that he'd be recognised, and that the police were still looking for him."

Grant had been one of the island's most successful businessmen for decades. He'd worked for one of the local banks, eventually becoming head of the bank during his long career. What no one realised at the time was that he was also directing funds from the customers' accounts into his own pockets. He'd only just managed to escape from the island as the police were closing their net around him. All of his accounts had been frozen, but Bessie was fairy certain that Grant had had numerous accounts in other names to which he would still have had access. She'd assumed, when he'd disappeared, that he'd find himself a safe haven where he could live out the rest of his days in quiet luxury.

"Considering he stole from just about everyone on the island, the list of suspects is going to be a long one," Hugh speculated.

"I think the body has been there for a while, certainly for more than a day or two, anyway."

Hugh frowned. "That complicates things further," he sighed. "Just once I'd like to stumble across a crime scene where the suspect is immediately obvious."

"I suspect John will say the same thing when he gets here," Bessie replied.

"Hugh? Bessie?" They heard their names being called in a familiar voice.

"Speak of the devil," Bessie said.

Hugh laughed and then quickly sobered as John Rockwell came up the stairs. John was in his mid-forties, with brown hair that was streaked with grey and bright green eyes. Bessie believed he was one of the most handsome men she knew.

"I'm not sure why you thought you needed Bessie to help you find the body," John said to Hugh as a greeting.

"I just wanted to talk to her on her own, sir," Hugh replied, flushing. "I wanted to make sure she was okay, that's all."

John nodded and then turned his gaze to Bessie. "And are you okay?" he asked.

Bessie nodded. "I'm fine. Finding a body is always upsetting, but I'm fine."

"Where is the body, then?"

"In the last bedroom on the right side," Bessie told him. "It was the master bedroom, as such, when the Looneys lived here."

They'd left all of the doors open during their tour of the house, and now John glanced into each room as he headed for the master bedroom. When he reached it, he stood in the doorway for several seconds, just staring into the room.

"You said someone touched the body?" Hugh asked.

"Yes, Harold tried to wake him but obviously failed. When he touched the man's shoulder, the body rolled onto its back," Bessie replied.

"And that was when you recognised him?" John asked.

Bessie nodded. "There was something oddly familiar about him as soon as I saw him, but I didn't actually recognise him until he rolled over."

"What was familiar about him?" John demanded.

Bessie shut her eyes and tried to remember how she'd felt when she'd first seen the body on the bed. "His coat," she said after a moment. "He wore that coat to some social event that George and Mary hosted just before Grant disappeared. I remember him telling someone that it was very valuable. The colour is quite unusual. It's almost black, but not quite, if you see what I mean."

John looked back into the bedroom and then nodded. "I do see what you mean. So you recognised the coat?"

"Not consciously, but, as I said, I felt as if there was something familiar about the body. I didn't know it was a man, of course, but I assumed it was. The shape suggested a man, anyway."

"I have a crime scene team on the way, and the Chief Constable should be here any minute. This investigation is going to be a nightmare," John said in a low voice. "That Elizabeth Quayle was here when the body was found won't help."

"I'm sure she'd have rather been anywhere else in the world," Bessie replied.

"We'd better get you back downstairs," Hugh told Bessie. "You don't want to be up here when the Chief Constable arrives."

"No, I don't," Bessie said firmly.

Back in the sitting room, Elizabeth and Andy were sitting together on the battered couch. Harold had settled on one of the folding chairs. Bessie sat on the other one and gave the Elizabeth and Andy a small smile. Andy looked as if he had a dozen questions for her, but with two constables and an inspector in the room there was no way he was going to ask anything.

"Which estate agency is listing the house?" John asked suddenly.

Elizabeth replied with the name of one of the largest agencies on the island.

"Hugh, ring them and let them know that we have a situation," John said. "Why don't they have someone here, showing you around, actually?" he asked.

"They gave me the keys so that we could come and take a closer look ourselves," Elizabeth replied. "We've already made an offer on the property, although we'll be withdrawing it now, obviously."

"Why obviously?" John asked.

Elizabeth looked up the ceiling and shivered. "I don't want to own a house where someone was murdered, especially not that particular someone. Andy and I will find some other property to buy."

"We'll talk about it later," Andy said.

"There's nothing to discuss," Elizabeth countered.

"You'll have to save that conversation for later," John said. "I need to question each of you individually before I let you go. I'll get started as soon as the Chief Constable arrives."

The words were barely out of John's mouth when the Chief Constable walked into the room. He nodded at the constables and John and then rushed over to Elizabeth.

"My dear girl, are you okay?" he asked, sounding genuinely concerned.

Bessie knew that the man was friendly with George, but she hadn't realised that the relationship extended to Elizabeth.

For her part, Elizabeth greeted the man warmly before assuring him that she was fine. "Just a bit shaken up, but otherwise okay," she told him.

"I rang your father for you," he replied. "He's sending his advocate over to sit with you during your session with Inspector Rockwell."

"That isn't necessary," Elizabeth said. "I've nothing to hide. I don't need an advocate sitting with me."

"The choice is yours, obviously," the Chief Constable said smoothly. "I just need to go and take a look at what you've found."

John led the man out of the room. In the uncomfortable silence that followed their departure, Bessie could hear their footsteps as they climbed the stairs. The Chief Constable was back a few minutes later. He glanced around the room and then looked at Elizabeth.

"Your advocate will be here soon," he said.

"As I said, I don't need him," Elizabeth replied.

The man shrugged. "I've instructed Inspector Rockwell to wait to interview you until your advocate arrives. You can make your decision at that point."

Elizabeth looked as if she wanted to argue, but she didn't get a chance. The Chief Constable nodded to the constable who was standing at attention near the door and then turned and left the room. To Bessie it seemed as if everyone let out a relieved sigh when they heard the house's door open and then close.

John was back a moment later. "Mr. Looney, if I could start with you, please," he said.

Harold looked surprised and then got to his feet. "Are we going to the police station?" he asked. "I've never been inside a police station."

"I'm going to be using the small office at the back of the property for interviews," John told him. "We just need to wait a moment. Someone is bringing some chairs and a table for us to use."

A moment later, Bessie watched as two constables carried a small folding table and several chairs through the house towards the office at the back. John and Harold followed them a minute later.

With nothing to do but wait, Bessie found herself listening to the various sounds of the people working around the house. As the sitting room was between the door and the stairs, every new arrival had to walk through it on his or her way to the crime scene. Some of the investigators seemed to stare at Bessie and her friends as they walked through the room, while others seemed to be doing their best to pretend they hadn't noticed that anyone was there. A short while later, a man in a dark grey suit was led into the room by a uniformed constable.

"Miss Quayle? I'm Jason Bergan-Hardy. Your father sent me," he announced.

Bessie studied the man, who was a stranger to her. He appeared to be in his mid-thirties, with dark brown hair that was almost black. His eyes were dark as well. He was carrying an expensive-looking briefcase, and Bessie was certain that his suit had cost a good deal more than anything she had in her wardrobe. She hadn't heard about any new advocates on the island, but the island's population was growing rapidly as many of the banks and insurance companies expanded. If Mr. Bergan-Hardy was working out of Douglas, he was probably just one of many new arrivals about whom Bessie had yet to hear.

"I don't need you, but thank you anyway," Elizabeth replied.

The advocate frowned. "You're going to be questioned in a murder investigation. Having a solicitor by your side is only sensible."

"We call solicitors advocates on the island," Elizabeth told him. "I'm going to guess that you haven't been here very long if you don't even know that much."

Flushing, he smiled tightly. "I did know that, but in my rush to get here to assist you, it escaped me. In fairness, I haven't been on the island for very long, either. I've only just moved across from Liverpool to join a law firm here."

"The one my father uses, presumably," Elizabeth said.

"Yes, that's correct. I'm the newest associate at Richard Hart's firm."

"Why did they send you, then? I know just about all of the other advocates at the firm. Daddy is one of their best customers."

"I'm an expert in criminal law. Most of the others in the firm deal with businesses, estates, and other noncriminal matters," he explained.

Elizabeth shrugged. "I don't need an expert in criminal law. I don't need anyone. John Rockwell is going to ask me a few questions about finding the body and then he'll let me go. I didn't know the dead man was on the island, although, if I had, I might have been tempted to stick a knife in his chest, actually."

Bessie frowned. While she understood why the girl felt that way, it wasn't a smart comment to make in front of a police constable.

"Miss Quayle, that's exactly the sort of thing that your father wants me here to prevent you from saying," the advocate said. "You do understand that my client is under considerable stress," he said to the constable. "She can't possibly be held accountable for anything she's saying right now."

Elizabeth laughed. "Thank you, Jason, but I'm happy to be held accountable for everything I say, whenever I say it. I hated Grant Robertson for the things that he did to my father and I'm happy that he's dead. I didn't kill him, but if I'd known he was on the island, I might have considered hiring someone else to do the job. As it is, I can only feel happy that someone eliminated the man before he could do anything else that might have hurt my father."

"I think we need to speak privately before you talk to the inspector," the advocate said. "You can arrange that, can't you?" he asked the constable.

"I'll have to check with Inspector Rockwell first," the constable replied.

He looked amused, and Bessie knew that he was looking forward to sharing every word of the exchange with John when he had a chance.

"Miss Quayle, I'm going to insist that we speak before you are interviewed. I'm not sure that you truly appreciate exactly what it means to be involved in a murder investigation. This isn't going to be like on the telly, you know."

Elizabeth laughed. "I'd be willing to bet that I've been involved in more murder investigations that you have," she replied. "Murders seem to happen with alarming regularity around here, actually. I know exactly what to expect and I'm absolutely certain that I don't need you interfering with any of this."

John walked back into the room escorting Harold Looney as the advocate opened his mouth to reply. "Mr. Looney, thank you again for your time," John said.

Harold glanced around the room and then shrugged. "I'm not really sure what to do with myself now," he said.

"You're free to go and do whatever you had planned for the day," John told him.

"Ah, yes, but I didn't have any plans," Harold said with a small chuckle. "Of course, I don't want to be in the way here, but I do feel as if I'll be missing out on something if I leave. Do you think you'll be making any arrests today?"

Bessie thought John looked as if he wanted to either laugh or shout. He took a deep breath. "I don't expect to make any arrests today," he said steadily. "Just processing the crime scene will take several days, as will the results of the autopsy. We're just barely getting started on our investigation."

Harold nodded. "I suppose I'll just have to keep listening to the local news if I want to find out anything more, then."

"I may need to speak to you again as the investigation continues," John replied. "Please let me know if you decide to move to a different hotel."

"I can't imagine why I would. The one I'm staying in is comfortable enough. I should be thinking about going back home, of course, but you said I can't leave the island, didn't you?"

"I'd appreciate it if you'd stay here for the next few days, anyway," John said. "I'll ring you and let you know when you're cleared to leave. If you need to go sooner, you can ring me. I gave you my card."

Harold nodded. "I suppose I'll go, then," he said. He glanced around the room and seemed disappointed when no one tried to stop him.

"Hugh, can you escort Mr. Looney out, please," John said, sounding a bit fed up.

Hugh grinned and then took Harold's arm. "Do you have a car here?" he asked as he started to lead him out of the room.

"Yes, it's a hire car. I parked it right outside," Harold replied.

The pair were still talking as they disappeared from view.

"Inspector Rockwell? I'm Jason Bergan-Hardy. Mr. George Quayle sent me to assist Miss Quayle during questioning," the advocate said, taking a step closer to John. He looked as if he was trying to challenge John's authority, but John didn't seem the least bit concerned.

"Miss Quayle, I'm ready to take your statement now," he said to Elizabeth, turning his back on the advocate.

"Good," she replied. "Unlike Mr. Looney, I do have things to do today."

John smiled as Elizabeth gave Andy a quick hug and then got to her feet. As she started to follow John out of the room, Jason Bergan-Hardy fell into step behind her.

"You can go," she told him firmly. "I don't need you to hold my hand."

"I'm sure your father would prefer..." the advocate began.

Elizabeth held up a hand. "Have you even met my father?" she demanded.

The advocate flushed. "I have not yet had that pleasure, no, but he did ring the firm and request..."

"Go," Elizabeth cut across his reply. "I can ring Daddy and tell him to tell you to go, if you prefer."

"I'm simply trying to do what's best for you," the man protested.

"Then go. I know Inspector Rockwell well enough to know that he's excellent at his job. I'll tell him everything I know, which is next to nothing, and then he'll go out and find the killer. You are completely superfluous to all of this," Elizabeth said.

The advocate flushed and then shrugged. "If that's your last word, then I'll go. I hope you won't live to regret that decision, young lady." He turned on his heel and marched out of the room with his head held high.

Elizabeth sighed. "I'm going to have to have words with Daddy," she said softly.

"Let's get our conversation out of the way first," John suggested.

Elizabeth nodded and then followed John out of the room. Bessie sat back in her chair, ready for another long wait. More people in lab coats and white clothing came into the house while she waited. After a while, Bessie began to wonder how they were all fitting into the small bedroom where the body had been found. The room had felt crowded when she and Harold and Elizabeth and Andy had been inside it. At least a dozen men and women had come through the sitting room and gone up the stairs. Maybe they were taking turns in the room, she thought. Or maybe some were busy investigating the other rooms rather than dealing with the body. John was back half an hour later.

"Andy? You're next," he said.

"I'm going to wait here for Andy, if I may," Elizabeth said.

John nodded. "Just don't talk to anyone, okay?"

"After all of your questions, I won't feel like talking again for at least an hour," Elizabeth joked.

John led Andy out of the room. Their conversation took about the same amount of time as John had spent with Elizabeth. While they were busy, Bessie counted another six investigators who came through the sitting room and went up the stairs. After a while, Bessie began to worry about the structural integrity of the floors above them. Surely they weren't designed to hold the number of people who were now stomping around overhead.

"Thank you for your time," John was saying to Andy as they walked back into the room a few minutes later. "Bessie? I'm ready for you now."

Bessie got to her feet and followed John through the house to the small office at the back.

CHAPTER 4

"*H*ave a seat," John told Bessie.

She sat down on the uncomfortable chair in front of the small table. "These chairs are terrible," she said.

"I know. I think they're worse than what we have in our interview rooms at the station, and before today I didn't think that was possible," John agreed.

"Where did they even come from? I can't believe that the Looneys had folding chairs in the house when they lived here."

"I've no idea, but there are a few more near the door at the back of the property. That's where we found this table, too," John replied, gesturing towards the small folding table.

"I was surprised to see furniture in any of the rooms, actually," Bessie said thoughtfully. "I suppose I'd simply assumed that Gary cleared out the house once the estate was settled. If he didn't want some of the furniture, he should have given it to the Looneys. I'm certain they would have appreciated it."

John shrugged. "Let's start by going through your day. Tell me everything that you did from the time that you woke up this morning."

Bessie had been expecting the request. She did her best to keep her reply as succinct as possible without missing out anything important. "And then we found a body in the last bedroom," she concluded after a while.

John looked up from his notebook. "Obviously, I'm going to be interviewing Susan Davison. Did she do or say anything that made you think she was at all interested in seeing more of the house?"

"Not at all. She didn't seem interested in the house. Her father only lived here for a short time, after all. She was surprised and upset by everything that I told her. She said, when she left, that she didn't want anything to do with the property."

"Because she thinks her father might have murdered Valerie Looney."

"From what she said, it sounded as if she suspects that he might have murdered more people than just Valerie Looney," Bessie replied. "She seemed to think that he might have had a hand in her own mother's death, and others."

"I had a brief telephone conversation with her, but we were interrupted by other things. I'm going to have to go and have a very long talk with her later today."

"You can't be thinking that she had anything to do with Grant's death, though, can you? She didn't know the man, after all."

"At this point, everyone on the island is a suspect. Once the coroner can give me an idea of when Grant died, I may be able to eliminate a few people from consideration."

"Susan and Harold are both simply visiting. They couldn't have known Grant, and I can't imagine that either of them had any motive for killing him, either. Anyway, they may not have even been on the island when Grant died."

"It's interesting that they're both visiting at the same time," John remarked.

Bessie frowned. "Now that you've mentioned it, it does seem odd. Susan may have come because Andy and Elizabeth made an offer on the house. As she and her brothers are the owners, they'd have been told, I'm sure."

"And Harold?"

"He said he saw the house being advertised for sale in the local paper. I didn't question it at the time, but the house has been on the market for well over a year. I wonder why he just now decided to visit."

"So do I."

"But he couldn't have had any motive for killing Grant, could he? He said he hadn't been on the island since his childhood, after all."

"We're still unravelling all the schemes in which Grant was involved. It's possible that Susan or Harold may have lost money from Grant's activities."

"How would they have known where to find him, though? The police have been looking for him for over a year and you didn't know he was back on the island."

"That's something we're going to be investigating thoroughly. Grant shouldn't have been able to fly or sail to the island without being discovered, but clearly he found a way to get here. I'm hoping when we find out how he managed that, we'll know more about why he was here and who was helping him stay hidden."

"Whoever was helping him probably killed him,' Bessie suggested.

"Maybe, or maybe Grant was careless and got discovered by someone else. There are about eighty thousand people on this island, and I believe at least twenty per cent of them lost money to Grant. That leaves me with a long list of possible suspects."

Bessie sighed. "He must have been being very careful, though. Staying here was a good idea, right up until Elizabeth and Andy decided to take a look at the house. Before that, it had been sitting empty for a really long time. The door at the back wasn't even locked. Grant could have just walked in and made himself at home."

"There's no evidence to suggest that he'd been staying here for any length of time, but if he was careful, there wouldn't be. After more than a year on the run, I suspect he'd learned to be careful."

"But someone killed him."

"And we'll talk about the possible suspects another time. I need to get back to the crime scene and then I need to talk to Susan again." John flipped through his notebook, asking Bessie a few questions as he went. "I think that's everything for now," he said eventually. "I don't think I'll be done in time for a gathering tonight, but maybe we could all meet at your cottage tomorrow night to talk things through."

"I'd like that. Let's say six o'clock. Do you want me to invite Doona and Hugh?"

"I can take care of that. Hugh is here, somewhere, and I'll see Doona at home tonight."

Bessie smiled at the casual reference to Doona and home. When she'd first met John, Bessie had thought that John and Doona would make a lovely couple. Doona was around John's age and had two failed marriages in her past. John had still been married to Sue, but it was quickly obvious to everyone that the marriage was struggling.

It had taken a long time for John and Doona to overcome the many obstacles that had been thrown in their path, but they seemed to be settling into a comfortable relationship now. Bessie knew that Doona did a great deal to help John look after his two children, Thomas and Amy, too. They were teenagers, and it seemed to Bessie as if they were never in one place for more than a few minutes at a time. Because neither was old enough to drive yet, either Doona or John had to spend time every day taking them back and forth to visit friends, play sports, or attend school functions. Bessie wasn't certain if Doona was actually staying at John's house now or not, but clearly John expected her to be there later that evening.

"So if I don't talk to you before tomorrow, I'll see you around six," Bessie said.

"I'll bring food, so don't worry about that," John told her.

"Andrew Cheatham is meant to be arriving on Saturday," she reminded John.

"It might be useful to have his thoughts on the case," John replied.

Andrew was a former Scotland Yard inspector who'd befriended Bessie when she'd been on holiday in the UK. He'd visited the island some months earlier, and together the duo had solved a pair of cold cases. Now he was returning to the island and Bessie was fairly certain that he was going to be bringing another cold case with him to discuss with her. Not only had Andrew been a very successful investigator, he'd also written several books on the subject. He could be a real help to John if the case hadn't been solved by the time he arrived.

Bessie nodded and then got to her feet. John stood up as well and then offered his arm. "I'll just walk you out," he said. "But how will you get home?"

"I suppose I could walk, although it would take a while," Bessie said. "I'll ring for a taxi."

"I'm sure I can spare a constable to take you home," John said.

When they got back to the sitting room, though, they discovered that neither was necessary.

"Miss Quayle asked me to tell you that she will be waiting outside to take you home," the constable in the sitting room told Bessie.

"Thank you," Bessie replied. She turned to John. "That takes care of that, then."

"I want you to ring me after you've spoken to Elizabeth, just in case she says something useful," he told her.

Bessie nodded and then continued on her way to the door. It had been a long afternoon and she was looking forward to getting home again.

Elizabeth was sitting on a bench in the corner of the front garden. She jumped to her feet as soon as Bessie walked out of the house.

"I'm sure you thought that I'd forgotten all about you," she called as Bessie walked towards her.

"Not at all, although I wouldn't have blamed you if you had. It's been a rather unusual day, after all."

Elizabeth laughed and then immediately sobered. "I shouldn't laugh, should I? Not when there's a dead man in the house behind you. Not even if I'm glad he's dead."

"You really shouldn't say that," Bessie suggested.

Elizabeth shrugged. "It's true, and anyone who knows me will already know that it's true. I hated Grant Robertson for what he did to my father. It was bad enough that he'd been stealing money from just about everyone on the island, to go and disappear, leaving my father to deal with the mess he'd left behind, was simply horrible. There are still some people on the island who won't speak to Daddy, because they think Daddy had to have known what Grant was doing. When word gets out about Grant's death, it's all going to start up again, as well. Daddy will be ostracised a second time."

Bessie patted the girl's arm. "Maybe it won't be as bad this time around."

"It won't be bad if the police find the killer quickly enough. Do you have plans for the rest of the afternoon?"

Finding the question a bit worrying, Bessie shook her head slowly. "Not really," she replied.

"Excellent. You can come back to Thie yn Traie with me. I sent Andy on ahead and told him to make something delicious for dinner, just in case I had to bribe you to come back with me. I don't know if Mum or Daddy will be there, but if they are, you can talk to them, too. Between us all, we should be able to work out who killed Grant. Then we'll just have to tell the police so that they can arrest the killer. If we're quick enough, maybe it won't be so bad for Daddy this time around."

Bessie wanted to argue, but Elizabeth hadn't waited for her to reply. Instead, the girl had turned and begun to walk away. Bessie rushed after her, walking through the gates at the front of the house and then stopping short.

"Miss Cubbon, how lovely."

The familiar voice made Bessie frown. "No comment," she snapped at Dan Ross, the reporter for the *Isle of Man Times* who always seemed to turn up at every murder investigation.

"My goodness, I haven't even asked you anything yet," Dan laughed. "Do let me get a rude question out before you refuse to speak to me."

"No matter what your question, the answer will be the same," Bessie replied as she tried to step around him.

"What happened in there?" Dan asked, nodding towards the house behind Bessie. "I know enough about the police to recognise a crime scene team when I see one. You found another body, didn't you?"

"No comment," Bessie said, swallowing a sigh.

"We have to go," Elizabeth said to Dan. She took Bessie's arm and tried to lead her away from the reporter.

"Ah, Miss Quayle, maybe you can tell me why you were at the Looney house today? Is there any truth to the rumours that you're moving out of Thie yn Traie because your parents don't approve of your relationship with young Andy Caine? I know he's worth some money, but only because he inherited it from the grandfather he never knew he had, isn't that right? I suppose I can understand your parents not wanting you to get involved with someone with his rather questionable past."

Bessie patted Elizabeth's arm as the girl took a deep breath. "The only possible reply is no comment," she whispered loudly.

Elizabeth looked at Bessie and then at Dan. "No comment," she said tightly.

"I'm sure the Looney house will be quite a change for you. I imagine you'll be remodelling and extending the house, won't you?" Dan asked.

Elizabeth didn't even bother to reply as she led Bessie towards her car.

"But none of that matters now, since you've found a dead body and all. Who have you found?" Dan demanded.

Bessie looked at Elizabeth and sighed. "Maybe, instead of harassing us, you should be looking at missing person reports," she suggested.

Dan frowned at her. "Are you actually trying to give me a useful tip, or are you simply trying to get rid of me?"

"There are so many more possibilities than just those two," Bessie remarked.

"At least you're admitting that you found a body," Dan said, making a note in the large notebook he was carrying.

"I've done no such thing," Bessie shot back. "If I were you, I'd be very careful about what I publish. I have a very good advocate, you know."

Dan flushed. Bessie was sure that he knew that her threat was not an idle one. Doncan Quayle, Bessie's advocate, had a solid reputation on the island.

"At least tell me if you found a man or a woman," Dan pleaded as Elizabeth unlocked her car.

"I'm sure John Rockwell will be making a statement at some point," Bessie replied.

"Sure, and everyone and their brother will be there to get the story by that time. I was hoping for an early exclusive with the woman who found the body."

Bessie shook her head. "Sorry, no comment."

"Miss Quayle, you were there. Did you see the body? Was it anyone you recognised? Your father sent his very expensive new advocate over to protect you, the one he brought from across to deal with criminal matters. Did your father bring this Jason Bergan-Hardy across because he knew he was about to get caught up in a criminal investigation? Are the police taking another look at your father's dealings with Grant Robertson, for instance? Does your father maybe know where to find Grant?"

Elizabeth helped Bessie into the car and then walked around to the driver's door. "No comment," she said as she climbed inside the vehicle.

"I've been told there was another man here when the police first arrived. A middle-aged man that my source didn't recognise. Surely you can tell me who that was?" Dan asked.

Bessie smiled to herself. Dan was getting desperate, throwing out questions about everything and hoping for at least one answer.

"Take care," Elizabeth said to Dan before she shut her door and started the car's engine.

Dan said something in reply, but his words were drowned out by the car's engine. Bessie waved at him as Elizabeth pulled away.

"That was awful. I dislike Dan Ross almost as much as I disliked Grant," Elizabeth said as she drove towards Thie yn Traie.

"I almost feel sorry for him. This is going to be a huge news story when it breaks and poor Dan isn't going to be able to break the story any sooner than anyone else."

"You could have told him more," Elizabeth pointed out. "You could have told him a great deal more."

"And I'll buy the local paper regardless of what headline Dan decides to use after today. John asked me not to tell anyone what happened. I'm going to do my best to do as he asked."

"I hope that doesn't mean you won't talk to me and Andy about the case," Elizabeth replied. "We're really hoping you'll be able to solve the murder before we go to bed tonight."

"That's far too ambitious," Bessie protested. "I'm happy to talk to you about the case, but I can't imagine solving it."

"You're just being modest. You've solved hundreds of murders before this one. You probably have more experience with how a homicide investigation goes than most of the constables in Laxey."

Bessie frowned. "It hasn't been hundreds," she said in a low voice.

Elizabeth laughed. A moment later, she pulled her car into the huge garage behind Thie yn Traie. "It looks as if Daddy is out," she said as she and Bessie got out of the car. "His car is gone, anyway. Mum might be home, though. Do you think Inspector Rockwell will be very upset if I tell her whom we found?"

"He'd probably rather we didn't talk about the case with anyone," Bessie replied with a frown. She was eager to hear what Mary and George thought about Grant's reappearance on the island and his death. No doubt John had a number of questions for them as well, and Bessie knew that he'd prefer to be the one breaking the news of Grant's death to the Quayles.

Bessie followed Elizabeth into the house. The butler met them in the foyer.

"Miss Cubbon, how lovely to see you today," he said formally.

"Jack, really," Bessie sighed as she pulled the man into a hug. She'd known Jack Hooper since childhood and she still thought of him as the freckle-faced, ginger-haired boy who'd eaten biscuits in her kitchen. To the Quayle family, he was Jonathan, a classically trained butler who continued to impress them.

"Is Mum here?" Elizabeth asked.

"Mrs. Quayle is at home, but she's speaking with the Chief

Constable at the moment," Jonathan replied. "I took tea and biscuits to them a short time ago."

"So she'll know what's happened by the time he leaves," Elizabeth said. "What about Daddy?"

"Your father had a meeting in Douglas about the new retail park. I believe the Chief Constable is going to try to speak to him in his office there once he leaves here," Jonathan replied.

Bessie could see the suppressed curiosity in the butler's eyes, but there was no way that she could satisfy it.

"Is Andy in the kitchen?" Elizabeth asked next.

"Mr. Caine arrived here about half an hour ago with a number of shopping bags. He's been in the kitchen ever since," Jonathan confirmed.

Elizabeth nodded. "And is the chef very upset?"

"I believe Mr. Caine told her that you'd suggested that she have a night off. He said something about her working too hard lately and deserving a night for herself."

Elizabeth giggled. "He's very clever, is Andy," she told Bessie.

Bessie nodded. Before she could speak, she heard voices in the corridor behind them.

"Thank you again," the Chief Constable was saying as he and Mary walked into the foyer. "I appreciate your time. I'll head down to Douglas now to speak to George."

Mary nodded. "He'll be as shocked and upset as I am, of course, but you know George. He may well seem pleased by the sad news."

The Chief Constable nodded. "In his place, it's entirely possible that I'd be pleased as well."

Mary smiled tightly and then watched as the man turned and walked away. Jonathan followed, opening the door to let the Chief Constable out.

"Are you okay?" Elizabeth asked her mother as the door swung shut behind the police officer.

"I've been better," Mary said flatly. "But how are you? You found the body. It must have been horrible for both of you."

Bessie glanced at Jonathan, who was clearly listening intently. "Maybe we should go and see how Andy is doing," she suggested.

Jonathan frowned at her. "Things were just getting interesting," he whispered in a voice that only Bessie could hear.

She winked at him. "You'll hear the whole story soon," she promised.

He nodded and then disappeared into the house.

"We shouldn't talk about anything in front of the staff, should we?" Mary asked.

"I'm sure the local news will have something about what's happened soon, but for now I think John would prefer if we kept things as quiet as possible," Bessie replied.

"Let's go and talk in the kitchen, then," Mary suggested. "Andy has given the entire kitchen staff the rest of the day off, with my blessing, of course. I know whatever he's making will be much nicer than what our chef was planning."

"And we can talk freely there," Elizabeth said.

The trio made their way down the corridor towards the kitchen. Bessie took several deep breaths, her mouth watering, as she smelled whatever it was that Andy was preparing in the kitchen.

"Something smells good in here," Elizabeth said as they walked into the kitchen.

"Just trying out a few new recipes for the restaurant," Andy replied. "After everything that happened today, I felt the need to be creative tonight."

Elizabeth gave him a hug and then, as he moved to stir something, she turned and hugged her mother tightly.

"Was it very awful?" Mary asked in a low voice.

"It was pretty bad," Elizabeth replied. "At first, I thought it was a squatter, sleeping, and that was upsetting enough, but when the body rolled back and I saw the knife, well, that was terrible. A moment later, I recognised the victim, too, which made things even worse."

"I hate to ask, but who was he?" Andy said.

Bessie looked at him for a minute. "Were you already away at culinary school when he disappeared?" she asked.

Andy shrugged. "I can't answer that, as I don't know who he was."

"Sorry," Bessie said with a rueful grin. "He was Grant Robertson. He worked in banking on the island for many years, retiring as head of one of the banks. Then he began investing in local companies. He was incredibly wealthy, and it wasn't until he disappeared that the police were able to prove that most of his wealth had come through dishonest means."

"He was Daddy's partner on a number of different projects," Elizabeth added. "Daddy was supposed to be retired. Grant promised that he'd do all of the work if Daddy invested, but then Grant ran away and left Daddy with tons of work and lots of very worried business associates. Many people refused to believe that Daddy hadn't know what Grant was doing, and the police even investigated Daddy for months and months. It was awful."

Andy frowned. "Some of this sounds familiar, but I didn't really pay that much attention to the story. I was still trying to come to grips with the idea that I'd inherited a good deal of money and that I could finally go to culinary school. The things that Grant did didn't impact me in any way."

"You were one of the lucky ones, then," Bessie said. "There are thousands of people on the island who lost money to Grant."

"And thus, thousands of suspects in his murder?" Andy asked.

"But who even knew he was here?" Mary wondered. "And why was he here, for that matter?"

"He must have had a reason for coming back," Bessie said. "Surely, doing so was incredibly dangerous for him. The police reckoned that he left the island with more than enough money to buy a little house somewhere and live comfortably. Why risk that to come back to the island?"

"Maybe he didn't have as much money as everyone thought," Andy said. "Maybe he came back to get money or something else that he'd left behind."

"Just before he left, he told me that he'd been planning his escape for some time," Bessie replied. "I can't believe he'd left anything behind."

"Scott had to know he was back," Mary said quietly.

"Scott?" Andy repeated.

"Scott Meyers. He was Grant's advocate. He worked for Grant, and only for Grant, for thirty years or more. I never believed him when he said that he didn't know where Grant had gone, and I'm certain Grant will have told Scott that he was coming back, as well," Mary told him.

"That has to make Scott the main suspect," Elizabeth said.

Mary shrugged. "Maybe. I don't care for Scott, but I'm not sure I can see him as a murderer."

"So who can you see as the murderer?" Andy asked.

Mary looked at him and then slowly shook her head. "That's an impossible question. There are probably thousands of people on the island who were cheated out of money by Grant Robertson. They all had a motive, but none of them could have known that Grant was here. He was a criminal and a horrible person, but I will admit that Grant was smart, smart enough to avoid getting caught coming back to the island."

"So whoever killed him must have been someone that he trusted," Elizabeth suggested. "Scott Meyers, for example."

Mary frowned. "I've never cared for Scott, but he was very good to your father during all of the difficulties when Grant disappeared. He did a lot to persuade the police that your father hadn't been involved in any of Grant's illegal schemes."

"Which was only fair, because Daddy never would have done anything illegal," Elizabeth said stoutly.

Mary opened her mouth and then shut it again. After a moment, she sighed. "There must be other suspects beside Scott. Of course, I'm sure George and I will be suspects."

Elizabeth laughed. "As if either of you would do anything like that."

"Your father was certainly incredibly angry at Grant when he disappeared, especially after he'd learned what Grant had been doing," Mary said. "And George made no secret of the fact that he was furious. I'm sure Dan Ross at the newspaper has several quotes from your father about what he'd do to Grant if the man returned to the island."

Bessie winced. George was never shy about expressing his opinion, and Dan Ross would have been more than happy to quote every angry word that George had said.

"Richard will keep Daddy out of the papers," Elizabeth said confidently.

"Richard is off the island," Mary told her. "I've not been terribly impressed with the associates he's left running the firm in his absence, either. He's brought several men and women over from the UK in the last six months or so. I'm afraid they don't know enough about the island and how it differs from the UK to be useful to us under the current circumstances."

Bessie frowned. "Everything is going to be okay," she told her friend. "Things might get awkward again for a few days, but once the police arrest the killer, they will calm down very quickly."

"I just hope the police can solve the case in a few days," Mary replied. "I can't help but feel as if it's going to be a very complicated investigation."

Bessie nodded. There was little doubt in her mind that Mary was right about that.

"Everything is just about ready," Andy announced. "I've done three different choices, but only two portions of each option. I hope everyone will be able to find something they'll enjoy."

"We can always share portions if we want to try more than one thing," Bessie said. "I always love everything you prepare, though, so I don't really mind what I get."

Elizabeth nodded. "You know I'll eat anything you make," she told Andy.

A few minutes later they were all sitting around the small table in the corner of the room. Bessie had small helpings of each of the three choices. Mary and Elizabeth had each chosen two different options and Andy had a plate full of various bits and pieces that had been left over after the other plates had been filled.

"Everything is delicious," Bessie said after a moment.

"The chicken dish is wonderful," Mary said. "It should definitely go on the menu when you open your restaurant."

"I'm not sure about the beef option," Andy said thoughtfully. "It's not come out exactly the way I'd expected."

"It isn't my favourite," Bessie admitted. "But it's still better than anything I could have made."

"But would you order it at a restaurant?" Andy asked.

Bessie took another bite and then slowly shook her head. "No, probably not, even though it is good. I simply like the other two options more."

Andy nodded. "I think the sauce on the chicken worked well and I think the pork tenderloin came out very nicely. They're both on the short list for the restaurant." He sighed. "Of course, I still need to find a location and do a thousand other things before I even start on the menu."

"I thought you were considering a space in George's new retail park," Bessie said, trying to remember what she'd heard.

"That's probably going to take rather longer than I want to wait," Andy replied, looking down at the table.

"Which simply means that he'll have to open his second restaurant in the retail park once it's built," Elizabeth said. She reached over and patted Andy's hand. "It's all good."

He looked up at her and smiled.

Bessie could see how much the pair cared for one another. She looked over at Mary, who was beaming at the couple, clearly delighted that they were so happy together.

"The weather has been very odd for April," Bessie said, determined to keep the conversation light for the remainder of the evening.

Elizabeth insisted on driving Bessie home after dinner.

"I wish I knew where Daddy was," she said with a sigh as she stopped her car in the parking area next to Bessie's cottage. "I was hoping you could talk to him about Grant's murder."

"Maybe another time," Bessie said, hoping that other time would never arrive. George was loud and boisterous, and Bessie preferred to spend as little time with the man as possible. It wasn't that she disliked him, just that she didn't really enjoy his company.

"I'll have him ring you," Elizabeth said as Bessie reached for the handle on the door.

"Great," she muttered as she climbed out of the car.

She crossed to her door and then waved to Elizabeth, who was clearly waiting to see that Bessie was safely inside before she was going to drive away.

Bessie let herself into her cottage and then locked the door behind herself. Sighing, she switched on the lights and then looked at the answering machine. Of course, it was flashing frantically. No doubt half of the island had rung to find out what Bessie knew about the goings-on at the Looney house. Bessie was halfway through listening and deleting messages when someone knocked on her door.

Frowning, Bessie crossed the room while debating with herself about opening the door. It was only eight o'clock, but it was dark and she wasn't expecting any visitors. Another knock, this one loud and rather insistent, had her grabbing her mobile phone. She dialled 999 but didn't push the call button. Instead, she cautiously opened her door.

"George? This is a surprise," she said.

"Bessie, you have to help me," George replied.

CHAPTER 5

"Come in," Bessie said almost instinctively, as she took a step backwards.

George rushed into the room and then stopped short and looked around. "Have I ever been here before?" he asked. "It's smaller than I remember."

"I'm not certain that you have been here before," Bessie replied, trying to recall.

"It hardly matters. I'm here now, and you have to help me."

"Let me put the kettle on. I think you could do with a cuppa."

George nodded. "Or some gin."

"I'm afraid I don't have any gin."

George frowned. "Tea will have to do, then."

"Sit down," Bessie told him. "It won't take long for the kettle to boil."

While she waited for the kettle, Bessie piled some biscuits onto a plate. She set it in the centre of the table at which George was sitting, looking uncomfortable. "Help yourself," she told him, handing him a smaller plate for his selections.

George put the plate on the table and then stared at the biscuits as if unable to decide what he wanted. The kettle boiled and Bessie quickly made tea for two. When she sat down across from George, having put the teacups on the table, he was still staring at the biscuits.

"Are you okay?" Bessie asked.

George looked up at her and then slowly shook his head. "You found the body," he said in a strained voice. "And my baby girl, she was there. She saw Grant dead with a knife stuck in his heart."

For a moment Bessie was concerned that George knew more than he should have about the crime scene. His next words put her mind at ease.

"The Chief Constable told me everything," he said in a dull voice. "He probably shouldn't have. Inspector Rockwell wasn't very happy that I knew as much as I did."

Bessie frowned. The Chief Constable had a history of telling George too much. He'd also warned Grant when John had started his investigation into the man's business interests, which had given Grant the opportunity to plan his escape. Bessie had hoped that the Chief Constable had learned something from his past indiscretions, but it didn't seem as if he had.

"Elizabeth is coping very well," Bessie assured him.

George nodded. "She's pretty tough, really. She's a lot like her mother in that regard. She looks fragile, but she's strong when she needs to be. It isn't as if this is the first time she's found a dead body, either."

Bessie grimaced. "That's true," she said with a sigh.

"Anyway, I'm in a terrible predicament and I didn't know where to turn. Then I thought of you. I know you can help me."

"What's wrong?" Bessie asked, suddenly worried.

George glanced around the room and then slid forward in his seat. He leaned as close to Bessie as he could and then whispered loudly. "I knew Grant was back on the island."

Bessie was sure that she looked as stunned as she felt. "You knew Grant was back on the island?" she repeated, unable to process what George had said.

"I did. He rang me a few weeks ago and told me he was coming back."

63

"You should have rung the police," Bessie said.

"But Grant begged me not to, you see. He told me that everything that had happened was all just a big misunderstanding. According to Grant, the real criminal behind everything was his advocate, Scott Meyers. Grant told me that Scott was the one who'd stolen all the money and that he'd been clever enough to frame Grant for everything."

"Surely you didn't believe him."

George sighed. "I didn't know what to believe. Grant and I had known each other for years. I truly hated the idea that he was a criminal and that I'd never suspected anything. I've never been terribly fond of Scott Meyers, though."

"But Grant confessed to everything when he spoke to me before he left," Bessie said. "I told you everything that he said, remember?"

"Yes, but he told me that he'd only done that because he felt he'd had no choice. He'd found out what was happening and he'd confronted Scott. Scott had shown him everything he'd done, all the fabricated evidence against Grant, and told Grant that the only thing he could do was flee. He set up the getaway boat and everything for Grant. He let Grant take enough money with him to get himself a small house and to live quietly for the rest of his life."

"If that were true, and I don't believe it for a minute, that still doesn't explain why he confessed to all those crimes when he talked to me."

"Scott gave him access to a bank account that would pay his living expenses, but he made Grant agree to confess to everything before he left. That way Scott would be in the clear, you see. Grant agreed to take the blame in exchange for access to that bank account."

"So why come back?" Bessie wondered.

"Grant told me that his conscience wouldn't let him stay away any longer. He felt guilty for what he'd done to me, leaving me to deal with all those businesses that we'd agreed to help, and he felt terrible about living off of money that he knew had been stolen by Scott. He'd decided to come back and confront Scott, even if it meant that he'd be spending the rest of his life in prison."

"Surely it would have made more sense for him to contact the police and tell them the whole story."

"Maybe, but Grant wanted to do things his own way. He wanted to confront Scott and make sure that Scott knew that he wasn't afraid of him anymore."

Bessie shook her head. None of what George was saying made any sense, but she could almost accept that he'd believed it. George was a genius at making money, but sometimes she thought he wasn't very smart.

"What do I do now?" George demanded.

"When did you see Grant last?" Bessie asked.

"Just before he left the island," George said, looking confused.

"So you didn't see him once he came back?"

"No, I didn't. He rang me several weeks ago to tell me he was coming, but he hadn't made his travel plans yet. He told me that he'd ring me before he came across. I was going to help him find a safe place to stay."

Which would have been illegally assisting a wanted man, Bessie thought. She bit her tongue. There was no point in scolding George. "And he never rang you back?"

"He did. He rang about a fortnight ago and told me he was going to be on the last ferry that night. I offered to meet him at the ferry terminal, but he told me that he had everything arranged and that it would be best if I didn't know where he was staying."

"Did you hear from him again after that?"

"He rang again the next day. He told me that he was on the island and that he was working on arranging to speak to Scott. I told him to make sure that they met in a public place, as it would be safer, but he just laughed and reminded me that he would be arrested if he appeared in public. We never spoke again after that."

"Did you try to ring him?"

"I did, actually," George admitted, sounding slightly sheepish. "A few days later, I rang the number that he'd rung me from the last time I'd spoken to him. No one answered." He looked down at the table and then took a sip of tea.

"There's something else you aren't telling me," Bessie said.

George nodded. "About a week ago, I rang Scott Meyers. I asked him if he'd heard anything from Grant. He just laughed and said that he hadn't spoken to Grant since he'd left the island, and that if Grant did try to contact him, he'd simply turn him over to the police."

"And did you believe him?"

George shrugged. "I've no idea what to believe. I thought I knew Grant. We were friends when we were young and I thought I knew him and could trust him. I wanted to believe what he said about Scott, I really did. I may have let that colour my judgment."

"If there was any truth in anything that Grant told you, that has to make Scott the most likely suspect for Grant's murder."

"That's what I was thinking," George agreed. "If Grant was telling me the truth, Scott had a strong motive for wanting Grant dead."

"You have to tell the police everything you just told me," Bessie said firmly.

George looked surprised. "The police? But I've already told them everything I told you. I talked to both the Chief Constable and Inspector Rockwell and I told them both everything."

Bessie frowned. "So what are you so concerned about?"

"I told the police everything. I needed to do that. But I haven't told Mary any of this. She's going to be furious with me when she finds out that I heard from Grant and didn't tell her. How can I tell Mary and not upset her?"

Sighing, Bessie sat back in her seat. "I'm not sure you can tell Mary without upsetting her," she said after a minute.

George shook his head. "You don't understand. Mary is my whole world." He sighed and sat back in his chair. "I'm going to bore you now, but you need to understand. I can't lose her, and when she finds out that I kept this from her, she might be angry enough to leave me."

"You should be having this conversation with Mary," Bessie said.

"We met in the sixties," George said, seemingly ignoring Bessie's words. "I'd been in the UK for a few years, running various businesses with varying degrees of success. I'd had a few girlfriends, but nothing serious. I felt as if I was waiting for someone special. I started a secondhand car dealership, and it turned out I was pretty good at selling cars. I hired a few more salesmen and then I decided that I needed a pretty girl at the front desk. A pretty girl in a short skirt could bring in a lot of business, so I put an advert in the papers. I had a dozen applicants, but I only interviewed two of them: Mary and some girl who was called Betty or something like that."

"You don't remember?"

George laughed. "She even got the job," he said. "She worked for me for two or three years, sitting at reception, flirting with every man who came in to look at cars. She was very good for the business, actually, and she was much smarter than she ever let on to the customers. I'm sure she was called Betty. She ended up marrying one of men who'd come in to buy a car. He was a very successful businessman and the last I heard they were very happy together."

"And Mary didn't get the job?"

"No, she didn't. I knew, as soon as I saw her, that she was the only woman in the world for me. She isn't beautiful, but she was beautiful to me. I could tell that she was terrified, talking to me, but she made herself smile and laugh at my jokes. She had a steel core, even though I could see that she was painfully shy and a little bit insecure."

"You seem to be opposites in many ways," Bessie said.

George nodded. "I'm good at making money. I can sell just about anything to just about anybody. I'm also aware of my weaknesses, though. I'm not very smart." He stopped and looked away. "I can't believe I just said that out loud. It took me years to admit it to myself and I've never admitted it to another person, aside from Mary, of course."

"You're smart enough to have made a considerable fortune."

"I wish I could take the credit, but, really, I'm just smart enough to surround myself with other, smarter people," George told her. "Mary was the first, though. I could tell the day we met that she was smart. Not just average smart, either, but brilliantly smart. I fell madly in love with her, but I also realised that she was going to be incredibly useful to me, which sounds awful, doesn't it?"

"You fell in love with her, though."

"I did, and I still love her just as much today as I ever did, more, really, because we've built an amazing life together. She's been my inspiration and she's also been my sounding board. I tell her everything that I'm thinking of doing and she tells me whether it's a good idea or not. I don't always take her advice, but I'm always sorry when I don't."

"And you didn't take her advice about Grant?"

George flushed. "She never cared for Grant. I should have known better than to trust him, really, just because of that, but I met Grant years before I met Mary. We'd worked together at the bank on the island and he'd helped me with some of my earliest business ventures. He got the bank to lend me money when they probably shouldn't have and he got me very favourable interest rates, as well. I wouldn't have been able to start my first business if it weren't for Grant."

"So you trusted him."

"I did trust him. We didn't see much of each other when I lived across. I still did all of my banking through the bank here on the island, but I mostly dealt with Grant by phone. He came across once in a while and we sometimes had lunch or dinner, but it wasn't often."

"And you didn't include Mary in those meetings?"

"No," George mumbled, looking away again. "I was pretty certain that she wouldn't like Grant, so I never introduced them to one another. They didn't actually meet until we moved to the island. By that time, Grant was retired, and I imagined that we'd meet to play golf together once in a while or maybe have lunch, but nothing more."

"It didn't work out that way, though."

"No, not at all. As soon as Mary and I were settled, Grant started ringing to talk about different schemes in which he was investing. He kept encouraging me to join him in this one or that one and, after a while, I yielded to temptation and put some money into one of the businesses with which he was working. Within a few months, I found myself tangled up in dozens of Grant's projects."

"Why?"

George blinked at her. "Why?"

"Why keep saying yes?"

"It was complicated. I wasn't enjoying being retired, and Grant knew that. He kept reminding me, every time we spoke, that I was bored at home. The first few projects I joined in with were simply to give me something to do, really. Once I'd committed to those, though, Grant kept finding new things. Grant was very persuasive and he knew exactly how to get me to agree."

Bessie wondered if there had been an element of blackmail in any of this, but she didn't want to ask.

"Anyway, Mary was furious, of course. We'd come to the island to enjoy my retirement and now I was working more than I ever had. She didn't like Grant and she didn't think most of his projects were smart investments, either. For the first time in many years, I was investing in things without discussing them with Mary first, and I know that I made some very bad choices. I was scrambling to keep everything going, even hiring my son to help handle the workload. Then Grant disappeared."

"And everyone discovered what he'd been doing."

"Yes, and everyone thought that I'd been involved or at least known what he'd been doing." George sighed. "I said it before, but it bears repeating. Sometimes I'm not very smart. I should have realised that Grant was far more financially successful than he should have been. I should have asked him where all of the money he had came from. I should have done a lot of things differently. I thought I knew him. I thought we were friends. I thought I could trust him."

"A lot of other people trusted him, too. That was part of the problem."

"Yes, of course, but once he'd vanished, I was the one who had to deal with the mess he'd left behind. We'd made commitments to dozens of businesses here on the island and also further afield. When Grant left, he took his share of the funding with him. Suddenly, I had to find a lot more money to help out businesses, some of which I didn't even know I'd agreed to assist."

"Oh, dear."

"Mary was beside herself, really. She went across to visit some family, and I really thought she wasn't going to come back. I finally went over and begged her to give me another chance. We sat down together and went over every deal that I'd made through Grant. She found ways to make everything work, even when I was certain we were going to lose everything. We would have lost everything if it weren't for her."

"I'm glad it all worked out for you."

"It was a very difficult time. Many of our friends stopped speaking to us because they believed that I was a part of what Grant had done. Mary wanted to move back to the UK for a long while. It was only after she found Thie yn Traie that she agreed to stay on the island."

"I hadn't realised that," Bessie said, grateful that her friend had found the mansion that she and George now called home.

"Anyway, it took ages for us to recover from everything that had happened. Things were settling back down though. Mary and I were happier than we'd been in years. Elizabeth has finally found a wonderful young man and something to do with her life. Our sons are both doing well, as are the grandchildren. I've finally been able to give more responsibility to my son so that I can work fewer hours every week. Mary and I were even talking about taking a long holiday somewhere, maybe to the US, as we've never been there."

"And then Grant rang."

"Exactly," George sighed. "He rang my mobile. As I said before, he told me that Scott had set him up and that he was innocent of any wrongdoing. I didn't want to believe him, but he was very convincing."

"You should have spoken to Mary and to the police immediately. If Grant were telling the truth, the police would have been able to find proof."

"Grant made me promise not to tell anyone that he'd rung. He was worried that Scott would hear that he was coming back. He told me that he was afraid Scott would kill him if he returned to the island."

"And then someone murdered him."

"Exactly. And when the police arrest Scott, the whole story will come out and Mary will discover that I was keeping things from her again. I promised her, when everything went wrong, that I wouldn't do that anymore."

"You have to tell her."

"I was wondering if you and Mary wouldn't like to go away for a long holiday. Have you ever been to Australia? I've heard it's a very interesting place to visit. I'd happily pay for you and Mary to go for a few months."

"Australia?" Bessie repeated. "I don't think so."

"America? Canada? New Zealand? Where would you like to go? I'll pay, of course, as long as you take Mary with you and keep her away until things have settled down here."

"You can't send Mary away. You have to tell her what happened."

"I can't tell her. What if she leaves me? I can't live without her."

"Maybe you should have thought of that before you kept Grant's return a secret from her," Bessie suggested.

George nodded grimly. "Of course I should have told her at the time, but I was trying to be a loyal friend to Grant. He was convinced that his life was going to be in danger when he returned. I was trying to protect him."

"I still don't understand why he was coming back."

"He wanted to clear his name. I think he wanted his old life back, really."

"There was an awful lot of evidence against him."

"But Scott could have fabricated all of it. According to Grant, the only thing he was guilty of was trusting Scott too much."

"Don't forget that Grant confessed to me. He was very convincing."

"Because he felt as if he had to be, not because it was all true."

"You sound as if you really believed Grant."

"I wanted to believe Grant," George said with a sigh. "I wanted him to come back and clear his name. After everything that had happened, it would have been enormously satisfying if everyone had had to admit that Grant was innocent."

"But did you believe him?" Bessie asked.

George looked at her for a minute and then slowly shrugged. "I didn't know what to believe. He said he was bringing evidence with

71

him that would prove that Scott was the one behind everything criminal that had happened."

"What sort of evidence? Why didn't he just produce his evidence when he found out he was being investigated before he left? None of this makes any sense."

"I suppose you're right. I suppose I simply wanted to believe him, so I did. He asked me to keep his return a secret for his protection. I should have rung Inspector Rockwell and I should have told Mary. Now I've made a terrible mess of everything."

"Did you tell anyone that he was coming back?" Bessie asked.

"No, not really."

"Not really?"

"I may have mentioned it to my advocate, Richard Hart, but only in passing."

"Anyone else?"

"My assistant, Carolyn, may have overhead some of the conversations, either with Grant or with Richard."

"How long has Carolyn worked for you?"

"Nine, no, maybe ten years now. She worked in my office across and then I hired her to help me make the transition from working across to being retired on the island. She moved here just before Mary and I came. She helped us find the house in Douglas and did many other jobs for us, and then she went back across to help wrap up all of my business concerns there. By the time that was done, things were getting busy here with Grant's projects, so she came back over here to help me with them. She's been my son Michael's assistant more than mine, really, for the last year or two."

"Michael is the one who works for you?"

"Yes, Junior works for one of the insurance companies on the island. He's very happy where he is and not at all interested in working for me. Michael had been working in banking when we all lived across, but he had some difficulties finding work here on the island. I offered him the job with me as things grew increasingly complicated with Grant and he's been working for me ever since."

"Doing what?"

"Oh, everything. I'm training him to take over for me, really, hope-fully soon. Since Grant left, I've been working on cutting back on my business investments. For a year or more, Michael and I were both working forty or fifty hours a week to keep on top of everything, but now I'm only working a few hours each day. Michael is still doing forty hours a week, but things have slowed down for him, too. Carolyn helps him much more than she helps me these days."

"Did you tell Michael when Grant contacted you?"

"No, but I can't promise that Carolyn didn't tell him. As I said, I'm pretty sure she overheard at least one of the phone conversations. She was probably upset to hear the news, too. She knew just how much trouble Grant had caused me, of course."

"So she might have told Michael?"

"She might have."

"And she might have told a dozen other people, including Scott Meyers."

George looked shocked. "She wouldn't have done that." He frowned and sat back in his seat. "I can't be certain what she might have overheard. I just remember her being in the room during one of the conversations that I had with Grant. She may not have heard Grant making his accusations against Scott. I'd hate to think that she told him that Grant was coming, though. Scott might have murdered Grant and it might be my fault that he knew Grant was here."

Bessie swallowed a sigh. George was right about one thing, anyway: he wasn't very smart. "I hope you told the police all of this."

"I may have forgotten to mention that Carolyn may have over-heard one of my conversations with Grant," he said sheepishly. "I believe I told them that I didn't tell anyone about Grant."

"I'll ring John. You need to tell him."

"Now?"

"The sooner the better, I think."

George glanced at the clock. "Maybe he could come here to talk to me. And maybe he could take his time driving over. Mary should be going to bed before too much longer."

Bessie made a face as she picked up the phone. Spending time with

George was exhausting. She'd been hoping that he'd head for home soon.

She tried the nonemergency number for the station first, but the call was transferred to the Douglas constabulary, as the Laxey station didn't have reception staff on duty after six. Reluctantly, she rang John's mobile number.

"John, it's Bessie. I've just been having a lovely chat with George Quayle and he's remembered a few things that I thought you should know."

John sighed deeply. "I spent two hours talking with George today. I thought I was very thorough in my questioning."

"We've been talking about who else might have known that Grant was coming back to the island. George has just remembered that his assistant, Carolyn, might have overheard one of the conversations he had with Grant."

"Just remembered or just made up," John muttered. "What's Carolyn's surname?"

"George, what's Carolyn's surname?"

He blinked several times. "She's Carolyn White. Sorry, I had to think about that for a minute. I never call her anything other than Carolyn."

"I'm going to send a car to collect George and bring him to the station," John said. "Under the circumstances, I want to do everything strictly by the book. Please tell him that I'll have a car there for him in the next ten minutes or so."

"John's going to send a car for you. He wants to talk to you at the station."

"But what about my car? I drove myself here."

"You can leave it outside my cottage for now," Bessie assured him. "I'm sure that John will have someone bring you back again."

"I will," John confirmed.

George nodded. "I do hope that Carolyn didn't say anything to Scott Meyers. I'd hate to think that I did something that contributed to Grant's death."

Bessie heard John sigh again. "It's all turning into something of a nightmare," she suggested.

"You can say that again. We've far too many suspects and plenty of motives. Now it seems as if there may have been a number of people who knew that Grant was on the island, as well. It's a good thing we're already planning a gathering for tomorrow night. I think we need to talk through everything."

"I'm looking forward to it."

"You never rang me after Elizabeth drove you home from the Looney mansion. Was anything said that can't wait for tomorrow night?"

"I don't think so," Bessie replied, trying to think back to the conversation that seemed to have taken place a long time earlier.

"I'll see you tomorrow, then" John said.

She put the phone down and smiled sympathetically at George. "I'm sorry you're going to have to talk to the police again."

"I'm not," George told her. "I hope Inspector Rockwell takes his time. Mary will be in bed after ten, at least."

Bessie glanced at the clock. It seemed likely, knowing how thorough John liked to be, that George would be out well past ten. "You'll have to talk to her in the morning, then. The sooner the better, really."

"I suppose you're right," he sighed. "She's going to be furious."

A knock kept Bessie from having to reply. She opened the door to the uniformed constable. George was already on his feet, seemingly eager to go. He gave Bessie an awkward hug before he left.

"I was trying to protect her, really," he said in a low voice. "She hated Grant. I thought she would be happier not knowing that he was coming back."

Bessie bit her tongue and then watched as the constable led George out to his car. As they drove away, Bessie shut her door and locked it.

CHAPTER 6

*B*essie tidied up the kitchen and then headed for the stairs, still thinking about George and Mary. She'd never understood how the marriage between two such opposite personalities worked. Now she was concerned that the pair might end up separating over George's behaviour. From everything that George had said, Scott Meyers seemed to have had a very strong motive for Grant's murder. As Bessie slid under her duvet, she wondered if the police would have Scott behind bars before breakfast.

After her shower the next morning, she switched on the radio, something she rarely did. It was tuned to a local station and she was eager to catch the local news to see if any arrests had been made overnight. The reporter seemed very excited to break the news of exactly whose body had been found, something Bessie hadn't realised hadn't been released previously, but otherwise, he didn't have anything new to share. Bessie washed the last of her toast down with some tea and then headed out for her morning walk.

The holiday cottages were still empty, but Bessie knew that some guests were booked for the upcoming weekend, including her friend Andrew Cheatham. She glanced into a few of the cottages as she walked. The owners, Thomas and Maggie Shimmin, had been working all hours to get them ready for their first guests. Thomas had been ill for much of the winter, which meant they'd fallen behind schedule. Now, though, as Bessie glanced through sliding doors into each cottage, every one looked freshly painted and spotlessly clean. When she reached the last cottage, she looked away.

The last cottage hadn't been painted and wouldn't be used for guests this season. After a terrible accident and a murder had taken place there, Maggie and Thomas had decided to tear down the existing cottage and replace it with a larger one. While they'd been waiting for planning permission, a second man had been murdered in the cottage. Bessie knew that when permission for the larger cottage had been denied, the pair had gone back to the drawing board to try to work out the best thing to do with the cottage that everyone considered uninhabitable.

When Bessie reached the stairs to Thie yn Traie, she hesitated. It was cool, almost cold, on the beach and she thought about turning back. That there was a gathering planned for the evening kept her walking, though. Whenever she and her friends met to discuss a case, they always ate too much delicious food, which always seemed to include a pudding. Bessie knew she needed the extra exercise that a longer walk would give her.

She walked about half of the distance between Thie yn Traie and the new houses that had been built on the beach in the past year. That was far enough for now, she decided. Another walk later in the day would probably be a good idea, though. Turning for home, she found herself watching the waves as she tried to work out who might have killed Grant Robertson.

"Bessie? Hello." A loud voice cut through the quiet morning.

Forcing a smile onto her lips, Bessie turned towards Maggie Shimmin, who was marching down the beach towards her. "Good morning, Maggie," she said.

"Good morning. Although it isn't a good morning for your friend George Quayle, is it?" Maggie demanded, a small smirk on her lips.

"No? Is something wrong with George? I hadn't heard."

Maggie smiled. There was nothing she liked better than gossip, and she truly loved knowing things that other people didn't. "He spent the night at the police station," she told Bessie. "I thought you would know, since he was collected from your cottage."

Bessie swallowed a sigh. "I didn't realise he'd spent the night."

"He's still there, last I heard. My friend, Jane, lives near the station and she saw them taking George in last night right after Inspector Rockwell arrived. She's been watching for him to come out ever since."

Bessie knew Jane, too. She was another woman who thrived on gossiping about others. "Maybe George left through the back," Bessie suggested.

Maggie frowned. "Jane would have seen the car, anyway," she said after a moment.

"Doesn't Jane ever sleep?" Bessie wondered.

"She's a very light sleeper. She would have woken up if a car had started anywhere near the station."

"So you think Inspector Rockwell is still at the station, too?"

"He must be."

Bessie was very tempted to pull out her mobile and ring John, just to ask if he truly had spent the entire night at the station, questioning George. Instead, she changed the subject. "But how are you?" she asked Maggie.

"Mustn't complain," Maggie replied. "My back has been bothering me again, but the doctors don't seem to know what to do about it. They keep giving me different tablets to try, but none of them seem to help for more than a day or two. Thomas is finally feeling better, so what does he do? Goes off on a short holiday with one of his mates from school, that's what he does. They've gone across for three days to play golf or some such thing. Can you imagine? We've guests arriving on Saturday and I'm on my own, trying to get every last-minute thing done."

"That wasn't very kind of Thomas," Bessie said, feeling surprised that the man had done something that seemed out of character for him.

"He and his friend had been planning the trip for the last year and a half," Maggie admitted. "Thomas was determined to get well enough to go, and after everything he'd been through, I didn't have the heart to tell him that he couldn't go. I'm off to Ibiza with a few of my friends next month, anyway. I'll be going for an entire week and Thomas will have to deal with everything here by himself."

"You'll be a good deal busier in a month, too," Bessie remarked.

Maggie shrugged. "It's still stressful, trying to get everything ready on my own."

"I was looking at the cottages as I walked this morning. It's amazing how much better they all look with their fresh coat of paint. What else needs doing?"

"Not a lot," Maggie admitted. "I'll give each one a quick dust and polish before the first guests arrive. Otherwise, I think they're ready."

"And when does Thomas get back?"

"Tomorrow. He'll be here to help for a lot of the last-minute things, I suppose."

Bessie nodded. "That's nice for you."

"Well, the cottages were his idea, after all. He was meant to do all of the work, really."

Bessie knew that usually Thomas did the vast majority of the work involved with keeping the cottages running and the guests happy. Maggie had had to do a bit more when Thomas had fallen ill, but as far as Bessie could tell, Maggie complained more than she worked.

"We've been talking again, me and Thomas, about that last cottage," Maggie said.

"Oh?"

"Since we can't get planning permission to build a larger cottage in its place, we were thinking about tearing it down and replacing it with a smaller one."

"A smaller one?"

"Yes, but a very special smaller cottage. It would be a couples-only cottage with a fancy jetted tub, maybe even heart-shaped. It would have a single bedroom with a king-sized bed in it. We were thinking of advertising it for honeymoons and wedding anniversaries and that sort of thing."

"I'm not sure how many people want to honeymoon on Laxey Beach, but you may find it easier to get planning permission for that than you did for the larger cottage."

"That's what we were thinking." Maggie blushed. "We were thinking maybe we could stay in the new cottage once in a while, too. I'd love to have a jetted tub and a king-sized bed, but Thomas doesn't think we need those sorts of luxuries at home."

"I'm sure you know that I didn't object to your previous planning application. I can't imagine objecting to this one, either."

Maggie nodded. "We know who objected," she said darkly. "People who live in the village, nowhere near the beach, shouldn't be allowed to object, in my opinion, but the planning committee didn't ask me for my opinion."

"It is a public beach," Bessie replied.

"But never mind all of that," Maggie said. "I can't believe that Grant Robertson came back to the island, not after everyone had discovered what he'd done."

Bessie nodded. "It's difficult to imagine why he'd returned."

"He must have run out of stolen money and come back for more. I wonder if he knew that most of his property was auctioned off to repay the people he'd stolen from?"

"He must have known. I'm sure he must have kept up with island news, wherever he was in the world."

"George Quayle probably kept him informed. I'm sure the two stayed in touch. That's probably why he's been kept at the police station all this time. He must be the chief suspect, wouldn't you think?"

"I'm sure there are a number of people who had a motive for killing Grant."

"Including me and Thomas," Maggie said. "He stole some money from our bank accounts, although most of it was repaid after the auction. That's what the advocates said, anyway. We'll never know if we actually got back everything we deserved or not, of course."

"The accounts were audited by two separate firms, and then settlements were made based on their findings. I believe there was a system put into place if you wanted to challenge your settlement."

"To be honest," Maggie said in a low voice, "we hadn't even realised that Grant was taking money out of the account. He'd set it up so that he was stealing fractions of cents from each transaction, but it was so cleverly done that we'd never noticed. I say that because no one else noticed, either, of course. That was how he got away with it for such a long time."

Bessie nodded. "I was just happy that people got most of their money back."

"Yes, we were grateful, of course, but that doesn't mean that we'd forgiven Grant for what he'd done. I wouldn't have murdered him, of course, but if I'd known he was back on the island, I certainly would have enjoyed having a chance to give him a piece of my mind."

"I believe a lot of people felt that way."

"I know you're friends with George and Mary, but you have to admit that George had reasons to fear Grant's return."

"Did he?"

"I'm sure the police did a very thorough investigation into George's business practices once Grant disappeared, but I still find it hard to believe that George didn't know what Grant was doing. What if Grant threatened to tell the police the whole story unless George gave him money?"

"We could speculate all day about who might have had reasons to kill Grant. None of that will get my washing done, though. I'd better get it started."

Maggie frowned. "I have cottages to prepare, anyway. I haven't all day to stand around and chat."

Bessie nodded and took a step forwards, only to stop as again someone shouted her name. She looked up at the stairs to Thie yn Traie and then grinned as she spotted George making his way down them.

"They must have just let him go," Maggie hissed behind her.

"Bessie, my dear, I just had to rush down and thank you," George shouted across the beach. "I had a lovely chat with Inspector Rockwell last night, and then, when I got home, I had a wonderful talk with Mary. She was far more understanding that she should have been, I must say. Anyway, I slept better last night than I have in years, and when I woke up this morning I was determined to find you and thank you before I did anything else today."

"I'm glad I was able to help," Bessie replied.

George pulled her into an awkward hug and then seemed to notice Maggie for the first time.

"Mrs. Shimmin, what a lovely surprise. Are you ready for your busy season? It must be starting soon, mustn't it?"

"Our first guests of the year arrive on Saturday," Maggie replied.

"As soon as that?" George said. "I'll wish you much success again this year, then. Must dash."

He gave Bessie another quick hug and then began the long climb back up the stairs to his mansion home.

Bessie turned to Maggie. "Maybe Jane was mistaken," she suggested.

Maggie flushed. "She mustn't have noticed when George left the station. He probably went out the back and had a car waiting for him." Before Bessie could reply, she spun on her heel and began to walk rapidly back up the beach, slipping and sliding in the soft sand.

Bessie smiled to herself as she continued on her way back to her cottage. She was only a short distance from her door when she spotted the woman standing near her cottage. Frowning, she reached for her mobile phone. It was a public beach, but it was a cool and windy morning, and far too early for casual visitors during the off-season. With her phone in her hand, just in case she needed to ring 999, Bessie continued towards Treoghe Bwaane.

"Oh, I am sorry. I hope I'm not trespassing." The words rushed out as Bessie got close enough to recognise the visitor.

"Susan? Good morning. You aren't trespassing. The beach is a public beach."

Susan Davison looked confused for a moment. "I met you at the house, didn't I? The one that my father owned. I'm sorry, but I've forgotten your name."

"I'm Elizabeth Cubbon, but everyone calls me Bessie."

Susan nodded. "Now I remember. You were very kind to me, sharing everything about my father and his first wife. I'm not entirely sure Valerie Looney was his first wife, though, actually."

"Oh?"

"I'm trying to find out what I can, but it's difficult. My father never talked about his past, ever, and when he died, we didn't find a scrap of paper in the house, aside from a few recent bills."

"He left a will, though?"

"Yes, although he didn't have a copy of it at home. He'd told Ned, my older brother, when he'd had the will made so that we'd know where to find it."

"And his solicitor didn't know anything about his past?"

"He'd only met my father twice. Once when my father came to have the will drawn up and a second time when my father came to sign it. It was about the most basic will imaginable, too. He simply left everything he owned in equal shares to his three children, whom he named. If he hadn't attached a list of his assets, we never would have known about the house on the island at all."

"Was that the only surprise?"

Susan hesitated. "Not exactly."

Bessie looked up at the dark skies and shivered as the wind blew gustily. "Come in for some tea," she suggested. "You can tell me more or not, whichever you prefer. I'm sure you can use a cuppa, either way."

"I would love a cuppa."

Knowing that John wouldn't approve didn't stop Bessie from issuing the invitation. It was highly unlikely that Susan was a suspect in Grant's murder anyway. It wasn't as if she'd known Grant or had any connection to the island.

"Have a seat," Bessie suggested, nodding towards the chairs around the small table in the corner of the kitchen.

"What does it say and what does it mean?" Susan asked, pointing to the small sign just outside the cottage door as she walked into the room. She shut the door behind herself and then looked expectantly at Bessie.

"It says 'Treoghe Bwaane,' which is Manx for Widow's Cottage," Bessie told her.

"Oh, I am sorry," Susan replied as she made her way to the table and slid into a seat.

"I'm not a widow," Bessie replied. "I never married, actually."

"No? I'm not sure that I'll ever marry. It seems a very old-fashioned notion these days. Anyway, I don't know anyone who's happily married. It seems as if it's incredibly hard work for very little reward. I'm not sure I'd trust a man, anyway, not after what my father did."

Bessie nodded as she filled a plate with biscuits. The kettle boiled as she put the plate on the table. "Help yourself," she told the other woman.

Susan picked up a biscuit and nibbled on it as Bessie made the tea. Bessie put the cups on the table and then sat down opposite her guest.

"I assume you spoke to the police," she said tentatively.

"I did. Inspector Rockwell was lovely. I don't suppose he's available?"

"I don't believe so."

Susan sighed. "I shouldn't have even asked, really. As I said, I'm not sure I'd be able to trust anyone, not now that I've learned what I have about my father."

"I'm sure it was all a huge shock."

"Yes, it was. I rang my brothers after I'd spoken to the police. They don't want to believe that our father ever killed anyone, but it seems rather suspicious to me that both of his wives died in identical accidents."

"It is unusual," Bessie agreed.

"I think I told you that he sent us all to boarding school as soon as we were old enough to go. Ned and Neil went at ten and I went when I was eleven. Even when we'd lived at home, though, we didn't have a normal family life. Our father was rarely there. We had a succession of women who looked after us. They weren't exactly nannies, more like housekeepers who also took care of us when we weren't at school.

None of them ever lasted more than a few years, though. Now I wonder what happened to some of them. I wonder if my father killed them."

"Surely it's more likely that they simply found other jobs."

"Maybe, but I'm going to talk to someone with the local police where we formerly lived and suggest that they investigate. As I said before, a lot of the women with whom my father had relationships died in accidents. Some of them may have been genuine, I suppose, but now I'm questioning everything."

"I don't blame you. I don't want to pry, but I'm curious whether you and your brothers inherited anything else you weren't expecting, besides the house on the island?"

"There was a good deal more money than we thought our father should have had," Susan told her. "There was jewellery, women's jewellery. I thought, at the time, that it must have been my mother's, but now I wonder."

"I don't remember Valerie Looney having a great deal of jewellery," Bessie said thoughtfully. "She wore a plain gold wedding band when she was married to Sam. I seem to recall that Gary bought her something fancier, maybe with a diamond or a coloured gemstone in the band, but I could be misremembering."

"I tried to convince my brothers that we should give the house back to the Looney family, but they both refused to consider the idea," Susan sighed. "They both need the money more than I do, of course. I should have expected that, really."

"Whatever happened all those years ago, you and your brothers inherited the house legally," Bessie pointed out.

"But if my father killed Valerie Looney, he shouldn't have ever been allowed to own it."

"The police conducted an investigation at the time. He was never charged with anything."

"When I get home, I'm going to try to find out more about the case. If I end up believing that my father was responsible for Valerie Looney's death, I'll be giving my share of the sale of the house to the remaining Looney children, whatever my brothers think."

Bessie took a sip of her tea. "What do you do back in the UK?" she asked after a moment.

"I'm a teacher, actually. I've been teaching Reception for the past seventeen years, which is probably why I've never wanted children of my own." Susan laughed, but Bessie was pretty sure there was some truth behind her words.

"And what do your brothers do?" she asked next, feeling as if she was being nosy, but too curious to stop herself.

"Ned works for a trucking company, driving the big container lorries all over the UK and abroad. He's often on the Continent, actually, maybe even more than he's in the UK."

"Is he married?"

"He's been married and divorced three times. He has a child with each of his former wives, too, which means a lot of income goes to child maintenance. He was thrilled when I told him what the house here on the island might be worth."

"And Neil?"

"Neil is an artist who waits tables while he waits to be discovered. He and our father had a very difficult relationship, so he was happy to believe that our father killed any number of women. Our father wanted Neil to get a proper job, you see, while Neil just wants to paint. As our father refused to support him in any way, Neil's been waiting tables since he left school, but he doesn't consider that his job."

"And is he married?"

"He's been in and out of a dozen relationships in the past twenty years. None of them last for more than a few weeks, or a month, maybe. I think he was with one woman for six weeks, actually, but that was exceptional. He's just not good at commitment."

Bessie nodded. "Children?"

"Not that he knows of, anyway," Susan replied dryly.

"And you've never married, either?"

"I came close once, right after I'd finished teacher training, actually. He was another teacher at the school where I got my first job, and I thought we were perfect for one another. He proposed on our six-month anniversary and I started planning for a summer wedding. I caught him in the school's storage shed with a supply teacher about a month before the wedding. He told me it was just cold feet. I moved to another job in another town several hours away."

"I'm sorry."

"I'm not. Not really, anyway. With the benefit of hindsight, I can see that I was more in love with the idea of being in love than I ever was with Peter. I'd finished school and taken my first job. Getting married was next on my list of things to do. I was more disappointed that the plans for my life had gone off the track than I was about losing Peter."

"It's probably for the best that you didn't marry him, then."

"Definitely. He's had four wives since I ended things with him, and the last I heard, he was engaged again. My closest friend from teacher training still teaches at that same school with him, you see. She loves keeping me informed."

Bessie laughed. "I can't imagine marrying a man who'd failed at marriage four times previously."

"After things ended with Peter and I realised that my life wasn't necessarily going to go exactly the way I'd planned it, I gave myself some time to think. That's when I decided that I wasn't actually in any hurry to get married. I've been on my own ever since and I'm fairly happy that way."

"I've been on my own my entire life. It suits me."

Susan nodded and glanced around the room. "I have a little house near the school where I teach. Your cottage reminds me of home, actually. My house is full of everything that matters to me and my kitchen is very like yours. It's cosy, if a bit cluttered."

Bessie looked around at the room and shrugged. It didn't seem cluttered to her. It seemed just right.

"But I should be on my way. I came down here to take a walk on the beach, but I wasn't certain if it was allowed."

"As I said, it's a public beach. Even where there are houses, there is a public right of way along the water."

"Excellent. I shall try to get a few miles in, then."

Bessie had never measured the distance of her walks, but now she wondered how far she usually travelled. Miles sounded ambitious, though.

Susan got to her feet and headed for the door. "Do you think that your friends truly do want to buy the house, then?" she asked as she went.

"I'm not sure how they're feeling now, actually. Elizabeth was quite upset about the body."

Susan stopped and turned back around. "The body?" she repeated questioningly.

"You didn't hear?"

"Clearly not."

"After you left, we walked around the entire house. There was a dead man in the master bedroom."

Susan frowned and then slowly crossed back to her chair and sank into it. "A dead man?"

"Yes."

"Is there any way my father had anything to do with it?"

"I can't imagine how. Your father has been dead for over a year, hasn't he?"

"Yes, but, I mean, how long had the body been there?"

"Less than a year, certainly," Bessie told her. "Maybe more than a few days, but less than a month, I believe."

Susan nodded. "Have the police worked out who he was?"

"They have. He was a man called Grant Robertson. He was from the island and wanted by the police, actually."

"Wanted by the police? Why?"

"He'd stolen a great deal of money from the island's largest bank, and the police wanted to question him about a couple of murders, as well."

"I knew something awful had happened in that house," Susan said in a low voice. "I could feel the negative energy as soon as I stepped inside it. That man, Grant whoever, he was murdered in the house, wasn't he?"

"I'm not sure about that."

"I am," Susan said firmly. "He was murdered there in a house full of sadness. Houses don't like to be empty, you know. That house was built for children, to shelter them and to watch them grow. I'm angry that my father let it sit empty, that he didn't take proper care of it, and that his negligence allowed someone to be murdered there. Those are some of his lesser sins, of course."

"The name Grant Robertson isn't familiar to you?"

"I think I heard it on the radio today, actually. Something about a body being identified, but I wasn't paying attention. I never connected a random radio news story to my father's house, of course."

"Of course not."

"He was a thief and a killer, this Grant Robertson?"

"The police certainly seem to think so."

Susan shuddered. "I'd already decided that I didn't want anything to do with the house or the money from the sale of it. I wonder if my brothers will be less excited about getting money from a house where someone was murdered."

"The value of the property may well decline," Bessie warned her.

"I suppose it will. It was already in a terrible state, but this is even worse." She shook her head. "I need that walk. I need to clear my head."

Bessie stood up and followed her to the door.

"I'm probably going to walk for hours," Susan said in the doorway. "But I may come back for another chat when I'm done if you don't mind. I have a lot to think about, and it seems likely that I'll have more questions for you once I've had time to think."

"You're more than welcome to come back. I'm nearly always at home, unless I'm out walking on the beach myself."

"Thank you. I'll probably see you later."

Bessie watched as the woman pulled her coat around herself tightly and then began to walk briskly down the beach. The wind was blowing strongly, but Susan didn't appear to notice as she went.

After she'd shut the door, Bessie quickly rang John's mobile and told him about the conversation.

"I probably shouldn't have mentioned the body, but I'd assumed you'd already spoken to her about it," she said in the end.

"I rang her hotel and left a message, but she never rang me back," John explained. "As it seems unlikely that she knew Grant, she's pretty low on my list of people to interview. The name was released on the early news this morning anyway."

"Yes, I heard it and so did Susan, as I said earlier."

"I have to go," John told her. "We'll talk about her more tonight, along with everything else we have to go over."

"I'll see you at six," Bessie said before she put the phone down.

CHAPTER 7

$\mathcal{T}$here was still enough time before lunch for Bessie to get something productive done, she decided. The house was clean enough, she thought. Spending time with Onnee would be more interesting than vacuuming. She went up the stairs, heading for the bedroom she used as an office.

Having never had to work, over the years Bessie had filled some of her time doing research as an amateur historian. The Manx Museum archives were full of documents ranging from the earliest written records on the island to much more modern items. For many years Bessie had focussed on wills, transcribing them and studying what their contents revealed about life on the island in whatever period from which the will originated. Recently, Marjorie Stevens, the museum's librarian and archivist, had sent Bessie a collection of letters. The letters were more modern than some of the things Bessie had studied, but the writer had handwriting that was difficult to decipher.

Onnee had left the island at eighteen, newly married to Clarence, a man who'd come to visit the island with Onnee's distant cousin. She'd travelled across the Atlantic and then across the US to settle in Wisconsin with her new husband, the cousin having passed away on the sea crossing to the US.

There were fifty years' worth of letters from Onnee to her mother, for Bessie to transcribe. Thus far she'd worked her way through the first three years or so and she found herself getting increasingly caught up in Onnee's story. Besides the difficulty of moving to a new country far from home, where she knew no one, Onnee had been shocked to learn that Clarence had left a fiancée behind when he'd gone on his travels. Faith had been staying with Clarence's parents while he'd been travelling, and Faith had been equally shocked when she'd learned that Clarence had married someone else while they'd been apart.

Three years later, Faith was still living with Clarence's family. Onnee and Clarence had recently bought a small house for themselves and their small family. After a miscarriage, Onnee had given birth to a baby girl. There had been complications with the delivery and Onnee's doctors had told her that baby Alice would probably not survive for long or ever be able to reach any milestones. In each letter to her mother, Onnee bragged about every little thing that Alice accomplished. Bessie didn't know enough about babies to know if the little girl was behind where she should have been, but in the last letter she'd read, Alice was walking and had started saying a word or two as well.

Just over a year later, Onnee had given birth to a second child, a boy they had named William. Perhaps most surprising to Bessie was that Faith and Onnee seemed to be working towards some sort of friendship. Faith was even helping to look after Alice and baby William, and Bessie was sure that Onnee, who still knew very few people in her adopted country, was grateful to finally have a friend.

Now Bessie pulled out the next letter in the pile and settled in with a sheet of blank paper and a favourite pen. It generally took her about an hour to painstakingly transcribe each letter, word by word, before she could sit back and read what Onnee had written. Bessie found herself trying to rush, but every time she thought she was getting somewhere, it seemed as if Onnee changed the way she made a letter or two, forcing Bessie to slow down and really concentrate.

When she finally sat back, having reached the end, Bessie had a pounding headache. Taking tablets took priority over reading the transcribed letter. Once she'd washed two tablets down with a glass of water, Bessie went back to her office and read through her neat copy of the letter.

She was pleased to learn that the baby was doing well and that Alice seemed to be adjusting to being an older sister. She was talking more, saying her version of the baby's name every time the baby cried, which delighted Onnee. Faith was now spending many hours each day at the house, helping with the children and keeping Onnee company. According to Onnee, she usually arrived not long after Clarence went to work and left just before he was due to return home. At the start of the letter, Onnee hadn't worked up the nerve to ask Faith about her relationship with Clarence, but she confided to her mother that she thought the pair had had some sort of falling-out.

Faith had been working for one of the small shops in the town where they were living, but the shop had gone out of business and Faith was having difficulty finding a new job. She had no more than a high school education, and jobs were scarce in the small town. Onnee wrote to her mother that she wasn't sure what Faith was going to do if she didn't find work soon, but that Faith's health still wasn't good following an extended illness a year or so earlier. She wasn't strong enough for many of the jobs that she might have tried had her health been better.

Onnee added to her letter a few days later, telling her mother that she and Faith had had a long talk. Faith had explained that she'd been raised to expect that she'd get married young and be a wife and mother and nothing more. She'd been engaged to Clarence at sixteen, and Onnee speculated that Faith may have been relieved when Clarence came home from his travels married to someone else. It seemed to Onnee as if the pair hadn't been particularly well suited. Anyway, Faith was now in her early twenties and still unmarried. She was in danger of becoming an old maid, which worried both Onnee and Faith. If she'd had some extra money, Onnee said, she might have encouraged Faith to visit the island. No doubt the pretty American girl would have been popular with the island's men, she suggested.

Bessie put the letter down and sighed. For months she'd been worried about Onnee, on her own in a strange land. Now she was worried about Faith and where her life might lead her in the future. As she put away the letters, Bessie thought about how much things had already changed in Onnee's world. When she'd first moved to the US, she'd been distrustful of Faith and, at one point, been convinced that Faith was having an affair with Clarence. Those fears seemed to have been unfounded, though, and it now seemed as if Onnee and Faith were well on their way to becoming friends.

The work had taken Bessie longer than she'd intended. Back in the kitchen, she threw together a quick, late lunch. John was going to be bringing something for dinner that night for everyone. She didn't want to fill up on lunch. She was tidying after her meal when someone knocked on her door.

"Mary? This is a surprise."

Mary Quayle nodded and then flushed. "I should have rung first. I'm so very sorry."

"Not at all. You're always welcome to visit."

"I was out walking, you see, just strolling on the beach, and then I thought maybe you would have time for a quick chat. Things are, well, complicated right now."

"I always have time for my friends," Bessie assured her. "Come in and I'll put the kettle on."

As Bessie followed Mary away from the door, she was suddenly sorry that she hadn't taken the time that morning to clean the cottage. Thie yn Traie was always spotless and, as Mary crossed the kitchen to sit at the table, Bessie remembered that she hadn't vacuumed in a few days. Still, there was nothing she could do about it now, so Bessie got on with making tea and adding biscuits to a plate. When she sat down opposite Mary, she patted her friend's hand.

"What's wrong?" she asked sympathetically.

Mary shrugged. "You talked to George last night. You must know why I'm upset."

Bessie hesitated. Was it possible that George had told Mary something other than what he'd told her? Surely George wouldn't have done anything that foolish?

Mary was watching her closely. "You aren't sure how much George has told me, are you?"

"I'm sure George told you everything. I'm just not sure which bit of it has upset you."

Mary laughed. "Yes, I suppose I can see your point." She took a deep breath and then a sip of her tea.

Bessie watched as her friend nibbled her way through a biscuit and drank more tea before she spoke again.

"I consider you an excellent judge of character," Mary said eventually.

"I'm not sure about that," Bessie replied.

"I have to ask you something. You know George. You've known him for years now. Did you know him when he was growing up on the island?"

"No, I don't believe that I did."

"That's a shame. Nevertheless, you've known him for years now. I want your honest opinion. Did George kill Grant Robertson?"

Bessie nearly dropped her teacup. She set it down carefully before she stared at Mary. "He's your husband. Surely you know him better than anyone in the world does."

Mary shrugged. "I know him well, of course, but he's different when it comes to Grant. He's always been, I don't know, oddly protective of the man, maybe. I wasn't surprised last night when he told me that Grant had contacted him and that he hadn't told me. He'd always do things for Grant that he'd never do for anyone else. He was supposed to be retired, but every time Grant asked him to do more, he always agreed. It was an odd relationship, really."

"If he was that devoted to Grant, surely he wouldn't have done anything to hurt him?"

"I keep thinking that, but then I wonder. What if Grant knew something about George that would have ruined him? George loves his money and his position in Manx society. That was why it was so difficult when Grant first left and so many people ostracised George.

He had to work hard to get back to where he wanted to be. What if he found out that Grant was coming back and he knew that his position would be in jeopardy again?"

"I can't believe that George would murder someone just to stay on the guest list for certain parties."

"But it was more than that. What if Grant had evidence that George had been a part of some of the criminal activities? George would have lost his money, his social standing, and maybe even his freedom. I can't imagine George surviving in prison, can you?"

Bessie took a sip of her drink so that she could have time to think. "No," she said eventually. "But I also can't see George being involved in Grant's schemes. He was investigated by the police, after all. They didn't find any evidence of any wrongdoing."

"No, but that doesn't mean that Grant didn't have something that he was able to use to threaten George."

"Maybe, but it seems more as if Scott Meyers was the one that Grant was threatening."

"What if everything that George told you about Scott was what Grant really said about George?" Mary asked.

Bessie took another deep breath. "Then Grant would have rung someone else for help. He never would have asked George to help him if he were threatening George with exposure."

Mary nodded slowly. "I suppose that makes sense. But do you think that George might have killed him?"

"The police have to take him seriously as a suspect. I don't," Bessie replied. "I don't feel as if I know George well, but, really, if I had to guess, I think that if he truly felt threatened by Grant's return he would have either run away or, well, ended his own life. I can't see George murdering anyone."

After a long and shaky breath, Mary gave her a small smile. "You may be right. George is probably too much of a coward to kill anyone. I never thought I'd be happy that my husband is somewhat cowardly, but in this case, I think I prefer that to the alternative."

"That isn't exactly what I said."

"No, but it's what you meant. And you're right. George never stood up to Grant when they worked together and he wouldn't have stood up to him now, either."

"Are you very angry with him for not telling you that Grant was coming back to the island?"

"Not very angry. Not even very surprised. As I said, he always did whatever Grant wanted. George would have known that I would have made him ring the police if he'd told me about Grant. He was trying to protect both me and Grant, something he'd done many times before."

"You didn't seriously think that he might have killed Grant?"

"I didn't know what to think. I still don't know what to think. It worries me that George knew that Grant was back on the island. While I'm not surprised that Grant told him a string of lies, I do wish that my husband had been smart enough to see through those lies. I know that he really wanted to believe them, though. George had a terrible time believing that Grant truly had done all the things that he was accused of doing. I'm sure he was happy to believe that his unscrupulous advocate had set Grant up. George has never cared for Scott Meyers anyway."

"And George never said anything to you about Grant coming back?"

Mary laughed and then shook her head. "I'm laughing at myself, because I should have seen through George, really. A few weeks ago, he said something in passing about Grant. It was an odd remark, one that suggested he'd spoken to him recently. I immediately questioned him, but he denied having had any contact with him. I shouldn't have believed him. It was the first time he'd mentioned Grant in over a year, but I wanted to believe him, so I didn't push him."

"Was anyone else there when you had the conversation?"

Mary looked surprised and then thoughtful. "I don't think so. We were having a quiet night at home. Someone from the staff may have been in the room, but I don't remember anyone being there."

Bessie frowned. "Did George tell you that he'd told anyone about Grant's return?"

"He told me that he'd told Richard, our advocate. Richard has been working with George for more years than I've known him. He handled all of George's accounts on the island while George lived in the UK. I'm pretty sure that George confides things to Richard that he wouldn't ever tell anyone else, even me."

"And Richard could have told anyone," Bessie sighed.

"He wouldn't have, though. He isn't my favourite person, but he's very careful with his clients. He only has a few clients and most of them are in my family. He has a few others with whom he has worked for many years, but he hasn't taken on any new clients in decades. I do believe he's expanding the firm at the moment, though, bringing in new people from across."

"Even if he didn't tell anyone, someone might have overheard George's conversation with Richard," Bessie suggested.

"That's more likely. Carolyn is a good possibility. I'm sure George told you that. He never notices when Carolyn is in the room."

"Carolyn is his assistant?"

Mary hesitated and then nodded slowly. "I suppose you could call her that. She's, well, she does a little bit of everything for George. She's worked for him for about ten years now. If I didn't know the woman well, I'd probably be jealous of her place in George's life."

"I've never really had a chance to speak to her. I've only met her on one or two occasions over the years."

"I'm sure you've seen her at quite a few events since we've been on the island. She was at the barbecue and she was at the art auction, too. She has a way of blending into the background, though. I shouldn't be surprised that George rarely notices her presence. She's an expert at being invisible, really."

"Did she know Grant?"

"Of course she did. She even worked for both men for a short while when Grant started dragging George into some of his schemes. George thought that maybe Carolyn could handle some of the things that Grant wanted doing, but Grant was never happy unless George did the work himself."

Bessie wondered if that gave Carolyn a motive for murder. She frowned. "How well do you know Carolyn?"

"Pretty well. I don't think she killed Grant, if that's what you're asking. She works hard for George and she's very well compensated, but she'd leave him tomorrow if she got a better offer or if George suddenly went to prison or some such thing. She's dedicated but not devoted, if you see what I mean."

"And now she mostly works for Michael, is that correct?"

"I suppose so. George told me that, anyway. He should know."

"Tell me about her," Bessie requested.

"She's in her mid-fifties, I believe. If she were younger, she'd probably be running her own very successful company, but she was born into a generation that still believed that women were best suited to being wives and mothers. Carolyn tried marriage, but things didn't work out. She never talks about her short-lived marriage, but I get the feeling that her husband was abusive in some way. Anyway, after her divorce, she began working for a man who was starting a small business. She helped him make a success of that business and then moved on to someone else. She's quite brilliant, and I'm sure George has been more successful for the last decade in large part due to her hard work."

"And you aren't jealous?"

"I'm jealous of the time she gets to spend with George, which can be more hours than he spends with me. I'm also jealous that she understands his business in ways that I don't. I think I could have been a good assistant myself, given the opportunity."

Bessie nodded. "I'm sure you were, in the early days of your marriage."

"Yes, rather," Mary nodded. "I did a lot of what Carolyn now does up until the children started arriving. Then George hired a young man, who worked with him for many years. He was, sadly, killed in a car accident about ten years ago. That was when he found Carolyn."

"Do you remember where he found her?"

Mary sighed and then sat back in her seat. "Someone recommended her, I believe, but I'm not certain who. A lot of things have happened in the last ten years. Sometimes I'm surprised that I remember my own name these days."

"It wasn't Grant who recommended her?"

Mary gasped. "What a thought. I, no, but…" She took a deep breath and then slowly exhaled. "I don't know. I suppose it's possible. I simply don't know."

"You hadn't met Grant yet at that point, I believe."

"No, I didn't meet him until we moved to the island. I was, well, shocked by how important he seemed to be to George, seeing as how George had never mentioned him over the years."

"You've never been worried about George and Carolyn developing a personal relationship?" Bessie asked, trying to phrase things carefully.

"Never. George flirts too much, but I truly don't think he'd ever cheat on me. Regardless, Carolyn wouldn't give him the chance. As I said, I'm not sure what went wrong with her marriage, but I do know that it soured her on the idea of having a man in her life. She's simply not interested in getting involved again."

"I think I'd quite like to have a chat with Carolyn."

"The next time you're at one of our parties, you'll have to look for her. She's always there, somewhere."

"Was she at the groundbreaking for the retail park?" Bessie asked, trying to think of other events she'd attended with George and Mary.

Mary thought for a minute and then shook her head. "She wasn't at the actual groundbreaking. Alastair's team dealt with most of that, pretty much sidelining Carolyn, which caused some problems between George and Alastair."

"Did it?" Bessie wasn't really surprised. No doubt Alastair Farthington had wanted to keep as much control over the project as he possible could, right up until he'd decided he was no longer interested in being a part of the retail park project.

"It wasn't anything terribly serious, but it did cause some hard feelings. I think she was secretly delighted when Alastair decided not to continue with the project."

"How well do you know Scott, then?" Bessie asked.

"I don't really know him at all. He was Grant's advocate. Richard generally handled any dealings he had with George. We sometimes include him in social occasions, both he and Richard were at the barbecue, for instance, but then we invited about half the island to that stupid barbecue."

"It was a lovely evening,"

"It was not lovely. George got the idea in his head that he had to have an American barbecue, and no one could persuade him otherwise. I can't tell you how much that one evening cost us, but it was a significant amount of money. George had Carolyn find some party planning people from London to handle everything, and they simply kept running up more and more bills until everything was exactly the way George had envisioned." She sighed. "I understand that some people had an enjoyable evening, anyway. For me, it was something of an ordeal."

"I had an enjoyable evening, " Bessie told her.

Mary shrugged. "You may have noticed that we haven't had another party on that scale since."

Bessie frowned. "I hadn't noticed, actually."

"One of the reasons I wanted to move to Thie yn Traie is that it's smaller than the Douglas house. I was hoping that might discourage George from doing any more lavish entertaining. So far, it seems to be working, anyway."

Bessie knew that Mary was painfully shy. No doubt the sort of huge parties that George loved were nothing but difficult for Mary. "Can you think of any reason why anyone would have wanted to kill Grant?" she asked.

Mary stared at her for a minute and then chuckled. "Is that a serious question? How long do you have?"

Bessie sighed. "It was a badly worded question," she admitted. "Of course there were quite a few people who were angry with Grant and, arguably, might have wanted him dead. I suppose I was hoping you might be able to suggest a few suspects about which the police might not be aware?"

"I don't know. I mean, if I were Inspector Rockwell, I'd be looking at both George and myself. Grant probably could have ruined George, regardless of whether George is actually guilty of anything or not. I'm sure Grant was more than clever enough to fabricate some sort of evidence that George was involved in his schemes, whether he was or not. And I hated Grant and made no secret of that fact. Anyway, I'd do just about anything to protect George. For better or worse, I still love that man far too much."

Bessie took a sip of her tea. "What about Michael?"

"Michael? What about him? He's my son. I won't consider him as a suspect. Don't even mention George Junior or Elizabeth either. I won't consider them or discuss them."

"We've already discussed Carolyn, Richard, and Scott. Can you add anyone else to the list?"

"I could probably name a few men who worked with Grant during the years we were on the island. Any one of them could have been involved in his less-than-legal schemes, but I'm sure the police investigated all of them."

"So where does that leave us?" Bessie asked.

"It leaves me feeling a little bit better, anyway," Mary told her. "As I said, I wasn't all that surprised that George hadn't told me that Grant had been in touch. I was more shocked that Grant had come back, really. I'm still not sure why he would have come back."

"Someone suggested to me that he needed money."

Mary made a face. "And George would have given him some, if he'd asked," she sighed. "As far as I know, Grant got away with quite a bit of money, but knowing him, he probably spent it all as if he were still making more. It wouldn't surprise me in the least to learn that he came back because he was broke, now that you've said it."

"George said that Grant told him that everything illegal was actually Scott's doing. Do you believe that?"

"No, although I'm prepared to believe that Scott had a hand in everything that Grant did. I thought he was lucky not be charged with anything after Grant disappeared. He did cooperate with the investigation, of course, but I'd be willing to bet that he was able to hide just how much he knew about what Grant was doing."

"Do you think they stayed in touch after Grant left?"

"Probably. I believe I said before that I don't like Scott. I wouldn't trust him with a single penny of my money."

Bessie nodded. "So Grant may have told Scott that he was coming back."

"Maybe he told Scott that everything that had happened was all George's fault," Mary sighed. "Scott had to know better, of course, but I would have thought that George knew better than to trust Grant as well."

"Let's hope that the police can find something that will help them narrow down the suspects."

"I just hope they find something that clears George. I don't think the children are really suspects, although maybe I should be more worried about Michael, as he works for George. I'd be quite happy if Scott were arrested and the case was closed. Tell John Rockwell that, won't you?"

Bessie smiled. "I'll tell him, but I'm not certain that he'll be able to oblige."

"He will insist on evidence, won't he?" Mary asked. She glanced at the clock and then frowned. "I need to go. George may well have come back and noticed that I'm gone. I promised to help Elizabeth with a few things this afternoon, too. She'll have definitely noticed that I'm gone."

"She seems to be doing well with her business."

"She is, although she isn't charging enough for her time, which is one of the things we're going to discuss today, actually. As she doesn't really need to the money, she feels odd about charging a fair price for her services. I've suggested in the past that George and I could end her allowance and then she would need the money, but she wasn't fond of the idea."

Bessie laughed. "She and Andy seem well suited."

"They do, which continues to surprise me. He had a very different upbringing to hers, and I'm often surprised that they get along as well as they do. He sometimes reminds her of just how fortunate she's been, actually, when she's acting particularly spoiled. Of course, now he has a fortune of his own, which I believe he's finding useful but challenging."

"I hope they continue to be happy together. I like Andy a great deal and I think they're good for one another."

"I feel the same, but it's early days yet. Elizabeth was hinting the other day about the possibility of a wedding in the future. Andy told her that he wasn't prepared to even consider marriage until he'd opened his restaurant. And he can't do that until he's found a place to live. I'm not sure the Looney house is the right choice, though."

"Why not?"

"I haven't been there, obviously, but from what Elizabeth has told me, it's in a terrible state. I'm not sure that Andy should be putting that much time and money into a house when he still hasn't found a restaurant, that's all."

Bessie hid a smile. It seemed possible that Mary was at least as eager as Elizabeth for a wedding.

"I'd better get home," Mary said with a sigh as she got to her feet. "Thank you for the conversation. I feel better, even though I don't think we actually solved any of the world's problems."

"You know where to find me whenever you want to talk."

"I do. And you know where to find me, as well. You know you're always more than welcome at Thie yn Traie."

Bessie nodded and then followed Mary to the door. She gave her a quick hug before she let her out. The wind had picked up a bit more, but Mary didn't seem to notice as she turned and headed back down the beach towards Thie yn Traie. After a moment, Bessie pushed the door shut and then leaned against it. Her friends were due in less than a hour. John had offered to bring dinner, but he hadn't said anything about pudding. It was likely that he'd bring something anyway, but just in case, Bessie decided to make something.

There were a few apples in the bowl on the table, so Bessie threw together an apple crumble. The house filled with smells of baking apples and cinnamon as the crumble baked. With that job out of the way, Bessie found a logic puzzle magazine and went to work on one of the puzzles while she waited for her friends.

104

CHAPTER 8

*I*t was still five minutes before six when the first knock on the door came. Bessie put down her pencil and crossed the room.

"Doona, hello," she said, pulling her closest friend into a hug.

Doona hugged her back and then walked into the house behind Bessie.

"You've cut your hair," Bessie exclaimed as she studied the other woman.

Doona flushed. "I'd been wearing it in the same bob for years. I thought maybe I'd try something different."

Her new cut was much shorter, with layers throughout. The brown colour remained the same and Bessie could see traces of the blonde highlights that Doona nearly always had. "It's different," Bessie said slowly.

"I hate it," Doona said with a rueful grin. "I'm stuck with it now, of course, but I'm hoping it will grow in quickly." She sighed. "It was something to try, anyway, and it's only hair. I keep reminding myself that it doesn't really matter."

"I don't hate it," Bessie told her. "It's just very different, that's all. I believe I prefer it to when you tried dying your hair red, anyway."

Now Doona laughed. "That was pretty awful, though. Anyway, John doesn't hate it, either, although I think he may just be telling me that because I was rather upset right after I'd had it done."

"John wouldn't lie to you, not even to spare your feelings."

"I don't know. We're still struggling to understand how our relationship is going to work."

"But it is working, isn't it?"

"It's working most of the time. The children are a complication, but also a huge blessing. I do wonder if John and I will find we don't actually care for one another after all once the children have both gone to uni, though."

"I can't see that happening."

"But how are you? Were you terribly upset when you found the body?"

Bessie shook her head. "It wasn't the worst one that I've found, which is a terrible thing to say, but true. I think I was more shocked at the victim's identity than anything else."

"What could have brought Grant back to the island? I can't see him putting himself in danger in that way, not unless he had a very good reason."

"Someone suggested to me that he might have needed money."

"Surely he didn't think that anyone on the island would give him money?"

"Mary seems to think that George might have."

Doona made a face. "We should wait and talk about this once the others are here. I didn't realise I was so early."

"You know you're always welcome. I was just doing logic puzzles."

"Really? I bought a book of them once, but I didn't really understand how they work."

"I can show you, if you're interested. The one I'm working on is all about sweets."

Doona laughed. "Maybe not, as I'm already starving."

"I made an apple crumble for pudding."

"That's good news."

John and Hugh arrived a short while later. Hugh had followed

John from the station to Bessie's cottage. They each carried a box of food inside.

"What did you bring?" Bessie asked.

"A little bit of everything from the restaurant across from the station," John told her.

"Is it still an Italian restaurant?" was Bessie's next question, although the mouthwatering smells of tomato sauce and garlic suggested that it was.

"Yes, it's still Mama's Italian Kitchen. I'm really hoping they stay there for a long time. Grace and I both love their food, and it isn't terribly dear, either," Hugh answered for John.

A few minutes later, Bessie's guests were sitting at the table with plates full of food in front of them. Bessie passed around cold drinks before she joined them and began to eat.

"Delicious," she said a short time later.

"It's always been good, every time I've had their food," Doona said. "No doubt they'll go out of business in another week or two, though. Nothing ever stays in that location for long."

"I hope you're wrong," John said. "I've been doing my best to support them by getting lunch there nearly every day. I thought maybe I'd take a pizza home tomorrow night. I think the kids will both be home for a change."

"Amy has tennis at six," Doona told him.

John frowned. "I forgot about tennis. It starts again tomorrow?"

"It does," Doona replied.

"Well, Thomas and I both like pizza, anyway," John said.

"And Amy can reheat her share when she gets home," Doona added. "You know she'll be starving when she finishes."

"She's always starving these days. I think she's about to grow again," John said.

"How's the baby?" Bessie asked Hugh as Doona and John's conversation ended.

"She's great. She's always hungry, too, but she isn't eating pizza yet. It's impossible for me to imagine that she'll ever eat pizza, really. She isn't even allowed solid food yet, not even baby food, which isn't really solid, is it?" he replied.

"And how is Grace?" was Bessie next question.

"She's good. She's decided not to take any supply teaching jobs until Aalish is at least six months old. I suspect that might get pushed back, as well, but we were originally planning for her to stay home for two years, so it won't matter if it does. It makes things easier for me, too, as I'm starting my classes in June."

"Are you looking forward to going back to school?" Bessie wondered.

Hugh shrugged. "I'm not sure how I feel, really. I didn't care for school when I was younger, but that was because it felt as if I was wasting my time being there. I was young and stupid, and I thought I wanted to get out of school and get a job and actually do things rather than just sit and study all day. Now that I'm going back, I'm worried that I'm not going to be able to manage the workload on top of everything else that I'm doing, but I'm determined to do everything that I can to get my degree so that I can provide the best possible life for Grace and Aalish."

Bessie looked at Hugh's flushed face. It was clear that he was worried about returning to school. "You're going to do brilliantly well," she told him. "I always knew that you were smarter than you ever gave yourself credit for."

Hugh shrugged. "I hope you're right."

"I have a confession to make," John said a moment later. "I forgot to bring a pudding."

Hugh looked incredibly disappointed as Bessie grinned. "I made an apple crumble," she announced.

Hugh's eyes lit up and Bessie thought that he'd very nearly applauded her words.

"Thanks, Bessie," John said. "We've a lot to discuss and our conversations always go better with something sweet to eat."

"That was my thinking exactly," Bessie told him. "I assumed, if you did bring pudding, that Hugh could take my crumble home with him."

Hugh looked disappointed again, but he smiled brightly when Bessie served up the crumble a minute later.

"Where do we start?" Bessie asked after her first bite.

"We always talk about motive, means, and opportunity, but I'm not sure that's going to work in this case," Hugh said.

John shook his head. "We're still waiting for the final report from the coroner, but it doesn't seem as if he's going to be able to pin down the time of death to much more than a fairly wide range of dates."

"Range of dates?" Bessie repeated.

"The last time I spoke to him, he was hoping to narrow that down to a twenty-four-hour period, but all he can say for sure at the moment is that Grant had been dead for at least a week, but probably not much more than that," John told her. "He gave Dan Ross the same information, so expect to see it in tomorrow's paper."

"Let's start with motive," Doona suggested. "Although that's a tough one, as so many people on the island were cheated by the man."

"Many of those who were cheated by Grant got most of their money back, though. I can see some of them still being angry with him, but murder takes a great deal more than simple anger," John replied.

"Was there anyone who didn't get his or her money back?" Bessie asked.

"There were a few people who gave up their claims to the funds that were raised from the sale of Grant's assets. George and Mary Quayle are the first that spring to mind," John told her.

"Grant stole from George and Mary?" Doona sounded shocked.

"The way he'd set things up, he stole from every single account in the bank," John explained. "It was automatic and it was only a tiny amount, but it was on every single transaction. We're talking about fractions of pence on a single transaction, multiplied by millions of transactions every year."

"And George and Mary opted not to be repaid?" Bessie checked.

"They instructed the advocate handling the sale to put their funds back into the disbursement so that everyone else could have more money back. Scott Meyers and Richard Hart did the same thing, as did the Quayle children."

"Does that mean that most of the people on the island no longer had a motive for killing Grant?" Bessie wondered.

John shrugged. "People were still upset, even once they'd received their money back, money that they hadn't realised had been taken, I should add. We're keeping in mind the angry mobs, but we're working on the more likely suspects first."

"Like George and Mary," Bessie suggested.

"Mary comes pretty far down on the list," John replied.

Which suggested that George was rather higher, Bessie thought. "I can't see George as a murderer. Maybe because I've known him for so long. I don't know. He's not my favourite person in the world, but I don't think he killed Grant."

"Who else is on the list of suspects?" Doona asked. "I don't feel as if I know anything about this case, for some reason."

"Mary seems to think that her children are suspects, especially her younger son, Michael, as he works for George and had worked with Grant," Bessie told her.

"No comment," John said firmly.

"I don't believe I've ever met Michael," Doona said thoughtfully.

"I've met him once or twice, but only in passing. I don't know enough about him to have an opinion of him, really," Bessie told her.

"And there's another son?" Doona asked.

"Yes, he's George Junior," Bessie replied. "He works in banking and isn't involved in his father's businesses, though. I must say, after I spoke to George, I thought that Scott Meyers was going to get arrested, really."

John frowned. "We're taking a close look at him, of course, but it's possible that he has an alibi, actually."

"An alibi? How?" Bessie demanded.

"He was off the island for several weeks and only just returned about six days ago," John explained. "He may have been away when Grant died, although we can't be certain until the coroner makes his final ruling."

"Did you believe anything that Grant told George?" Bessie asked.

"What did Grant tell George?" Doona interjected.

"I forgot that you haven't heard all of this," Bessie said. She quickly told her friend about her conversation with George. "I should add that I had tea with Mary this afternoon. She had some interesting things to say, too," she added before she told them all everything she could remember from her talk with Mary.

"My goodness, was George truly dumb enough to believe Grant?" was Doona's first question when Bessie was done.

"I don't know whether he believed him or he simply wanted to believe him," Bessie replied. "Remember that he'd known Grant for a great many years and that he'd trusted him completely. Believing that Scott was actually the one behind all of the illegalities must have made George feel better."

"While it's entirely possible that Scott knew a great deal more about what Grant was doing than he'll ever admit, there's no way he was behind it all," John told them. "For a start, Grant was stealing from the bank for years before he hired Scott. Additionally, as everything was being unravelled after Grant's disappearance, even Scott was shocked at the extent of what Grant had done."

"Or so he claimed," Hugh suggested.

John shrugged. "Even if he was aware, there's no evidence that any of the stolen money ever made its way into Scott's pocket, aside from what he was being paid by Grant to act on his behalf. I will add that he donated a fairly large sum to the reimbursement project, and that he's been doing a great deal of volunteer work on the island since Grant's disappearance."

"None of which means he didn't kill Grant," Doona said stoutly.

John nodded. "I'm sure he wouldn't have been happy to hear that Grant was coming back to the island. Even if he truly is completely innocent of any wrongdoing, I suspect Grant could have provided evidence to the contrary that could have ruined Scott's reputation and his business."

"I don't think he needed to worry about his reputation," Bessie said dryly. "From what I could tell, everyone assumed he was guilty of helping Grant, even if he hadn't."

"You may be right about that," John agreed. "But he has been working hard to rebuild his business. Grant's return would have done possibly irreparable damage."

"Any other suspects?" Doona asked.

"What do you think about George's advocate, Richard Hart?" Bessie asked John.

"He's not on the island at the moment," John replied. "He went across last week for a conference and then a holiday. He's not due back for another eight days."

"That seems convenient timing," Hugh said.

"Again, we're waiting to see what the coroner says. It's possible that Mr. Hart has an alibi, but at this point I'm assuming he doesn't. George has admitted that he told Mr. Hart about Grant's return. I'm sure you can understand why I'm eager to talk to the man," John said.

"Can you make him return early?" Bessie asked.

"I can't make him do anything," John replied. "I've had an inspector in London interview him and politely request that he consider cutting his holiday short. Beyond that, my hands are tied, unless we find any evidence to connect him to the murder."

"Is that likely?" Doona wondered.

"The killer was either smart or lucky," John replied. "He or she didn't leave any prints on the knife that killed Grant. Our experts tried to take prints from elsewhere in the house, but it was impossible. Grant didn't have anything in his pockets, and his clothes had all been bought recently from a chain shop in the UK."

"His coat was valuable, though, wasn't it? That was what I recognised when I first saw the body," Bessie said.

"Yes, it was a very expensive coat," John agreed. "Grant had it made about ten years ago."

"George said that Grant arrived on the island a fortnight ago," Bessie said. "Had he been staying at the Looney house for all that time?"

"We don't believe so. If he did get killed about a week ago, that leaves an entire week unaccounted for. If we can find out where Grant was for that week, we may have a lead on the killer," John said.

"George said that he offered to help Grant find a place to stay. Do you know where George was thinking of putting him?" Bessie asked.

"He told me that he was planning to put him in their Douglas house. No one is living there at the moment, and the house is meant to be on the market, but it hasn't attracted much interest from buyers. It's huge and very expensive, of course. It's going to need a very particular type of buyer," John replied.

"Maybe Grant simply broke into George's house in Douglas," Bessie suggested.

"We had George check, and there's no evidence that anyone had been staying there," John said.

Bessie frowned. She'd thought it was a clever idea. "What about George's assistant, Carolyn? Did she admit to overhearing what George said about Grant coming back?"

John frowned. "I can't repeat what I was told in interviews," he said.

"Did she have any motive for killing Grant?" was Bessie's next question. "Did he steal any of her money?"

"She wasn't living on the island during Grant's years with the bank," John told her.

"I barely know the woman," Bessie said thoughtfully.

"You'll have seen her dozens of times at parties and other events that George and Mary have hosted. She simply blends into the background and keeps her head down," John replied. "That's what she's paid to do, of course."

"How old is she?" Doona asked.

"I believe she's in her fifties," John replied.

"Maybe she had a personal relationship with Grant," Doona suggested.

"That's one possibility," John said.

"Mary told me that Carolyn had a failed marriage in her past and that the experience had put her off men completely," Bessie interjected.

"Now I want to speak with her," Doona said. "Having said that, I want to talk to all of the suspects, really."

"Let's call them witnesses," John suggested with a grin.

"At Bessie's we can call them what they truly are, suspects," Doona argued. "At work we'll call them witnesses."

John and Hugh both laughed.

"Who needs more crumble?" Bessie asked. She got up and gave everyone a second helping of pudding, along with cups of tea. The process gave her a short break from thinking about the murder, anyway.

"Is it possible that the murder is connected in some way to the Looney house, aside from the body being found there?" Bessie asked when they were all at the table again.

"We're looking into connections between the Looney family and Grant," John told her. "Sam and Valerie had some accounts with the bank where Grant worked, but then so did most of the island. That's all we've found thus far."

"What about Gary Davison?" Bessie wondered. "I'm not sure what he did for a job while he was living on the island."

John made a note. "What did you think of Harold Looney?" he asked Bessie.

She shrugged. "He seemed pleasant enough. I believe he found going through the house a bit overwhelming, and he seemed weirdly excited about being involved in a murder investigation."

"There are too many police shows on telly," Hugh said. "Now everyone thinks murder investigations are exciting. Sometimes I think they expect someone famous to come along and solve everything just before an advert break."

Bessie chuckled. "So maybe Harold watches too much telly. I don't know. We didn't really speak, aside from talking about his family and the house."

"Can you think of any reason why he might have killed Grant?" John asked.

"I can think of several unlikely reasons, but nothing that seems likely," Bessie replied. "I doubt he had any connection to Grant, being that he'd left the island so long ago."

"Grant had taken some money from his parents," Doona said thoughtfully.

"I assume that was paid back to their heirs?" Bessie asked.

John frowned. "Actually, any money that was returned would have gone into Gary Davison's estate. Sam left everything to Valerie and she left everything to Gary."

"That hardly seems fair," Bessie said. "But it does weaken Harold's motive for murdering Grant, I suppose."

"Maybe Harold broke into the house and found Grant there," Hugh suggested. "He got very emotional when he was telling me about the house. Maybe, when he found a stranger there, he went a bit crazy and killed him."

"A remote possibility, I suppose," John said.

Hugh flushed. "I know it's unlikely, but the whole situation seems unlikely to me. Grant Robertson managed to get away from the island with a fortune. He disappeared so successfully that we've never received a single tip as to where he might have gone. He had no reason to come back here and no reason to go into the Looney house. It's also odd that both one of the Looney children and one of the Davison children chose now to visit the island. Harold was vague as to why he'd decided to visit now. What did Susan say?"

"I believe she decided to visit once she'd heard there was an offer on the property," Bessie replied, trying to remember her conversation with the woman. "If the house had been sold, she might never have had a chance to take a look around it. She was curious, as she hadn't even known that her father had ever lived on the island."

"Are we certain that he did?" Hugh asked. "Maybe the man who married Valerie Looney wasn't actually Gary Davison, or at least not the same Gary Davison who later fathered Susan."

"Let's not overcomplicate things," John suggested. "While I was talking with Susan, I had someone go through the newspaper archives, and he managed to find a photograph of Valerie and Gary. It had been published when Valerie died, actually, but it was from their wedding day. Susan recognised her father in the photograph."

"Have you learned anything further about Gary's second wife or any of the other women with whom he was involved?" Bessie asked.

"I've spoken to several different inspectors across the UK. We're coordinating an effort to reexamine a number of different cases. Susan was able to provide the names of some of the women her father had known. So far, we've found four that died in, well, let's just say questionable accidents," John replied.

"So Gary might have been a serial killer," Doona said.

"Yes, but we're certain he didn't kill Grant," Hugh laughed.

"Is that sort of thing hereditary?" Doona asked. "I mean, is it possible that Susan has murderous tendencies?"

"She seemed genuinely shocked and upset when she found out about Valerie," Bessie told her. "Besides, I doubt she was even on the island when Grant was killed."

"Actually, she's been on the island for over a week," John told her. "She's been staying in a hotel in Douglas and exploring the island. She told me that she left Laxey for last, wanting to get to know the island before she tried to find out why her father had a house here."

"How very odd," Bessie mused.

"What about Harold?" Doona asked. "We talked about him, but has he actually been on the island long enough to have killed Grant?"

"He's been here for a fortnight," John replied. "He's a widower who's mostly retired. His children are both married and live some distance from him. When he decided to come back to the island, he booked the hotel for a full month. They've given him a very good rate because he's staying for so long."

Bessie sighed. "I don't feel as if we're getting anywhere. There are too many suspects and I'm not sure about motives. Do you know anything about the knife that was used?"

John shook his head. "It was a cheap kitchen knife. There are several shops on the island that sell identical knives, and it's available just about everywhere in the UK, too. I tried to get a few of the local shops to check their records to see when they'd last sold one, but none of them keep that sort of information."

"What a shame," Bessie sighed.

"Whoever killed him had to be someone that Grant trusted," Hugh said. "He was killed in the bed in the Looney house."

"Was he?" Bessie asked.

John frowned. "That isn't to be repeated," he said sternly. "I suspect it will hit the local papers in another day or two, but until then, it's confidential."

Hugh flushed. "Sorry," he said.

"It's fine," John assured him. "I know Bessie and Doona didn't have anything to do with Grant's death."

"Neither of us had a motive," Bessie said.

"He'd offered Doona a job and hinted at wanting a personal relationship as well," John reminded her. "Maybe she was angry when he left without telling her."

"I am sitting right here," Doona interrupted. "And I was nothing but grateful when Grant left. His job offer was tempting, because he'd offered me a lot of money, but I was never interested in a personal relationship with him."

"So whom would Grant have trusted?" Bessie dragged the subject back to Hugh's earlier remark.

"George," Doona said.

"But George claims he didn't know where Grant was," Bessie replied. "He may be lying, of course, but I believed him."

"Mary?" Hugh made it a question.

"Maybe. They didn't get along well, though. I'm not sure why he'd have told her where to find him," Bessie said.

"Maybe he rang Thie yn Traie and Mary answered," Hugh suggested. "Maybe he asked her to arrange a meeting between him and George, but Mary went, armed with a knife."

Bessie frowned. The idea had some merit, but she didn't want to think that her dear friend would have done any such thing. "Unlikely," she said after a moment.

"The same argument goes for anyone at Thie yn Traie," John said.

"If Grant rang the house, he might have spoken to Mary, Elizabeth, or maybe even Michael."

"And Grant probably would have agreed to meet any one of them in the Looney house," Bessie added.

"The same would go for Carolyn," Doona said. "I'm less certain about the two advocates, though."

"I can see George arranging a meeting and then sending Richard in his place," Bessie said. "But George insists that he never spoke to Grant again after Grant arrived on the island."

"As Grant had told George that Scott was actually responsible for everything criminal that had happened, I can't see him agreeing to meet Scott in an empty house," John said.

"Except we don't know what he might have been telling Scott," Bessie sighed. "They'd worked together for a very long time before Grant left. Grant may have trusted him, or he may have believed that he was stronger and smarter than Scott and that he didn't have anything to fear from him."

"That sounds like Grant," Doona said. "I can see him agreeing to meet just about anyone, full of confidence that he'd be able to handle whatever happened next."

"But he had to be worried that someone was going to ring the police," Hugh said. "He was taking an enormous risk telling anyone where he was."

"He'd have known that Mary would have gone straight to the police," Bessie said firmly. "I don't know Michael well enough to comment on what he might have done."

"Maybe he didn't tell anyone where he was. Maybe someone found him by accident or maybe someone came with him from across," Hugh said.

"I suppose it's possible that someone came over with him," John replied. "We haven't yet discovered how he got to the island, although George said that Grant had told him that he was coming on the ferry. It's a shame George didn't ring us, of course. We could have searched the ferry, arrested Grant, and seen him properly dealt with for all the things that he'd done."

"I don't think he'd have brought anyone with him," Bessie said. "He was hiding, and that was dangerous enough for one person. Trying to hide two people on a small island would have been nearly impossible, I believe."

"Unless the other person isn't hiding at all," Hugh said. "Maybe he met Susan or Harold somewhere in the UK. Maybe they were working together on some sort of scam or something when Grant decided to come back to the island. One of them might have travelled with Grant or even just followed him here."

"We're checking ferry records for around the date that George believes that Grant arrived," John said.

"Did Susan and Harold both arrive around that same date?" Bessie asked.

"Harold arrived on that date, but he flew in from London. Susan arrived later, but she did take the ferry," John replied.

"This is all just getting muddled up in my head," Doona complained. "We've no shortage of motives, even if some of them are somewhat far-fetched. The knife was available anywhere, and Grant was here for an entire week, no doubt meeting with people and planning something. That gave lots of people the opportunity to kill him."

"And on that note, I think I should get home," Hugh said, getting to his feet. "It's my turn to be up with the baby tonight, so I need to get to bed as early as possible."

"Your turn?" Bessie repeated.

"We take it in turns to get up during the night," Hugh explained. "Grace feeds Aalish around ten and then she goes to bed. Aalish is usually awake around three for another feed and that's the one that Grace and I take turns doing. Then, when Aalish wakes up at seven or so, one of us has had several good hours of sleep."

"It sounds complicated," Doona remarked.

"It's working, though," Hugh told her. "Whichever of us isn't getting up sleeps in the spare bedroom, so he or she can shut the door and block out everything that's happening elsewhere in the house. When it's my turn to sleep, I wear earplugs and everything. Grace usually ends up getting up anyway, when she's supposed to be sleeping, though. I'm hoping tonight she'll sleep through. She really needs it."

Bessie walked him to the door. "Give both Grace and Aalish hugs from me," she told Hugh as she hugged him.

"I will, of course," he replied before he walked away.

Bessie turned around. Doona had started on the washing-up.

"I can get that," Bessie said.

"I know, but it won't take a minute. It's the least I can do after you had us all here for the evening and made such a delicious pudding," Doona replied.

"I'm grateful for your input," John said as he rose. "Talking to you always gives me ideas for new avenues to explore."

Bessie thought back through the evening. She wasn't certain what new avenues John was talking about, but she didn't question his words. A few minutes later, the dishes all washed and put away, Doona and John got ready to leave.

"Coming back to the house tonight?" John asked Doona in the doorway.

"Maybe for a short while. It isn't too late. I know Amy wanted to talk about a few things with me," she replied.

John nodded. "She's been thinking about doing something with her hair, but my opinion isn't wanted, apparently."

Doona laughed. "She doesn't really want mine, either. She just wants me to agree with her."

"You're probably right about that," John replied.

Bessie watched as the pair walked back to their respective cars. Things seemed to be going well for them, and she hoped that would continue. No doubt there would be more bumps in the road ahead, but for now it looked promising.

CHAPTER 9

*D*oona had done a good job tidying the kitchen. Bessie moved the kettle a fraction of inch sideways and then slid the bottle of washing-up liquid closer to the sink. There was nothing else that needed to be done. It wasn't quite late enough for her to head to bed, so she grabbed her logic puzzle book and went back to work.

She had nearly worked out which sweets had been eaten on which day when her telephone rang. It was too late at night for double-glazing salesmen, she thought as she reached for the receiver.

"Ah, Bessie, it's George, er, George Quayle," the unmistakable voice boomed down the line.

"Good evening, George."

"Mary and I were just talking and I thought we should do something to mark Grant's passing. We're having some people around for drinks tomorrow evening. Nothing formal, just a chance for everyone to, well, talk about Grant, I suppose. I feel as if we have to do something, you understand."

Bessie wasn't certain that she did understand, but she wasn't about to question George. "Have you mentioned this to the police?" she asked.

"Oh, well, not exactly, but we have invited the Chief Constable, so

I suppose that's technically a yes, isn't it? Do you think we should invite John Rockwell, too?"

"It might be a good idea."

"Do you have a telephone number for him? I don't believe that I do."

"I can let him know about it, if you'd prefer," Bessie offered.

"That would be splendid. I'm rather tired of ringing people tonight, really. You were the last one on the list and I'm very glad to be done with it."

"So you're inviting me?"

"Yes, of course, wasn't that clear? I really should have had Mary do this. I'm not very good at such things, am I?" He laughed heartily. "Anyway, we'd love to have you come for drinks tomorrow evening. I expect things to start around seven. Andy is going to do some food for us, but not a proper meal, just little things to nibble on. You know what I mean."

"Yes, of course."

"Anyway, Mary wants you to come earlier, if you can. She said to tell you that you're welcome as early as midday, but she'll understand if you'd rather not spend the entire day with her."

Bessie swallowed a sigh. "It isn't that I don't want to spend the day with her, but I do have other plans for some of it," she said. "I'll come over after my dinner, maybe around six, if that suits you."

"I'm sure that will be perfect."

"So, I'll see you then," Bessie said.

"Yes, and, well…" George trailed off.

"Well, what?" Bessie asked after a moment.

"The thing is, we're inviting a number of people who might have had motives for killing Grant. I thought maybe you could speak to all of them while you're here. You're good at solving murders. Maybe you could solve this one for us."

This time Bessie didn't bother to try to hide her sigh. "I do my best to help the police, but solving murders is their job, not mine. As I said, I'll invite John to come along. Maybe he'll be able to learn something that will help."

"But you'll be talking to everyone, won't you? I'm certain someone will make a mistake and tell you something that turns out to be the key to the whole case. Mary and I are ever so anxious for it to be solved."

"I'll see you around six," Bessie told him, waiting until she'd put the phone down to sigh again. Spending an evening at Thie yn Traie remembering Grant Robertson sounded awful, but she cared too much about Mary to make the woman suffer through it on her own.

She glanced at the clock. It wasn't ten yet, so she picked the phone back up and rang John's home number.

"Hello?"

"Doona? It's Bessie."

"Oh, hello. Is something wrong?"

"No, not at all. George Quayle just rang me and invited me to come over to Thie yn Traie for drinks tomorrow night. He said it's in memory of Grant."

"I see."

"Anyway, he told me that I could invite John to come along. Things are meant to be starting around seven. The Chief Constable has also been invited."

Doona took a deep breath. "Lovely," she muttered.

"I'm going over around six, as Mary has asked me to come early," Bessie continued.

"John isn't going to be happy about that."

"No, but I'm doing it anyway."

Doona laughed. "I'll tell him that you said that. Was there anything else?"

"No, nothing else. I'm going back to my logic problems before bed. I'm going to work out whether the wine gums were eaten on Tuesday or Wednesday if it kills me."

"And you wonder why I don't do logic problems," Doona replied.

In the end, the wine gums had been eaten on Thursday. The gummy bears were on Tuesday and the chocolate truffles were on Wednesday. Bessie finished the puzzle and checked her answers. Feeling satisfied that she'd managed it, she put the book back in the dining room, where it would probably sit, untouched, for another month or two, and took herself off to bed. As she crawled under the duvet, she briefly wondered why Susan hadn't come back for a second visit.

It was clear and cool the next morning, and Bessie set out on her walk determined to walk to the new houses and maybe beyond. Andy was making food for that evening, and Bessie knew that she'd probably eat far too much, given the opportunity. She passed the holiday cottages and Thie yn Traie quickly, marching with determination. When the new houses came into view, she told herself that she wasn't the least bit tired and kept going.

Some distance past the new houses was a long stretch of beach where another cluster of homes were due to be built. The large sign advertising the plots of land had been covered with "Sold Out" stickers. Once the weather improved a bit, no doubt construction would begin.

Bessie stopped next to the sign and studied the drawings again. Every time she looked at them, she wondered at how close together the houses were and at their small size. From what she could see, it seemed likely that her tiny cottage was larger than any of these new homes were going to be.

"Pardon me, but it's Betsy, isn't it?"

The voice made Bessie jump. She turned around and then smiled at Harold Looney, whose approach had been drowned out by the wind and waves.

"It's Bessie, actually, but you were close."

He flushed. "It was something of an unusual day."

"It was indeed," Bessie agreed, although finding dead bodies wasn't as unusual for her as it undoubtably was for him.

"What brings you down here this early in the morning?" she asked.

He looked up and down the beach and then sighed. "When I was a small child, we used to come and play on Laxey Beach. I wanted to revisit the beach, but I can't seem to find the right spot. I've walked up and down several times now, but nothing looks at all familiar."

"You used to come to the stretch of beach by my cottage," Bessie told him. "I can give you directions, or you can simply walk there with me. I'm heading back there now, but it might be a longer walk than you wanted to take."

He shook his head. "I'd love a long walk. I wasn't certain how far I could go, you see. There are houses scattered along different sections of the beach. They're even building some here, I see."

"Yes, they are. But the beach itself is still public. You can walk all along it, although it's best to stay close to the water." She turned and began the long walk back to Treoghe Bwaane.

"I try to walk ten miles every day," Harold said as he fell into step beside her. "I don't walk very quickly, but I enjoy the exercise. At home, I have a treadmill, so I do some of my walking on that, especially when the weather isn't good. Since I've been here, I've been walking on the various footpaths, though. It's more difficult than walking on the treadmill, but much more satisfying."

"Ten miles is a long way."

"It is, but I'm retired now and I've nothing else to do with my days. I usually walk for two hours in the morning when I first wake up, and then another hour after lunch and a fourth hour in the evening after my dinner. That gets me about eight miles, anyway. Most days, if I do some shopping or visit a mall, I get another mile or two in without even trying."

"And you measure it all?"

"I have a pedometer, yes," he said, showing her the device that was clipped to his belt. "It's very satisfying watching the numbers add up."

They walked in silence for a short while. Bessie had a dozen questions for him, but she wasn't sure how best to bring up the murder.

"The police haven't said much about the man who died in my old house," Harold interrupted Bessie's thoughts. "The local paper said he was a criminal who'd been hiding from the police for the last year or more."

"Yes, that's right. Grant Robertson worked for one of the local banks. He'd managed to steal a great deal of money from its customers over the years."

"My goodness. It's hardly surprising that he was murdered, then, really."

"What's surprising is that he was even on the island," Bessie told him.

"He'd run away, had he?"

"Yes, the police were starting to investigate the bank's accounts, so he disappeared with a large amount of stolen money."

"Why would he have come back, then? Did he leave a wife or a girlfriend behind?"

"Not a wife. If he had a girlfriend, I didn't know about her," Bessie said, giving the idea some thought. Was it possible that Grant had been romantically involved with someone, someone that he'd found that he missed once he'd gone?

"If it wasn't for love, it must have been for money," Harold said. "Those are the only two things that I can imagine anyone putting themselves at risk for in that way, anyway. There may be more. Maybe I just don't have enough imagination."

Bessie shook her head. "I think you're probably right. Love and/or money seem to be the primary motivations behind most actions."

"Whatever the reason that he came back, why was he hiding in my house?"

Before Bessie could reply, Harold held up a hand. "Obviously, it isn't my house. It never was, of course, but I can't help but feel slightly possessive of it. I hate that something awful has happened there, and it worries me that that nice young couple no longer want to buy it because of the murder."

"I'm sure someone will buy it eventually."

"Yes, but I truly liked Andy and Elizabeth. I think they really wanted to restore the house to its former glory, which would make me very happy. It would have made my father happy, too. He'd have hated to see the state that it's in now. It wasn't the biggest house or the nicest house, but it was the happiest house in Laxey."

He turned his head to stare out at the sea, and Bessie watched as a tear slid down Harold's cheek.

"You asked why Grant was hiding in your house," Bessie said after a short while. "I don't think anyone knows the answer to that at the moment, but he may simply have chosen it because he knew it was empty. He may not have known that Andy and Elizabeth were thinking about buying it."

"I suppose that makes sense," Harold sighed. "That's better than thinking that there was a connection between Gary and the dead man. My mother loved Gary. I don't want to believe that he was a criminal."

Bessie bit her tongue. Now wasn't the time to question Valerie's untimely death. "I'm sure the police are looking for a link between Gary and Grant as part of their investigation. They'll be looking for links between Grant and everyone, really."

"Even me?" he asked, sounding surprised.

"Yes, even you."

"Oh, I suppose I never really considered that I might be a suspect. Surely, if I'd killed the man, I would have made sure I wasn't there when the body was found?"

"Maybe, or maybe you made sure you were there for some reason."

Harold stopped walking and stared at Bessie for a moment. "That would have been very clever of me, wouldn't it? Maybe, after I killed him, I realised that I'd left something with the body that would identify me. Maybe, when I went over to him in the bedroom, I was really retrieving something that I'd dropped when I murdered him."

Bessie nodded. "That's the sort of thing the police have to consider." She wasn't too concerned that that was the case, though, as she'd been watching Harold very closely in the dimly lit bedroom. As soon as she'd seen the body, she'd been fairly certain that the person on the bed was dead. She was reasonably certain that Harold had done nothing more than touch Grant's shoulder before backing away rapidly as Grant had rolled towards him.

"It must be a fascinating job. I sometimes regret going into accountancy. It provided a good living for my little family and me, but it was incredibly dull. I used to dream of travelling one day after I'd retired. My wife and I were going to see the world, but then she passed away unexpectedly. The children are busy with their own lives, of course. They aren't interested in travelling anywhere with me."

"That doesn't mean you can't travel on your own," Bessie pointed out. She took a few steps forwards, hoping that Harold would start walking again.

He sighed and then began to follow her down the beach again. "I'm afraid I'm just not that adventurous. I read a lot. That was always what I did to combat the boredom of my work. I'd read about James Bond's adventures in exotic locations and imagine that one day I'd see them for myself. The idea of actually travelling anywhere, though, well, that's rather scary."

"You came to the island," Bessie pointed out.

"Yes, and stumbled into a murder investigation. I'm not sure that's the best thing to encourage me to travel more."

They'd reached the new houses now, and Bessie slowed her pace as they walked behind them.

"These are lovely homes," Harold said. "Being right on the beach, they're probably very dear, aren't they?"

Bessie gave him a rough idea of what the houses had sold for when they'd been built. "I'm not sure what their value is now, though. They haven't been here for very long. I don't know that anyone who lives here is thinking of moving."

"I don't blame them. If I could live on the beach, I'd never leave, either."

Bessie waved to one of the residents that she knew. He was just letting his dog, Spotty, out onto the beach for a run. He waved back and then ducked back into the house. Spotty ran straight into the ocean, jumping happily over the waves.

"Do you have any pets?" Harold asked Bessie.

The sudden change in subject surprised her. "No, I don't," she said after a moment. "I'm not really an animal person."

"We had a dog when the children were small. It was one of the things that came with having children, really, or so my wife insisted. He was very much my wife's dog, though. We had a cordial relationship, but it wasn't warm."

Bessie grinned at the description. "And you've never been tempted to get another one?"

"Not in the slightest. I was sad when we lost him, but he'd had a good life and he died peacefully in his sleep. My wife was devastated, but we lost him at the same time as our youngest went away to uni. Her whole world changed at that time. It was all very difficult for her."

"I'm sure."

He shrugged. "She had an affair with one of our neighbours," he said in a matter-of-fact tone. "She was much happier after that."

Bessie wasn't often left speechless, but for several minutes she had no idea what to say.

"Where do the stairs go?" he asked as they approached Thie yn Traie.

"Up to Thie yn Traie," Bessie explained. She waved a hand at the mansion on the cliff above them. Only one wall, mostly windows, was visible from the beach.

"Oh, the Pierce mansion. I'd forgotten all about that place."

"The Pierce family sold it a few years ago," Bessie told him.

He nodded. "I saw something about that in the island newspaper at the time." He took another few steps and then stopped and turned in a very slow circle. "This is it," he said in a low voice. "This is the beach from my childhood. Those cottages didn't used to be there, though."

"No, the holiday cottages have only been there for a few years."

"They're holiday cottages? I could stay here?"

"They open on Saturday for the season. I don't think they're fully booked for the next week or two. You might be able to stay there."

Harold looked shocked. "I could stay in a cottage on Laxey Beach," he said in a dazed voice.

"I can give you the number for the booking agent," Bessie offered. Maggie and Thomas used an estate agent in Douglas to handle bookings.

"Yes, please," he said excitedly.

Bessie continued down the beach, heading for home. Harold followed more slowly.

"You probably think I'm crazy," he said after a minute. "I don't actually have that many memories of the island, but this beach, this beach I remember. We didn't come down here very often. I'm sure it

129

was a lot of work for my mother, getting all of us down here. We didn't have a car, of course, and getting seven children onto the bus must have been an ordeal. Other children were going across on holidays, but for me a day on Laxey Beach was better than anything else."

Bessie nodded. Cheap air travel had made family holidays much more elaborate now than they had been years ago. For many children in Laxey, a day at the beach was about as exciting as their summers ever got.

Harold clapped his hands together suddenly. "It's the magical cottage," he said, gesturing towards Treoghe Bwaane.

"The magical cottage?"

"It certainly seemed magical," he told her. "An older woman lived there. She always had biscuits for the children playing on the beach. We used to take it in turns to visit her because my mother wouldn't let all seven of us turn up on her doorstep at the same time. I used to go with my littlest sister, Sarah. Sarah had all this gorgeous curly blonde hair. She looked like an angel, really, when she was small. The lady in the cottage always used to give her an extra biscuit, and Sarah always gave me half."

Bessie smiled. She didn't specifically remember Harold and Sarah visiting her, but she had no doubt that the story was true.

"I used to daydream about running away from home and moving into that cottage. In my dreams, I ate nothing but biscuits and didn't have to go to school anymore. I had my own bedroom, too, which was the best part. After my mother died, I used to wish more than anything that I could move down to the beach with Aunt Bessie." He stopped and then turned and stared at Bessie. "You're Aunt Bessie," he said after a moment.

She nodded. "I have biscuits," she told him.

His face lit up. "I can't believe you're still alive," he said. As soon as the words left his lips, he turned bright red. "I can't believe I just said that out loud," he said.

Bessie just laughed. "I'm sure I seemed quite old to you all those years ago. You were a small child, after all."

"Yes, of course," he agreed quickly.

She unlocked the cottage door and led him inside.

"It's exactly the same," he said happily. "It even smells the same, like the sea and roses."

Every morning since Matthew's death, Bessie had patted on rose-scented dusting powder after her shower. The scent reminded her of the man who'd surprised her with roses during their courtship. She didn't really notice, but it was hardly surprising that the scent had spread throughout the cottage over the years.

Harold sat at the kitchen table while Bessie filled the kettle. She piled different types of biscuits onto a plate and put it in the middle of the table. After handing Harold a small plate for his selections, she made the tea and then joined him at the table.

"This doesn't quite feel real," he said after a moment. "I can't quite believe that you gave me tea. You used to give me milk because I was too young for tea. Once, when my mother came with me, you gave her tea and I thought it smelled incredibly delicious. Everything smelled and tasted better in the magical cottage, though."

"I never knew that anyone thought of my cottage as magical."

"I may have been the only one," Harold said, blushing. "I had quite an active imagination as a child. I loved to read books about witches and wizards and fairies. Tales of King Arthur and Camelot were a real favourite for a while. I was somewhat obsessed with Merlin, you see. That may well have been when I decided that your cottage was magic."

"I'm sorry that it isn't."

"But it is," he said softly. "I'm sitting here with you today, but in my head it's a great many years ago. Sarah is here, looking angelic, and my mum is just out on the beach with the others. My father is out at work, of course. He never had time to come to the beach with us, but that was what fathers did in those days. He had seven children to take care of, of course."

Bessie took a sip of tea, sitting back in her chair and deliberately not speaking. Harold was lost in his memories and she didn't want to interrupt.

"The sun was always shining on Laxey Beach," he said after a minute. "I'm sure we only came when it was sunny. Mum wouldn't have wanted to get all of us over here and then deal with rain on top of everything else. But when I was five or six, I wouldn't have thought about it that way. In my mind, it was always sunny at the beach."

Bessie looked out the window. It was overcast and it looked as if it might rain at any moment. Poor Harold still had to walk all the way back past the new houses to get back to his car.

"I still can't quite believe that you're still here. This little plot of land must be worth a fortune."

"I believe it's worth quite a lot, yes."

"You could move into a nice modern house somewhere."

"This is my home. It's been my home since I was eighteen."

Harold sighed. "That's sort of how I feel about my old house, except it was only my home for a very few years, really. This cottage feels as much like home as that house did, really. They're both parts of my past and, no matter how much I'd like to, I can't go back."

"There's nothing to stop you from moving back to the island."

He shrugged. "Being here has been, well, bittersweet may be the best way to put it. Right now, sitting here, I want to move back in the worst way. When I think about what happened in my house, that someone was murdered there, well, that makes me want to leave and never return. Maybe I should say that this visit has been a roller coaster."

"I hope you'll take away good memories when you go."

"I'll never forget today. Being here again has brought my mother and my baby sister back to me in a way I never expected. I'll be forever grateful to you for that."

"I didn't do anything except not move house," Bessie laughed.

After a moment, Harold laughed, too. "You gave me tea and biscuits, though," he said. "And that means the world to me."

"If you could travel, where would you go?" Bessie asked after a moment.

He frowned. "I don't know. I've always wanted to visit Narnia and Camelot, but I can't find them in any travel brochures."

"Fictional places are always much more interesting than real ones," Bessie said. "Actually, that isn't fair. There are many fascinating places to visit all around the world, and anywhere you go can be both amazing and educational, if you give it a chance."

"I know you're right, but I'd still rather visit Narnia."

Bessie laughed. "Me too. When I visit estate sales, I always check the wardrobes, just in case."

Harold nodded. "I do the same thing. If Elizabeth hadn't checked the one in my old house, I would have, even though I know there was no doorway to Narnia there when we owned the house."

"Have you done much travelling in your life?"

He shook his head. "Before we got married, my wife and I talked about travelling, but she fell pregnant almost immediately. We used to take the children to Wales to camp every summer, which wasn't really travelling, was it? As the children got older, we used to discuss taking them to Paris or Rome, but there were piano lessons and replacement windows and a dozen other things that used up all of our money. As I said, eventually we decided that we'd travel once I retired, but, well, that never happened."

"You're here."

"Yes, I am," he said, sounding slightly surprised. "I suppose, if I'm honest, revisiting the island was always on the top of my list of places to go. In my memories, the entire island was almost magical. My memories are hazy, of course, and everything is coloured by how I remember being a happy family before my father's death."

"Maybe you should try Paris next."

"Paris is for lovers," he countered. "I think I'd feel lonely there. Here, I'm surrounded by my memories, but there, I'd be all alone."

Bessie nodded. Maybe he was better off not travelling, not for a while, anyway. She'd never done as much travelling as she'd wanted to do, either. Money had always been tight, and now that it wasn't, she found that she was happy at home.

"I've taken up far too much of your time," Harold said abruptly. "Thank you so much for everything." He got to his feet and headed for the door.

Bessie followed quickly, grabbing a small bag and dropping a few biscuits into it. "For the walk back," she explained as she handed him the bag.

"Thank you so much," he said, swallowing hard. "For everything." He blinked several times and then rushed out the door before Bessie could reply.

She watched him as he hurried back down the beach, almost seeming to be trying to run away from the memories the visit had brought back to him.

As she washed the cups and plates, Bessie wondered if she should ring John and tell him about her conversation with Harold. No matter how hard she tried, she couldn't imagine that anything he'd said was at all relevant to Grant's murder, but she still decided to ring the inspector.

"Thank you," John said when she was done. "I'll see you later tonight."

"Yes, I'm looking forward to it."

"I'm not sure that I am, but I am bringing Doona with me. Mary rang this morning to invite me properly and she insisted that I was welcome to bring a guest."

"That was kind of her."

"I'm surprised she didn't ring you as well."

Bessie glanced at her answering machine. The light blinked back at her. "She may have done," she laughed.

After the call ended, Bessie pushed play on her messages. She deleted three from nosy friends and one from Dan Ross.

"You'd think he'd have learned by now," Bessie muttered as she pushed the erase button.

"Bessie, it's Mary. I know that George mentioned our little gathering tonight to you, but I wanted to make sure that you were invited properly. You're more than welcome to bring a guest, as well. The party, well, let's not call it a party, the evening starts at seven. I'm sure George told you that you were welcome to arrive earlier. He told me you'd said you could be here by six, which would be splendid. Ring me back if you have any questions or concerns. Otherwise, I'll see you around six."

Bessie smiled at the answering machine. Mary hated social occasions, even small gatherings in her own home. She'd probably rung just to make sure that Bessie truly was going to arrive at six. Her presence would help settle Mary's nerves. If nothing else, once Bessie had arrived, Mary would have a good excuse to open a bottle of wine. Wine always seemed to help Mary relax.

It had been an odd morning, and it was already nearly time for lunch. Bessie found a book that she'd recently purchased on a trip into Douglas. She nearly always enjoyed cosy mysteries, but this one was by an author she'd never read before. She read the first two chapters before she quickly made herself a sandwich for lunch. The book was proving nearly impossible to put down, and Bessie read the next chapter as she ate the sandwich, washing it down with tea.

With plenty of time to fill before she was due at Thie yn Traie, she carried the book into her sitting room and curled up, determined to finish it before she had to leave for what might be a very difficult evening of remembering Grant Robertson.

CHAPTER 10

*H*ours later Bessie put the book down with a frown on her face. The killer hadn't been the disagreeable next-door neighbour. Although the author's solution to the murder had been very cleverly done, Bessie had greatly disliked the neighbour and had spent the last hundred or so pages hoping that he was the killer. At the very least, he could have been another victim, she thought as she got up and stuck the book on one of her shelves. It was very likely that she'd donate it to a charity shop in the near future, but she didn't want to be hasty. There had been things she'd enjoyed about the story, even if she hadn't cared for the ending.

After a light snack, leaving plenty of room for whatever Andy would be making, she changed into a dark grey dress and matching shoes. While the evening wasn't actually a funeral or a memorial service, grey felt most appropriate. She moved everything she might need into a black handbag before she powdered her nose and added a coat of lipstick to her lips. She frowned as she walked back into the kitchen. It was raining, which meant the walk to Thie yn Traie would be a wet one. As she tried to find an umbrella, someone knocked on her door.

"Jack, what are you doing here?" she exclaimed.

"Mrs. Quayle sent me to collect you," Jack replied with a small bow.

Bessie grinned. "I was just complaining to myself about the rain."

"It isn't all that bad. It's fairly light, but it's also on the chilly side."

After putting on a coat, Bessie grabbed her handbag and was ready to go. Jack offered his arm and led her to the small sporty car he'd left outside.

"I was expecting something rather more grand," Bessie told him after he'd settled her in the passenger seat and climbed behind the steering wheel.

"This is my personal car," he explained. "I've only had it for a few days and I love having any excuse to drive it. When you live where you work, you don't have many reasons to drive anywhere."

Bessie laughed. "I'd never thought about that. It's a lovely little car."

"It's exactly what I need for popping around the island. Mostly I visit my mum. She isn't terribly fond of it, as I used to visit her with the various staff cars, which are all huge with leather seats and every other sort of option. Still, she's happy for me that I could afford a car of my own."

"She should be very proud of you."

"Oh, aye, she is, really. I think she's a little worried right now because of the most recent murder, though."

"It's very sad."

"Sad? I'm not sure that many people are feeling sad about it, actually. He'd hurt a lot of people, including my mum. She got most of her money back, but she felt very betrayed. She used to think the world of Mr. Robertson. It really upset her when she found out that her trust in him had been completely misplaced."

Bessie nodded. "I believe a lot of people felt that way about Grant when the truth came out."

"I can't help but wonder why he came back to the island. Considering his past, he must have expected to either be arrested or murdered if he returned."

"I can't imagine why he came back, either. He was a very smart man and coming back was a very foolish thing for him to do."

137

While they'd been talking, Jack had been driving the short distance between Bessie's cottage and Thie yn Traie. He'd pulled his car into the huge garage there and switched off the engine.

"Do you have any idea who might have killed him?" he asked as he turned to face Bessie.

"None at all."

"I can't help but wonder if it wasn't someone who'll be at tonight's gathering. It worries me that we might be entertaining a murderer."

"John Rockwell and the Chief Constable will both be here."

"Yes, of course. It's not that I feel as if anyone will be in danger. It's more the idea of people socialising with a killer." He shook his head. "I'll be in the corner, watching everyone closely. Maybe I'll overhear something important."

"If you do, go straight to John," Bessie told him sternly. "Whatever you do, don't confront the killer."

"I'm not that brave. I'll be more than happy to turn everything over to Inspector Rockwell. I just hope he can work out the solution soon. Mrs. Quayle is terribly upset about everything that's happened. She's one of my favourite people in the world and I hate to see her upset."

"She's one of my favourite people, too," Bessie replied.

"I assume you're going to be questioning everyone tonight. I wish you luck."

"I don't plan to question people, but I will be talking to everyone," Bessie replied, feeling as if the distinction was important.

Jack chuckled. "Of course," he said as if he didn't believe her. He got out of the car and rushed around it to open Bessie's door for her. "Mrs. Quayle will probably be in the great room," he told her as he escorted her into the house.

Mary was sitting on one of the couches, staring out the huge floor-to-ceiling windows that looked out at the sea. Jack cleared his throat as he walked with Bessie into the room.

"Remember to call me Jonathan here," he whispered to Bessie before bowing deeply and leaving.

"Bessie, thank you so much for coming early," Mary said from her place. "I can't tell you how much I appreciate it."

"I'm always happy to spend time with you," Bessie replied. She crossed the room and sat down next to Mary on the couch.

"I should be rushing around, arranging things, but I can't help but feel as if this evening is a very bad idea," Mary sighed.

"It's only a few people coming for drinks, isn't it?"

"I suppose so, but George wants it to be a sort of memorial for Grant, which seems in bad taste somehow. I don't want to remember Grant and I don't particularly want to talk about him, either."

"Now, now," a loud voice said from the doorway. "I know Grant had his faults, but he was also my friend and my business partner for a very long time."

Bessie smiled at George as he made his way across the room. He was a large man who usually filled the room both physically and with his enormous personality. Today, he seemed somewhat subdued, even if he hadn't turned down his volume.

"How are you?" she asked as he dropped heavily onto the couch next to Mary.

"Sad," he replied. "At the end of the day, I've lost a friend. I know he caused a lot of harm to a great many people, but we were friends long before he'd ever stolen a single penny. I mourn for that man, the one who had the potential to do a lot of good, even if he never fulfilled that potential."

Bessie nodded. "It may be a difficult evening for everyone."

"Not if we keep the alcohol flowing," George countered.

Mary sighed. "I'd rather not have people getting drunk."

"Why ever not? It's what Grant would have wanted," George laughed.

"Exactly," Mary snapped.

George frowned and then took Mary's hand. When she looked at him, he tilted his head and gave her a small smile. "I'm sorry, my darling. I've been so caught up in my own feelings that I haven't been thinking about you. I'm afraid you're probably used to that by now, though. Do you want me to cancel tonight?"

Mary shook her head. "We've invited everyone, and they should start arriving in the next half hour. It's far too late to cancel. I may not stay for very long, though. I have a migraine coming on."

"Of course, of course. You don't even have to attend at all. Elizabeth can act as hostess in your absence," George told her.

"I'll stay until everyone has arrived, at least. We'll see how I feel after that," Mary replied.

"Bessie, please keep an eye on Mary for me," George said. "I'll be too busy with our guests to do so, of course, but if her headache gets worse, you must make her go to bed."

Before Bessie could reply, Mary shook her head. "I'm quite capable of looking after myself. I will leave if my headache gets worse. Let Bessie simply enjoy the evening."

"Ah, but I'm hoping Bessie will do a good deal more than that. I'm hoping she'll unmask the killer while she's here," George said in a dramatic voice. "She's ever so good at that very thing. I'm sure, once she's spoken to everyone, she'll be able to tell Inspector Rockwell who killed Grant."

"I don't think that's at all likely," Bessie said.

George shrugged. "But you're going to try, aren't you? All you have to do is talk to everyone and work out who knew Grant was coming back to the island. Then you simply have to discover which of those people had a motive for killing the man and you'll have solved it."

"Except it seems very likely that just about everyone who will be here tonight knew that Grant was coming back to the island, and I suspect that all of them had some sort of motive, even if it seems unlikely or obscure to us," Bessie countered.

"Let's see how the evening goes. Guests should start arriving soon," George said.

Mary looked at the clock and gasped. "We need to get the room ready," she said, jumping to her feet.

"We do?" George asked, looking around the room with a confused expression on his face.

The great room was a huge space full of couches, chairs, and low tables that were currently scattered randomly throughout the room. There were a few large tables in one corner and two round tables along the back wall. Bessie and George stood up, ready to help Mary with whatever needed doing. Before Mary could say anything, though, Andy and Elizabeth rushed into the room.

"Sorry to interrupt, but we need to get the room ready," Andy said.

Mary nodded. "We were just talking about that. We've a lot of furniture to move."

Andy grinned and then turned towards the door. "Jonathan? Is the crew ready?"

Several young men and women walked into the room, with Jonathan Hooper bringing up the rear.

"I've gone over your plans with them," he told Andy. "We should have the room done in five minutes or less."

Bessie very nearly found herself swept away as the small army of staff began to rush around the room. Mary took Bessie's arm and led her back towards the entrance door as Andy carried in a huge box. He started covering various tables with tablecloths as they were settled into place by the team. Less than five minutes later, the room was transformed.

The couches and chairs were now arranged into half a dozen small groupings that would allow for easy conversations. Low tables had been placed in each cluster to allow people to set down drinks and plates. The larger tables had all been covered in cloths and arranged in a line. Bessie assumed that they would hold the food when it was served. The round tables had also been covered, and as Bessie watched, Jonathan began to set them up as an extensive bar.

"That was amazing to watch," Bessie told Mary as the staff began to leave the room.

"Andy has a way of organising people and making such things look easy," she replied. "His restaurant is going to be very successful."

"I believe you're right about that," Bessie replied.

"Mrs. Quayle, Miss Cubbon? Would either of you care for a drink?" Jonathan asked.

"I'll have a glass of white wine," Mary replied. "I didn't take anything for my headache. Hopefully the wine will help."

"I'll have the same, but please call me Bessie," Bessie told him.

He winked at her. "I'll try to remember that."

Bessie knew that he'd continue to call her Miss Cubbon throughout the evening, as he felt that was the proper thing to do. At least when he spoke to her privately, she was always Bessie.

He handed them each a glass of wine and then took a few steps closer to George, who had found a seat on one of the couches. "Mr. Quayle? Would you care for a drink?"

"Scotch," George replied without looking up.

"Not too much of that," Mary said gently. "It's going to be a long evening."

George got up and walked over to Mary. "Yes, dear. I'll try to be good."

A few minutes later, Andy began to bring in the food. Bessie immediately crossed to the tables where he was working to inspect the offerings.

"Everything looks wonderful," she said. "And it all smells good, too."

He glanced around the room and then leaned close to Bessie. "The food on this table and the next one, I prepared. The family's chef made the things on the third table. I just thought you might like to know that."

Bessie grinned. "Thanks for letting me know. I'm sure I'll find plenty to enjoy on these two tables."

Jonathan left the room a minute later, leaving another man in a tuxedo in charge of the bar. "I'll be at the door," he told Mary before he bowed and left the room.

"Here we go," Mary said softly as she joined Bessie near the food.

"It's going to be fine," Bessie told her. "People will probably have one drink and lots of food and then leave."

"I hope so," Mary said anxiously.

The Chief Constable was the first to arrive. Bessie had no more than a nodding acquaintance with the man and no desire to change that, so she stayed where she was as Mary rushed forward to greet him. John and Doona weren't far behind.

"Would it be rude to start eating now?" Doona asked Bessie as they met near the centre of the room.

"You probably don't want to be the first at the food tables," Bessie told her. "But by all means get a drink. Everyone else is already drinking."

John nodded. "White wine?" he asked Doona.

"Just the one," she agreed.

As John headed towards the bar, Doona looked at Bessie. "I'm not sure I'm ready for this," she whispered.

"It's just a few drinks with friends," Bessie replied.

"Whatever it is, I'm sort of John's official escort. That's weird."

"It isn't weird. You two are a couple now. You should attend social events together."

"This is our first proper social event, though, and I'm not sure how I feel about it."

"Just relax. If you and John weren't together, you'd probably both have come anyway."

"That's true," Doona nodded. "Oh, heck, here comes the Chief Constable."

Bessie looked over and spotted the man, who seemed to be heading straight for them. Doona's face had lost its colour as she took Bessie's arm and squeezed tightly.

"Good evening, everyone," someone in the doorway said loudly.

Bessie turned and looked at the new arrival. Scott Meyers was probably in his sixties. To Bessie, he always looked as if he should be the senior attorney on some American drama about a law firm. As she didn't own a television, she was simply guessing what American television lawyers looked like, of course, but that didn't stop her from feeling as if Scott looked exactly as if he'd just strolled away from a television set somewhere. His suit was clearly bespoke and expensive and his hair, black with silver threads running through it, must have just been cut recently.

The Chief Constable changed direction, veering away from Doona and Bessie to intercept Scott as he walked further into the room.

143

Doona blew out a sigh of relief. "He'll keep the Chief Constable busy for a while, anyway. That's Scott Meyers, isn't it?"

"It is. I'm not sure how he managed to escape criminal charges after Grant disappeared, but obviously the Chief Constable doesn't think he's guilty of anything."

Doona nodded as they watched the two men chatting together like old friends. John returned a moment later with Doona's wine and a drink of his own.

"Soda?" Doona asked.

"I'm not drinking in front of the boss," John said, nodding towards the Chief Constable.

Half an hour later, as Bessie chatted with John and Doona in a corner, the room was starting to feel less empty. There were a dozen or more people standing or sitting together in small groups.

"I should go and try to talk to a few people," Bessie said as she took the last sip from her glass of wine.

"Why?" Doona asked flatly.

Bessie chuckled. "I haven't seen most of these people since Grant died. It might be interesting to hear what they think of everything that's happened."

"You know I don't like you questioning suspects," John said.

"I'm not going to be questioning anyone," Bessie told him. "I just want to talk to some of them and express my sympathies, as is appropriate."

Doona covered her laugh with a cough. "Sympathies? Really? I can't imagine anyone here is actually sad that Grant is dead."

"That's one of the things I intend to find out," Bessie said. She glanced around the room and then headed for the bar. Richard Hart, George's advocate, was having a conversation with the bartender, and she couldn't help but wonder what they were discussing.

"…single malt, actually," Richard was saying as she approached.

"There are other options available," the bartender replied.

Richard shrugged and picked up the glass on the table in front of him. He downed the contents in a single swallow and then held out the glass. "I'll just have more of this," he said.

Bessie put her empty wineglass down on the table and smiled at the bartender, who was pouring amber liquid into Richard's glass.

"What can I get you?" he asked her.

"White wine," she replied.

"Do you know which one you were enjoying?"

"They all taste pretty much the same to me," Bessie admitted.

The man chuckled. "That's a shame. If I had the time, I could teach you to tell the difference between the various varieties. Wine is my passion."

He handed Richard his drink and then found an open bottle of wine and poured some into Bessie's glass. Before he could launch into a discussion of what he'd given her, Bessie picked up her glass, murmured her thanks, and turned away.

"How are you?" she asked Richard.

He looked startled and then shrugged. "I'm okay, I suppose."

Where Scott looked like an American television attorney to Bessie, Richard more closely resembled a homeless man. His suits were always wrinkled and none of them seemed to fit his thin and angular frame very well. As usual, his hair appeared to be badly in need of a cut and his glasses had a large smudge across one of the lenses. Bessie knew he had a reputation on the island for being incredibly smart and ruthless to deal with, but she always thought he looked as if he needed someone to look after him.

"I'm sure you were shocked to hear about Grant's death," she said.

"Shocked and more than a little unhappy. I'm supposed to be on holiday," he replied.

"I did hear that you were away. If I were you, I think I would have stayed on my holiday."

Richard made a face. "George wanted me here tonight. He's my best client. One doesn't say no to one's best client."

"I see."

"I shall be leaving again in the morning and hoping to enjoy what's left of my holiday when I get back across."

"George told me that he'd told you that Grant was coming back to the island."

Richard frowned and then sighed deeply. "I won't talk about things that I discuss privately with my clients."

"Of course not. I'm sure you advised George to go straight to the police. It's a shame George didn't listen to you."

"That's very true. Grant would be in prison, where he belonged, rather than dead."

"If the police could have found him."

"Yes, well, of course someone had to have helped him hide. I can't help but wonder who that someone might have been." Richard glanced around the room, and to Bessie it seemed as if his eyes settled on Scott for several seconds.

"Scott might be the most obvious candidate," she said.

"I agree," was the unsurprising answer. "I'm sure, if he did help hide Grant, that he had solid reasons for doing so. Of course, he could very well go to prison anyway, but I'm sure he had his reasons."

Bessie was certain that she hadn't imagined the satisfaction she'd heard in the man's tone as he'd mentioned Scott going to prison. "But whoever was helping Grant, who do you think killed him?"

Richard looked at her and then sighed again. "You really must stop playing amateur detective. I'm surprised that asking those sorts of questions hasn't resulted in your murder yet, really."

Flushing, Bessie took a sip of her wine before she could say anything she might regret later.

"For what it's worth, I've no idea who killed Grant, but if I were the police, I'd be taking a very close look at the people who used to work with him."

There was no mistaking the way Richard was staring at Scott that time. "But not George," Bessie suggested.

"No, of course not," Richard agreed, sounding anything but convincing.

He looked down at the drink in his hand and then downed half of it. "It's been nice speaking with you," he told Bessie in the same tone.

Before she could reply, he walked away. Bessie took another sip of her drink as she studied the small crowd. The food tables were where her next target was standing.

"Everything looks so good," she said to Scott as she reached the tables.

"Skip the last table," he advised. "Nothing very good there."

Bessie smiled and then began to fill a plate. "I suppose I should tell you that I'm sorry for your loss. Grant was your client for a great many years. I assume you became friends during that long relationship."

"You assume incorrectly," he replied snappishly. "We were never anything more than business colleagues."

Bessie knew better than that, but she didn't argue. "Were you surprised when you heard that he was coming back to the island?" she asked after a moment.

He stared at her for a moment and then laughed. "That was almost very clever. You may well have caught me if I were actually guilty of anything. As I know everything I tell you will be repeated to the police and to every other nosy woman on the island, here's my official statement. I did not know that Grant was coming back. I did not have any contact with Grant from the day he left the island until I was informed of his death. I have never been inside the old Looney mansion and I have no plans to ever go inside it now. You can refer any additional questions to my advocate."

Bessie grinned. "Who's your advocate?" she asked.

Scott sighed. "That was mostly a figure of speech. I don't actually have an advocate myself. Do you think I need one?"

"I can't imagine why. If you didn't know Grant was back, you couldn't possibly have killed him."

"Exactly."

"You knew him better than most, though. Whom would he have trusted to find him a place to hide?"

"I haven't any idea," Scott said with a frown. "I will admit that Grant and I had a friendly working relationship. We were in the same social circle, if you like, and it wasn't unusual for us to have a drink together after we'd concluded a deal or some such thing. For all of that, though, Grant was a very private man. I don't know who he confided his secrets to, but it wasn't me. If he was as smart as I think he was, he didn't confide them to anyone."

"I find it hard to believe that he didn't have any help in finding a place to stay on the island," Bessie argued.

"You may be right about that. Perhaps Grant had a lover or a close friend about whom I knew nothing. It's entirely possible. I didn't even know that he knew George until George moved back to the island."

"Really?"

"Grant was a very private person," he said, repeating himself.

As Bessie nodded, Scott picked up his plate full of food. "I must go and talk to someone else," he said, not waiting for Bessie's reply.

She watched him walk across the room, eventually settling onto one of the couches by himself. With her mouth watering, she turned her attention to the food, filling a plate with a dozen different things that all looked delicious.

"The little brown things are the best," a voice to her left said.

Bessie smiled at Michael Quayle, George's younger son. She'd met him on a few different occasions, but didn't really feel as if she knew him. "I'm not sure I'll be able to choose a favourite."

"Lizzie is going to weigh twenty stone if she stays with Andy," Michael laughed. "And the rest of us won't be far behind."

"He's incredibly talented," Bessie agreed as she took a bite of something.

Michael glanced around and then took a step closer to her. "Dad said that you're going to be talking to everyone and trying to work out who killed Grant. Are you having any luck so far?"

Bessie nearly choked. She took a large sip of wine to wash down the food that was suddenly caught in her throat and then shook her head. "I'm afraid finding Grant's killer is a job for the police."

"I saw you talking to Richard and to Scott. I was hoping maybe one of them said something that solved the case for you."

"Neither of them said anything of the kind."

"I'm sorry if I seem pushy, but we're all very anxious to see Grant's murderer behind bars. Mum is terribly upset and Dad isn't at all himself."

"I understand, but I'm afraid there isn't very much that I can do."

"You've solved a lot of murders in the past. I'm sure you'll be able to solve this one."

"I wish I had your confidence," Bessie told him. "Did you know that Grant was coming back to the island?"

Michael looked shocked and then slowly shook his head. "For a moment there I thought maybe you were thinking that I was a suspect, but I suppose you have to ask everyone questions, don't you? I've never really been involved in a murder investigation before. I know Mum and Dad and Lizzie have been, but I've managed to avoid all of that until now."

"As far as I'm concerned, you aren't a suspect," Bessie assured him. "It's just helpful to know who actually knew that Grant was here, that's all."

"Dad didn't tell me anything. He doesn't usually confide in me, though. Sometimes that makes our working relationship a bit difficult, but in this case, I was grateful. If I'd known, I would have rung the police, and that would have upset my father."

Bessie nodded. "Did you know Grant well?"

"Not really. I worked for him for a while, although officially I was working for my father. Grant was giving me my orders, though, for a few months."

"How was he to work with?"

Michael made a face. "He seemed to think of me as a small child. He didn't want to trust me with anything important. Mostly, I think he was simply humouring my father, giving me little bits to do so that my father could feel as if I were involved in his business."

"Your father gives you more responsibility now?"

"Oh, yes, mostly, sometimes." Michael shrugged. "It's a work in progress, but we're getting there. I prefer working for him than I did working for Grant, anyway."

"Darling, the baby is still awake. I think I need to go home before the sitter flees screaming into the night," a pretty blonde said as she approached them.

"Bessie, you've met my wife, Jenny," Michael said.

"Yes, how are you?" Bessie asked.

"I'm fine, but our little one is a handful. I hate to break up the party, not that it feels as if it's a party, but I need to go home," she replied.

"I'll come with you," Michael said quickly. "As you say, it isn't much of a party."

Bessie watched as the pair found Mary and said their goodbyes. She refilled her plate and then found a quiet corner where she could enjoy the food. Once her plate was empty, she got to her feet and headed for the door. After she'd freshened up, she'd try to find someone else to ask about Grant, she decided.

In the corridor, she hesitated. There were loos in both directions and she wasn't sure which one might be more or less popular. Flipping a mental coin, she turned and headed down the corridor to the left.

"I don't think you realise with whom you are dealing," a female voice said. "If I can't have the signed contract on my desk by nine tomorrow morning, we'll take our business elsewhere."

CHAPTER 11

*B*essie stopped and then inched forward slowly, not wanting to walk into the middle of a business conversation, but curious who was speaking. There was a short pause before the voice came again.

"I should think so. I'll be in the office at eight. I'd prefer to have the paperwork there when I arrive."

After another moment, Bessie heard the sound of heels clicking on the tile floor. Trying to look completely casual and as if she hadn't heard a thing, Bessie took a big step forward and nearly crashed into the woman who was striding down the corridor that intersected with Bessie's.

"Oh, goodness, I am sorry," Bessie exclaimed.

"Not at all. It was at least as much my fault," the other woman said, smiling at Bessie. "I didn't think anyone else would be in this part of the house."

"I was looking for an available loo," Bessie told the woman she recognised at Carolyn White, George's assistant.

Carolyn chuckled. "That's always a challenge, even in a house this large. It doesn't help that all of the bedrooms are en suite. I'm sure that's why the builders only added a few extra loos around the place."

Bessie nodded at Carolyn, who didn't look a day over forty. The woman's blonde hair concealed any grey and went well with her bright blue eyes. Her hair was pulled back into a casual ponytail that suited her. She was wearing a dark grey business suit and low heels.

"There is a loo right down the corridor," she told Bessie.

"Thank you," Bessie replied. She took a few steps forwards and then stopped, wondering if she should take advantage of the opportunity to ask Carolyn a few questions. When she looked back, though, the other woman was gone.

As Bessie shut the door behind herself, she sighed. Her kitchen and sitting room both would have fit comfortably in the huge space. The bathtub was probably the size of her bed. Why was there even a bathtub in here, she wondered as she did what she needed to do. Every bedroom had its own en suite facilities, presumably with a bathtub or a shower. Why put a huge tub in here?

She was still wondering about the tub as she made her way back towards the great room a short while later.

"Ah, Miss Cubbon, we meet again," a cool voice said.

Bessie stopped and then smiled at Carolyn. "Hello. It's nice to see you at a party for a change. I don't know that I've ever seen you at any social events and we've never had a chance to actually get to know one another."

Carolyn nodded. "I probably should have made more of an effort to get to know you at some point over the years, but I always do my best to blend into the background. I'm at events to work, not socialise."

"That's a shame."

"It goes with the job."

"Well, it's nice to finally have a chance to speak with you."

"Likewise. George and Mary both speak very highly of you, as does Elizabeth, of course."

"We've all become friends over the years."

"Yes, and Mary rarely makes friends. It's a shame, as she truly needs them."

"We all need friends."

"I suppose so."

Did that mean that Carolyn didn't have any friends, Bessie wondered.

"I can't imagine how awful it must have been for you, finding Grant's body in that horrible house," Carolyn said before Bessie could speak.

"It wasn't pleasant."

"Of course, it wasn't the first body you'd ever found, but I doubt it gets easier."

"No, it doesn't. Were you surprised to learn that Grant was coming back to the island?"

Carolyn shrugged. "What do they say about bad pennies? Coming back seemed a very risky thing for the man to do, but Grant was nothing if not overconfident. I'm sure he wasn't the least bit worried about being caught."

"And he wasn't. Not by the police, anyway."

"Exactly. Clearly, he still had a friend or two on the island who were willing to help him. I'm sure that tiny and dark bedroom in the Looney mansion wouldn't have been his first choice of place to stay. The entire house is in a terrible condition."

"You've been there?" Bessie asked, surprised.

Carolyn laughed. "As odd as it sounds, yes, I have. When George and Mary were first planning their move to the island, I went around a number of houses on their behalf."

"Including the Looney house?" Bessie asked.

"Yes, believe it or not, the estate agent tried to convince me that it was larger on the inside."

Bessie laughed. "I believe that only works on television."

"Precisely. I could see that as soon as I arrived at the property, but I was too polite to refuse to take a tour."

"Which was a complete waste of your time."

"Indeed. I took a look around the house, and then fired that estate agent and found a new one."

"I don't blame you."

"I was able to suggest it to Elizabeth and Andy, though," Carolyn

153

added. "It's much more the sort of thing for which they've been look-ing, although I did tell them that I thought it needed far too much work."

"It does need a great deal of work."

"I believe Elizabeth has decided that she would rather find some-thing else now."

"I don't blame her."

Carolyn nodded. "I find it difficult to imagine Grant staying there for any length of time."

"It is hard to imagine, but goodness only knows what he'd gone through since he'd left the island."

"He left with quite a lot of money. I doubt he'd been suffering."

"So what would have brought him back?"

"Money, or a lack of it. That was all that Grant ever cared about."

The bitterness in the other woman's voice startled Bessie.

Carolyn flushed. "I'm sorry, but Grant reminded me very much of my former husband. It was sometimes difficult for me to be polite to him."

"You weren't sorry to see him go, then."

"Except that once he was gone the true extent of what he'd been doing came to light. That caused a great deal of difficulty for George. My job is to take care of the difficult things on his behalf. It took a long time to repair all of the damage that Grant caused."

"So when you heard that he was returning, you must have been worried."

"Angry is probably a better word," Carolyn replied. "George didn't tell me directly, but I overheard him speaking to Richard Hart, his advocate, about Grant's arrival. I wanted to ring the police as soon as I'd heard, but George refused to even consider the idea. After every-thing that had happened, George still felt some misguided loyalty towards Grant."

"Did you know where Grant was staying?"

"If I had, I would have sent the police," Carolyn snapped. "My loyalties to Grant ended when he disappeared."

Bessie nodded. "George said that he never heard from Grant again after his arrival on the island. Who would have helped him, if it wasn't George?"

"I've no idea," Carolyn replied, sounding amused. "I know you have a reputation for being an amateur detective, but I wasn't expecting you to question me, I have to say."

"I thought we were simply having a conversation," Bessie countered. "I've been asking everyone whom Grant might have trusted. George is the most obvious answer, but I believe him when he says he wasn't involved."

"I believe him, too, of course. I couldn't work for George if I didn't trust him. As for Grant, he had a great many secrets. I think that's obvious, really. He may have had any number of friends or even lovers on the island to whom he entrusted his safety."

"It seems as if he trusted the wrong person."

Carolyn laughed. "It does, indeed. That amuses me, even though it shouldn't. As I said earlier, I didn't care for Grant."

"You've been working for George for a long time now. When did you first meet Grant?"

"I can print you a copy of my CV if you want all of my particulars. I don't think that's really cocktail party conversation, do you?"

"Neither is murder," Bessie pointed out.

"Of course not, but Grant's demise is on everyone's mind, isn't it? I'm sure it's come up in every conversation you've had tonight, hasn't it?"

Bessie nodded. "As you say, it's on everyone's mind."

"Even mine, though I have a great many other things upon which I should be focussed."

"I'm sure George keeps you very busy."

"He's doing less these days, actually. It's Michael who is keeping me busy now, although I meet with George at least once a week to talk about what Michael is doing."

"It would be nice if George could finally actually retire."

"Yes, well, that will be George's decision to make, of course."

Bessie opened her mouth to reply, but she was interrupted as Mary walked out of the great room.

"I was wondering where you'd gone," she told Bessie. "Carolyn, George was looking for you. He wants everyone to say a few words about Grant, and he thought you could arrange things."

Carolyn made a face and then nodded. "Of course," she said tightly.

Mary watched as the woman disappeared into the great room before turning to Bessie. "The evening continues to drag on and on. Michael and Jenny left, and I find myself wishing that I had a baby at home who needed my attention."

"I'm sure you haven't felt that way in years," Bessie laughed.

Mary shrugged. "I loved my babies when they were small. George found them very hard work, but I enjoyed every single stage of watching them grow. It goes by incredibly quickly, you know. One day you have a tiny infant who can't even lift his own head and then, before you know it, you have a fully grown adult who wants to take over running his father's business, even if his father isn't quite ready to let go."

Bessie raised an eyebrow. "Oh?"

"George and Michael had words earlier. I shouldn't be talking about it, though. It's between the two of them and no one else, really, although Carolyn will, no doubt, get herself into the centre of the debate."

"Are you okay?"

Mary laughed shakily. "I am, really. I've had one too many glasses of wine and I still have that headache. I can't take anything for it, not after all the wine I've drunk, and now I find myself babbling and unable to stop myself."

"Maybe we should go back to the party."

"I just escaped," Mary said with a dramatic sigh. "As I said, George wants to have everyone say a few words about Grant, and I can't imagine anything more ghastly, really. What can I say? He didn't steal much from us, really, aside from my husband's time, energy, and devotion?"

"Maybe you should go to bed," Bessie suggested.

"I should, but I won't. I shall go and be the devoted wife that George needs, no matter how I really feel."

She took a deep breath, straightened her spine, and then marched back into the great room. Bessie followed, after a deep breath of her own. George and Carolyn were having a conversation in one corner of the room. Bessie spotted John and Doona standing with the Chief Constable. From what Bessie could see, the Chief Constable was the only one speaking. John and Doona were both nodding occasionally, and Bessie smiled as she watched Doona struggle to hide a yawn.

Scott was standing near the food and Richard was on the opposite side of the room near the bar. There were half a dozen other guests scattered around the room, most of whom Bessie didn't recognise. Elizabeth and Andy were standing together in a corner, talking quietly.

"I think I need another drink," Bessie said.

Mary nodded. "I do, too, but I don't dare."

Bessie was halfway to the bar when George suddenly cleared his throat. "Ah, good evening, everyone," he said loudly.

Conversations around the room stopped.

"Thank you all for coming. I know that this is an unusual situation, but I felt it appropriate to do something to mark the passing of Grant Robertson. I'll be the first to admit that Grant had faults and to acknowledge that his actions caused a great deal of harm to a number of people, some of whom are here tonight. But at the end of the day, Grant was my friend before he was a criminal and I couldn't let his passing go unremarked." He stopped and took a deep breath.

Mary crossed the room and put her hand on George's arm. He gave her a grateful smile.

"Anyway, I'd like to say a few things about Grant and then I'd like to invite the rest of you to speak as well. I'm sure most of you can think of at least one kind thing to say about the man, who was brutally murdered, after all."

Mary whispered something to him and he nodded. "Of course, only speak if you feel as if you want to speak," George added.

There was an awkward moment of silence before Carolyn leaned forward and said something to George. He nodded.

"Let's all take seats," Carolyn suggested. "You may want to get a drink before you find a place to sit."

As she was already halfway to the bar, Bessie decided that a drink was a good idea. After she got her glass of wine, she looked around, trying to decide where to sit. John and Doona were together on a couch near the food. Andy and one of the waiters were busy moving several other couches into a rough circle there. The Chief Constable had moved over to speak to George.

Bessie walked across and slid into the chair next to Doona. "This was already incredibly awkward," she whispered to her friend.

"I'd be willing to bet it's going to get worse," Doona replied.

As Bessie sipped her wine, the rest of the guests slowly found seats around the circle. Everyone had a glass in his or her hand, and Bessie noted that Scott had glasses in both hands.

George looked around the room and then smiled at everyone. "I really need to thank you all for coming tonight. My lovely wife thought that having any sort of gathering to remember Grant was a bad idea, but I knew that my friends and my family would support me. Whatever Grant's faults, and I know he had many, he was my friend. We met when we began working together. He loved working for the bank, but for me, the bank was simply a stepping-stone on to other things. I was too loud to be a banker." George laughed, and a few others chuckled softly.

Mary whispered something in her husband's ear. He looked at her for a moment and then nodded.

"Right, well, where was I? Grant and I worked together for a few years, and then I moved across. I was certain that I'd have more success there, and I even tried to persuade Grant to move with me, but he was happy here. The island was his home, and while he travelled occasionally, he used to tell me that he was always happy to get back home again. I have to believe that he came back because he still felt as if the island was home, in spite of everything."

Bessie exchanged glances with John. She'd not really given that idea much thought, but it was an interesting one. Having known

Grant, though, she couldn't really see him putting himself in danger simply because he missed the island.

George took a sip of his drink. "After I went across, Grant and I didn't see one another very often. He would ring me every so often when he was visiting somewhere near wherever I was living and we'd meet for a drink or dinner, but otherwise we rarely spoke. He was busy with his job and I was busy with mine. I was fortunate to have a lovely wife and three beautiful children, as well. Grant never found that sort of happiness in his lifetime."

He stopped and said something to Mary. She found a tissue in her handbag and handed it to George. He wiped his eyes and then looked up at everyone.

"Sorry, I'm finding this more difficult than I'd anticipated. As I said before, Grant had many faults, but he was my closest friend, even over the years when we rarely saw one another. Over time, we began to work together on some small projects. Eventually, when I decided to come back to the island, we started working together even more. For a short while, I think I was spending more time every day with Grant than I was with my family."

Mary nodded, but George didn't notice.

"We had a great many plans for the island, including the new retail park that I'm still developing. I have to believe that Grant truly loved the island and I know that I cared deeply about him."

He wiped his eyes again while everyone else exchanged glances. After emptying his drink, George patted Mary's arm. "Your turn, my dear."

Mary looked stunned. "I don't think..." she murmured.

"Please," George said.

Mary's eyes met Bessie's, and Bessie could almost see the woman struggling to work out what to say.

"I didn't meet Grant until we moved to the island," she said after an awkward pause. "He helped George in many ways, and offered him many unique business opportunities. While we didn't always see eye to eye on certain matters, I do believe that he was a good friend to George."

Bessie didn't think that Mary could have done any better if she'd had hours to prepare her words. They were simple and appropriate, and she'd managed to make them sound sincere, as well. Now George looked past Mary to the next couch, where Elizabeth and Andy were sitting.

"Elizabeth?" he said.

She sighed. "I barely knew Grant, but I appreciated that he was my father's friend. Daddy always worked too hard and he rarely had friends, so it was good that he'd found one. I hope he'll find another friend now, one who doesn't make him work so hard, maybe."

A few people chuckled, including George. "Andy, you didn't know Grant, did you?" George asked a moment later.

Andy hesitated for a moment and then shook his head. "No, I didn't."

Bessie wondered about the hesitation, but now wasn't the time to question it.

George kept moving around the circle, having people talk about Grant. His older son said something very similar to what Elizabeth had said. The next man was one of George's business associates. He told a long-winded story about how he'd met Grant through a mutual friend and how they'd developed a solid working relationship over several years. Bessie had to hide several yawns as the story dragged on for ten minutes or more.

"Scott?" George asked when the man was finally done.

The advocate swallowed the last of one of his drinks and then carefully put the empty glass on the table in front of him. "I'm not sure what to say," he said in slightly slurred speech. "Grant was my client for many years. For much of that time, he was my only client because he sent so much work my way."

"He's more than a little drunk," Doona whispered to Bessie as Scott stopped and took a sip from his second glass.

"I hope he didn't drive," Bessie hissed back.

Doona frowned and then whispered something to John.

"I wish I could say that Grant was my friend," Scott continued. "Grant was a very private person, though. I mean, we all know now why he was so private, don't we?" Scott chuckled as everyone else looked uncomfortable.

"Anyway," Scott said. "Grant and I had a good working relationship, within the boundaries that Grant set. He paid me well and promptly. Aside from getting me tangled up in a major police investigation that almost cost me my career, I can't complain about him."

Bessie hid a smile behind her glass. Scott was simply being honest, but she was certain that his words were not what George had been hoping to hear.

"Let's move on," George said sharply. The next man was another of George's colleagues. He kept his comments mercifully short before turning his attention back to his drink.

Bessie was next. She really wanted to refuse to say anything, but she felt obliged to be polite for Mary's sake.

"I didn't really know Grant, but I believe everyone on the island knew who he was. He was, among other things, a supporter of many of the island's charities. Over the years I worked with a number of charities who were grateful for his assistance."

George nodded vigorously. "I should have mentioned that. Not only did Grant do a lot for charity, but he always encouraged me to give generously. I'm sure I wouldn't have done nearly as much as I have without his encouragement."

Sitting back in her seat, Bessie was glad that her part in the ordeal was over. George looked at Doona next.

"Mrs. Moore, I don't believe that you knew Grant," he said.

Doona shook her head. "I met him a few times, but we didn't truly know one another."

George nodded. "And I won't ask Inspector Rockwell to speak, as I'm certain that he would have trouble separating the Grant that I knew from the man that he learned about during the investigation after Grant's disappearance."

"I appreciate that," John said.

Bessie could see the relief on both of her friends' faces as George moved on to the couple on the other side of them. After yet another of

George's businessmen friends had said something meaningless, it was Richard Hart's turn to speak.

"I didn't have a lot of dealings with Grant," he said. "Mostly, I worked on George's behalf with Scott, who was working on Grant's behalf. We knew one another socially, of course, but as someone has already pointed out, Grant was a very private man who didn't make friends easily. On the odd occasions when I did see him, I always found him perfectly pleasant, anyway."

"Perfectly pleasant?" Doona echoed, raising an eyebrow at Bessie.

Bessie just shrugged.

The Chief Constable was last. He looked around the circle with a serious expression on his face. "This is very difficult. I knew Grant for a great many years. I'm not ashamed to say that I enjoyed his company. Of course, what we later discovered about the man was shocking and disappointing, but it doesn't take away from the fact that Grant could be an interesting and entertaining person with whom to spend time."

Everyone sat in silence for a moment and then George rose to his feet. "Thank you all for that. I needed to hear all the kind things that people had to say about Grant. I'm mourning his death, even if I'm the only person who is genuinely sad that he's gone. Thank you all for coming tonight. Please, have some more to eat and drink. There's plenty more food."

Bessie looked over at the three tables. The first two were starting to look a bit empty, but the third appeared to have been barely touched. She wasn't feeling very hungry, though. Mostly, she simply felt sad.

"That was horrible," Doona said in a low voice as people began to get up and move around again.

"It was pretty bad," Bessie agreed.

"George truly is the only one who seems to be mourning for Grant," Doona added.

"Perhaps Grant had some other friends about whom we know nothing," Bessie suggested.

"He must have, as someone hid him at the Looney house."

"But was he truly hiding there?" Bessie asked. "While everyone was talking, I was thinking. We went all over that house, and there was nothing anywhere to suggest that anyone was staying there. I think he was hiding somewhere else and simply visiting the Looney place."

"I'm inclined to agree with you," John told quietly. "But we aren't releasing that information publicly, for a whole host of reasons."

Bessie nodded. "So where was he staying?"

"That's the big question, aside from who killed him, of course," Doona replied.

"I suspect if you find out the answer to the first question, you'll also discover the answer to the second," Bessie said.

She got to her feet and then stopped and stared at the doorway. "I wonder why Carolyn didn't join us," she said to Doona, who'd stood up next to her.

"Carolyn?"

"Carolyn White, George's assistant." Bessie gestured towards the woman who was standing in a corner, talking on a mobile phone.

"I didn't even realise she was here tonight," Doona replied. "I think I've only seen her one time, at the Seaview when George and Mary were entertaining the men who were interested in the retail park project."

"We spoke briefly earlier, after she'd finished shouting at someone about something."

"It looks as if she's going to start shouting again," Doona remarked.

Across the room, Carolyn was frowning as she spoke into her phone. After a moment she began to pace, swinging one arm back and forth as she continued to talk. Bessie wasn't surprised when, after another minute, Carolyn stomped out of the room.

"Bessie, I feel as if I should apologise for George," Mary said, as she joined them where they were still standing.

"Not at all," Bessie replied. "I can't imagine how difficult this must be for him. While Grant had faults, he and George were friends, and it's only natural for George to want to remember his friend's better qualities."

"It's very kind of you to say that," Mary told her. "I'm sure the last

DIANA XARISSA

hour was something of an ordeal, though. I'm rather hoping that people start leaving now, though I shouldn't admit it."

"I'll go and I'll do so loudly, if you think the others will take the hint," Bessie offered.

Mary chuckled. "I'd rather you stayed, actually, out of everyone here. Aside from my children, obviously."

"Doona and I can go, but I'd rather not leave before the Chief Constable leaves," John told her.

"You're more than welcome to stay as long as you like. There are actually only a few people I'd like to see go." Mary looked around the room and Bessie was sure that her gaze stopped on Scott for several seconds.

"Would you like me to go and spill my drink all over Scott?" Doona asked.

Mary looked shocked and then laughed. "It's a lovely and very tempting idea, but no. I think you're better off staying well away from the man, really."

Doona opened her mouth to reply, but Carolyn, who'd just rushed back into the room, interrupted her.

"Mary, where has George gone?" Carolyn demanded. "I need his agreement on something."

"Now?" Mary asked.

Carolyn nodded. "I've been working on this all evening and the other side has finally given me a decent offer. I just need George's approval."

"He was talking with Richard. I believe they left the room together. I'll go and see if I can find him," Mary said.

"Don't bother. I'll find him," Carolyn replied. She dashed away before Mary could reply.

"Does she always work so hard?" Bessie asked.

Mary shrugged. "I rarely see her, although she does ring the house at all hours of the day and night, so probably."

Movement on the other side of the room caught Bessie's attention. The Chief Constable walked over to join Scott. After a short conversation, he took the glass out of Scott's hand and put a hand on his arm.

164

The room fell silent as the senior policeman escorted Scott out of the room.

"Oh, dear," Mary said.

Scott's exit seemed to be what everyone else was waiting for, though. Moments later, people began saying polite goodbyes to Mary and disappearing out of the room. Within minutes, nearly everyone was gone.

Bessie, Doona, and John remained standing together with Mary. Elizabeth and Andy were near the food table, talking and seemingly unaware of anyone else in the room. Bessie picked up her handbag, ready to head for home, as George and Carolyn walked back into the room.

"Has everyone gone, then?" George asked.

"Nearly," Mary replied.

"Excellent," George said. "Now Bessie can tell us who killed Grant."

CHAPTER 12

*B*essie flushed. "I'm afraid I can't do anything of the kind," she said quickly.

"You must have your suspicions, though," George said firmly. "You spoke to nearly everyone tonight."

"I was simply being friendly," Bessie protested.

"You asked me a great many questions," Carolyn said. "If you did the same with everyone, you should have gathered quite a lot of information."

"Maybe we should all sit down," Mary suggested. "I'm sure Bessie was simply being friendly, but people do have a habit of confiding in her. Maybe she heard something useful."

Bessie wanted to protest, but George didn't give her a chance. He came and took her arm and pulled her down onto a couch next to him.

John dropped into the chair next to Bessie. "Are you okay with this?" he whispered.

She shrugged. "It's probably easier to humour George than argue with him."

John nodded. "A quick chat about the case won't hurt anything, but if it starts to drag out for too long, I'll put an end to things."

"Thank you," Bessie said, feeling grateful that the Chief Constable had left, anyway.

"Right, so, what did you learn tonight?" George demanded as soon as all of the others had taken seats in a circle.

"Nothing, really," Bessie said. She was annoyed with herself when she heard her apologetic tone.

"You must have learned something," George said. "Scott was quite drunk. I'm sure he said things he shouldn't have."

"He may well have done, but nothing that he said to me seemed to have anything to do with Grant's murder," Bessie replied.

"The way I see it, there are several different questions that need answering," Elizabeth interjected. "The first question is where Grant was staying while he was on the island."

"We already know the answer to that," George told her. "He was found at the Looney house. He must have been staying there."

Elizabeth shook her head. "We went all over that house, through every single room. There was nothing there to suggest that anyone was staying there."

"Really?" George asked.

"Every piece of furniture had layers of dust on top. There isn't any running water to the property, either. That's been turned off for ages. Andy and I paid to have the electricity turned back on so that we could take a look around, but they only did that a few days ago. If Grant came back nearly a fortnight ago, he would have been staying in the dark for the first week and a half that he'd been staying there."

"He was hiding. Staying in the dark was probably a good idea," Carolyn suggested.

"Even if he were hiding and being very careful, we still would have found traces of his stay," Elizabeth said. "There wasn't any rubbish anywhere in the house, for example."

"So you think he was staying somewhere else and then moved to the Looney house just before he was killed?" George asked.

"That's the only thing that makes sense, unless he was killed the day he arrived, before he'd had a chance to do anything in the house," Elizabeth replied.

167

Everyone turned to look at John, who sighed. "We don't have the official report yet, but I know Dan Ross will be publishing some initial findings that he got from one of his sources in the next day or two. Grant hadn't been dead for more than week when he was found."

"So he stayed somewhere for at least a week," Elizabeth mused.

"Or multiple places," George suggested.

"Moving around would have been very dangerous for him," Doona suggested. "Unless he had a very good disguise."

"He wasn't wearing any disguise when we found him," Bessie said.

"Could he really have had multiple friends who were willing to hide him?" Elizabeth asked. "He was a wanted criminal, after all. Surely, if he'd contacted any of his former friends, at least one of those friends would have simply rung the police."

Bessie glanced at George, who flushed. "I would have agreed to hide him for a short while," he said, sounding sheepish. "I wanted to give him a chance to explain himself, really."

"But you didn't hide him," Carolyn said. "So who else would he have trusted?"

"Scott," George said flatly. "You should search his house. Maybe you could find evidence that Grant stayed there," he told John.

"I've no grounds for a warrant," John told him. "Anyway, Scott has had at least a week to clear away any trace of Grant, if he ever was there."

"And that's true for everyone," Elizabeth sighed. "I did wonder if we should search our house. Knowing Grant, he probably could have found a way in and hidden himself in one of the spare rooms."

George looked stunned. "That's exactly the sort of thing he might have done," he exclaimed. "Why didn't you think of that?" he asked John.

"We did, actually," John replied. "I had a long discussion with Mr. Hooper about that very possibility."

"With Jonathan? I see. Does that mean that you searched the house?" was George's next question.

"Not at all. Mr. Hooper was certain that no one was staying here without his knowledge, although he did agree to conduct his own search of the entire property. He promised to contact me if he found anything," John told him.

"Where is he?" George demanded. He got to his feet and crossed the room. "Jonathan?" he bellowed into the corridor.

The butler appeared only a moment later. "Yes, sir?" he asked.

"Inspector Rockwell said that you agreed to search the house for any signs that Grant might have stayed here," George said.

"Yes, sir, that's correct," Jonathan replied.

"What did you find?" George demanded.

"Absolutely nothing, sir," Jonathan replied "I told the inspector that I thought that it was unlikely that Mr. Robertson had been staying here, as I do regular room inspections of all of the unused guest rooms. In light of what happened to Mr. Robertson, though, I was more than happy to check each room, just in case I'd missed something previously."

"So where was he staying?" George asked as he crossed back to his seat.

"Thank you, Jonathan," Mary called from her place.

George looked slightly confused and then nodded towards the butler. "Oh, yes, of course, thank you."

"He could have been staying anywhere," Elizabeth said. "Maybe he was staying in a hotel or a bed and breakfast."

"We've several constables checking with every site on the island," John told her. "As it's the quiet season, there aren't that many places where he could have taken a room. Under the circumstances, we're asking all of the owners or managers of closed properties to check that no one has been staying anywhere uninvited."

"What about the holiday cottages?" Bessie asked as the idea popped into her head.

"That was one of my first thoughts," John told her. "Maggie went through them for me and didn't find any evidence that anyone has been staying in any of them."

"Maybe he was just really careful," Carolyn suggested. "Maybe he was sleeping in one of the holiday cottages but taking care not to leave any trace."

John nodded. "That's possible, of course. It isn't easy to stay somewhere and not leave evidence of your visit behind, but Grant had been on the run for nearly two years. He may have picked many different skills while he was away."

"Someone had to have been helping him," Elizabeth said. "Someone had to have been taking him food, for instance."

"Unless he did have a good disguise," Carolyn countered.

"Even with a disguise, surely he'd have wanted to stay out of sight as much as possible," Doona said. "But taking food back to wherever he was staying would have meant leaving behind traces of his visit."

"I think he was staying with someone he trusted," George said. "Someone who was prepared to buy or make meals for him."

"Which brings us back to Scott," Mary said with a sigh.

"He does seem the most likely candidate, if not for murder, than at least for hiding Grant," George said.

"But Scott was off the island when Grant first arrived," John said. "If Grant truly did arrive on the day he told George that he'd arrived, then Scott wasn't on the island to hide him."

"Maybe Scott came back from his travels and found Grant staying in his house," Andy suggested.

"It would be like Grant to simply move in," George said with a small laugh.

"Obviously, he was staying with someone he trusted," Elizabeth said. "Whoever it was wouldn't have wanted to murder him in his or her own home, which is why Grant was in the Looney house, I'm sure."

"That's assuming that the person who was hiding Grant is also the person who killed him," Andy said.

"Surely that's the only person who knew where Grant was," Elizabeth argued.

"Grant could have arranged to meet someone at the Looney house and not even told the person he was staying with about the meeting," Andy suggested.

"I suppose so, but it would be much neater if it was the same person," Elizabeth replied.

Everyone laughed.

"Sadly, murder investigations are rarely neat," John told her.

"Where is his luggage?" Elizabeth asked. "I'm sure he must have come back with some luggage. Where is it now?"

"It must be wherever Grant was staying," was George's verdict. "All the more reason to search Scott's house."

"Surely, whoever he stayed with will have found a way to dispose of everything by now," Mary said.

"Maybe he didn't bring anything with him. Do we know how he got to the island?" Andy asked.

John shook his head. "His name doesn't appear on any passenger lists for flights or the ferry for the relevant date or for a week either side of it. He could have come on a private boat. We're still checking with various boat hire companies in Liverpool and Heysham, as well as from some Irish ports."

"He said he was coming by ferry," George said.

"And you've no reason to believe anything he told you," Mary said softly.

George frowned and then shrugged. "I can't see why he'd lie. He knew he could trust me."

"Too bad the reverse wasn't true," Mary sighed.

"We're simply talking in circles," Carolyn said. "I don't know about the rest of you, but I'm getting tired. Perhaps it's time to call an end to the evening."

"You go home and get some rest," George told her. "You worked very hard today on that deal, after all."

"It's my job," Carolyn replied.

George nodded. "And you're very good at it."

She shrugged. "I'll be going, then," she said, getting to her feet.

Bessie was quick to stand up as well. "Ms. White is correct," she said. "It is getting late and we aren't accomplishing anything."

George frowned. "But we've so many unanswered questions. Why did Grant even come back to the island? Why did he go to the

Looney house? Who wanted him dead? Where did the knife come from?"

Bessie held up a hand. "Those are all excellent questions and ones that the police are working hard to answer. I think we should let them do their job."

"Are you quite certain that you didn't work out who did it tonight?" George asked.

"I'm sorry, but I did not. I'll think about everything that everyone said to me, but I doubt very much that it will make any difference," Bessie replied.

"But it might," George said hopefully. "Maybe, once you've thought it all through, you'll be able to work everything out."

Bessie was pretty sure that George was going be disappointed, but she was too tired to argue. Instead, she nodded and then took a step towards the door.

Mary jumped up. "Let me find someone to take you home," she said.

"I can walk," Bessie replied, feeling as if some fresh air and exercise would do her good.

"It's late. I'm sure Jonathan will take you home," Mary replied. "Wait here while I find him."

"We can take Bessie home," John said.

Mary shook her head. "I'm sure Jonathan won't mind." She disappeared out of the room before anyone else could speak.

A few minutes later, Mary was back with Jonathan at her heels.

"I'm more than happy to take you home," he told Bessie.

"Thank you," Bessie said. She said a quick goodbye to George, who was still sitting in his place, frowning.

"I wish you'd have solved everything," he said. "I hate having this hanging over all of us."

"The police are doing their best," Bessie replied.

Elizabeth and Andy both gave Bessie hugs, as did Doona and John.

"It was a pleasure to have a chance to speak with you," she told Carolyn.

"Likewise. I'm surprised it never happened before," Carolyn replied.

Bessie and Jonathan headed for the door. With every step, Bessie found herself feeling increasingly tired. As Jonathan helped her into his car, she was grateful that Mary had insisted on the ride home. The walk back along the beach would have felt incredibly long in her tired state.

"I'll just come in and check that everything is okay," Jonathan said as he parked outside Bessie's cottage.

"I'm sure everything is fine," Bessie told him.

"I am, too, but I'm still going to check," he replied firmly.

Bessie was too tired to argue. Since her cottage had been broken into some months earlier, she'd found that she didn't mind people fussing over her as much as she had previously. Her advocate kept suggesting both better locks and a security system, but thus far she hadn't agreed to either.

She stood in the kitchen, wondering if she should make herself some tea, while Jonathan stomped around over her head. When he came back down the stairs and into the kitchen, she gave him a hug.

"I told you everything was fine," she said.

"Yes, and I'd have never slept tonight if I hadn't checked."

She sent him on his way with a few biscuits for a bedtime snack. After locking the door behind him, she checked her answering machine.

"Ah, Bessie, it's Andrew, Andrew Cheatham. I was just ringing to let you know that my flight on Saturday is scheduled to land at two in the afternoon. I'm going to hire a car and then I'll be on my way to Laxey. My plan is to come to your cottage once I've moved into mine. Please ring me back if that doesn't suit you. I'm looking forward to seeing you the day after tomorrow. We have much to discuss."

Bessie frowned at the phone. What did they have discuss? No doubt he wanted to talk about another cold case with her. She'd helped him with one on his previous visit, after all.

The other two messages on the machine were from nosy friends who'd heard about the gathering at Thie yn Traie. Both were simply hoping for some sort of interesting gossip from the evening. Feeling very much as if nothing at all interesting had happened, Bessie headed for the stairs. Tomorrow was another day.

It turned out to be a rainy one. Bessie frowned at the weather as she got dressed. She'd been hoping to take a long walk this morning, but decided against it as a heavier rain began to fall. Having breakfast before her walk would give the weather time to improve, she decided. Sadly, the weather didn't seem to want to cooperate. It was raining just as heavily when she'd finished her toast with honey as it had been when she'd started.

Frowning, she pulled on her waterproofs and her Wellington boots. A short walk in the rain was better than nothing, she reminded herself as she took her umbrella out of the small closet near the door. After stepping outside and locking her door, she opened the umbrella. A moment later, it blew inside out in the strong wind.

Bessie shut the umbrella. She'd check it later to see if the wind had caused any damage. Then she took a deep breath and began her walk. The wind fought against her, trying to force her back to Treoghe Bwaane, but she pressed onwards, not stopping until she'd reached the stairs to Thie yn Traie. There she stopped and caught her breath.

The rain was still heavy and the wind was cold, so Bessie turned around reluctantly. If things improved later in the day, she'd take another walk, of course, but she was still disappointed. She was nearly back to her own cottage when she heard her name being called.

"Bessie, come in out of the rain," Maggie Shimmin shouted from the dining room of the cottage nearest Bessie's home.

"I was nearly there," Bessie muttered to herself as she turned back around and walked up the beach towards Maggie.

"Oh, dear, you're quite sodden, aren't you?" Maggie asked as Bessie stepped into the holiday cottage.

"It's raining very heavily," Bessie pointed out.

"Yes, of course, and you will have had a long walk, too, in spite of the weather, won't you?"

"I nearly always do."

"Yes, well, please try not to drip on the floors too much," Maggie said, looking worriedly at Bessie's feet.

Bessie looked down and noticed that water was pooling around her as it dripped off of her waterproofs. "I should probably get home," she suggested.

"Oh, but I wanted to talk to you about a few things," Maggie said.

"I'm afraid I can't stop the rain from dripping off of me."

"Never mind. I'll clean it up once you've gone. What's this I hear about one of the Looney children coming back to the island to claim his rightful inheritance, though?"

"I believe the man is simply here to revisit his childhood home," Bessie countered. "That's what he told me, anyway."

"I've heard he's been consulting advocates and talking about suing Gary Davison's children for a share of the estate."

"That's news to me," Bessie said firmly, hiding a smile at the disappointed look on Maggie's face.

"He probably won't get much, anyway," Maggie said. "There were seven of them, weren't there? And the only thing left on the island is the house. They'll never get what they were asking for it now, not after someone was murdered in it. By the time he pays for his advocates his one-seventh share won't be worth more than a few pounds, I'd have thought."

"I've no idea."

"What's he like, then? I'm too young to remember when they lived on the island, of course."

Bessie hid a grin. Maggie always insisted that she was too young to remember things, even though Bessie knew exactly how old Maggie was. "He seemed very nice when I met him."

"I'm sure he suffered terribly, losing both of his parents in that way, and then being dragged away from everything he'd ever known as well."

"His grandparents and his siblings did go with him."

"Well, yes, of course, but I'm sure it was still very difficult."

"No doubt."

"Imagine coming back and then discovering that the house that

175

you grew up in, the one that your father lovingly built with his own hands, is for sale and in a terrible state."

"He knew the house was for sale. That was one of the reasons why he came back now."

"Really?"

Maggie looked delighted to have learned something new. Bessie immediately regretted telling her anything.

"I believe so, anyway," she said.

"I'm sure it was a shock to him, too, finding out that one of Gary Davison's children was also on the island."

Bessie bit her tongue. As far as she knew, Harold still didn't know that Susan was there, and the reverse was also true, but she wasn't about to share that information with Maggie.

"You've met her, too, haven't you?" Maggie asked.

"I have. She seems very nice."

"Aside from having the blood of a killer running through her veins," Maggie said darkly.

Bessie thought for a moment before she replied, choosing her words with care. "I don't believe Gary Davison was ever charged with any crime."

"No, but we all knew that he killed poor Valerie. It was partly her fault, of course. Imagine marrying a man that much younger than yourself, especially when you have seven children to look after. She had to know that he was only marrying her for her money."

"I don't recall Valerie having very much money, actually."

"She had the house. That was more than Gary Davison had. He didn't have a penny to his name when he took Valerie down the aisle. He was a handsome brute, though, and I'm sure he told her everything she wanted to hear."

"I do remember him being rather attractive," Bessie admitted. As she recalled, Gary had been young and handsome, much more attractive than Sam Looney, who'd been a hard-working but rather ordinary-looking middle-aged man when he'd died.

"He was gorgeous. He could have had his pick of women on the island. I've no idea why he chose Valerie Looney."

"Maybe they fell in love."

Maggie laughed. "I doubt that very much. I always wondered if Gary thought Valerie had more money than she actually did, though. All she really had was the house. If she didn't marry Gary because he was handsome and young, she married him because she thought he'd look after the house for her. I'm sure he didn't expect her to fall pregnant again, not at her age."

"She was still in her thirties. She could have had several more children."

"None of which Gary would have wanted. He didn't care for children."

"Really? What makes you think that?" Bessie had to ask.

"He left all seven of Valerie's kids here, didn't he? When she died, he never even came back to the island to collect his things. He simply stayed in the UK with the baby."

"Which suggests he cared about the baby, anyway."

"Sam's parents weren't going to take the baby, were they? They already had seven kids to look after and the baby wasn't any relative of Sam's. I always thought that it was a shame that Valerie's parents were both dead. I'm sure they would have kept all eight children if they'd still been around."

Bessie nodded. She'd known Valerie's parents well. They'd loved their daughter and doted on their grandchildren. They'd also had a bit of money, money that Valerie had inherited when they'd passed away suddenly within a few weeks of one another.

"I always wondered whatever happened to all of their money," Maggie said.

"I believe Sam and Valerie put most of it towards the house." Sam had already been working on the house when Valerie's parents had died, but the original plan had been for a smaller structure, all on one level. After Valerie's unexpected inheritance, the plans had been amended to something considerably larger. That was when Laxey residents had begun referring to the house as the Looney mansion, even though it wasn't actually that large.

"I think someone should simply tear the house down. No one is going to want to buy it, not after the murder. It's in a terrible state, anyway. I'm sure it would cost less to build a new house there than it would to make that one habitable again."

"We'll have to see what happens, I suppose."

"Thomas and I were looking at it, actually," Maggie said. "We don't want the house, of course. I won't even go inside. We just want the land. It's a good location, right in the centre of Laxey. Thomas reckons we could build a small block of flats on the site and make a fortune renting them out."

Bessie frowned. While the Looney house did need a lot of work, she was very fond of how it looked in its place on the street. A small block of flats sounded quite unattractive. "Yes, well, I suppose all you can do is make an offer."

"We're trying to work out how difficult it might be to get planning permission to tear the house down," Maggie confided. "It isn't that old, but it is something of a well-known property. If we can't tear it down, though, we don't want to buy it."

"I can understand that."

Maggie shrugged. "Of course, if Elizabeth Quayle still wants it, we don't have a chance anyway. Her father will make certain that she gets it no matter the price."

Bessie shrugged. "I've no idea what Elizabeth and Andy are planning now."

"Really? I thought, since you were invited to their little gathering last evening, that you were in George's inner circle now."

"Not at all," Bessie said, flushing.

"I don't believe he invited more than a handful of people to last night's event," Maggie continued. "I was told it was something akin to a memorial service for Grant, but I'm not certain that I believe that. I can't imagine anyone having anything good to say about Grant Robertson."

"George and Grant were friends many years ago, when they were both first starting out. I believe that George wanted to remember that man, the one with whom he worked so long ago."

Maggie made a face. "He was a thief and a murderer. George should remember that."

Bessie nodded slowly. She hadn't really thought about it, but Maggie was right. Although nothing had ever been proven against him, Grant was certainly a likely suspect in more than one murder that had happened when he'd been on the island. Was it possible that someone from one of the victim's families had taken revenge on the man?

"You're lost in thought," Maggie said after a moment.

"I was just thinking about Grant's victims, the men who died as a result of their association with him, whether Grant killed them or not."

"Of course Grant killed them. I'm sure he hated getting his hands dirty, but I can't see him trusting anyone else with the job, can you?"

Bessie shrugged. "We'll probably never know for certain now."

Maggie looked down at the floor and then sighed deeply. "My goodness, that's a lot of water," she said in a disapproving tone.

Bessie looked at the puddle at her feet. "It is, isn't it?" she replied, determined not to apologise for the mess that was not her fault. Maggie had insisted on speaking to her, after all.

"I'd better get it cleaned up. This cottage is booked starting on Saturday."

"Yes, I know. My friend, Andrew Cheatham, has booked it."

Maggie looked surprised. "I didn't realise that. As all of the bookings are handled for us in Douglas, I don't keep track of our guests the way I did formerly. He's stayed with us before, though, hasn't he?"

"He has, yes."

"And he's coming back again? How nice for you."

Bessie braced herself for the questions that were sure to follow.

"How do you know him again?"

"We met at Lakeview Holiday Park the first time that Doona and I visited."

"Oh, yes, when her husband was brutally murdered," Maggie said. "He was the former Scotland Yard inspector who was staying in the cottage next to yours, wasn't he?"

"Yes, that's right," Bessie replied, feeling annoyed at how much Maggie knew.

"Let's hope no one else gets brutally murdered while he's here. Maybe he can help John solve Grant's murder, though. If ever there was a case for Scotland Yard, this must be the one."

Bessie didn't agree, but she also didn't argue. Instead, she looked at her watch. "My goodness, the day is getting away from me," she exclaimed. "I'd better get home and get some work done."

"What are you doing today?" Maggie asked as Bessie zipped up her jacket.

"I may do some transcription work for the museum," she replied.

"It seems as I'll be mopping the floor all day," Maggie said sourly as Bessie opened the sliding door.

Biting her tongue, Bessie stepped outside into the wind and rain and then carefully slid the door shut behind her. She gave Maggie a casual wave and then quickly walked the short distance to Treoghe Bwaane. Even though it was still raining quite hard, she found herself reasonably dry when she got home.

"I must have left most of the rain on Maggie's floor," she said to herself as she hung up her waterproofs in the ground floor loo.

Feeling as if she ought to spend more time with Onnee, Bessie made herself a cup of tea to get rid of the chill that she felt from the weather. She read the first chapter in a new cosy mystery as she sipped her tea. When the tea was gone and the first chapter was finished, she told herself to go and work on her transcriptions. The second chapter was a short one, though, so she let herself continue with the story.

Six chapters later, she was starting to feel rather guilty. The story was excellent, however, and she couldn't seem to put the book down. Onnee's story was fascinating, too, of course, but reading it took a great deal of work and concentration, unlike the novel in her hands.

What she really needed was another cup of tea, she decided. She'd read until that was finished and then she'd go and do what she should have been doing all along.

She filled the kettle almost to the top without thinking. Aware that it would take a good deal longer to boil that way, she didn't bother to tip any of the extra water out. Instead, she sat down and got lost in her story again. The kettle did, eventually, boil, and Bessie found herself making her tea as quickly as she could so that she could get back to the story. She'd just sat down, teacup in hand, and found her place in the book, when someone knocked on the door.

Frowning, Bessie slid her bookmark back into place and crossed to the door.

"Elizabeth?"

"I hope this isn't a bad time," the girl replied. "I need some advice."

CHAPTER 13

*B*essie thought longingly of her book as she welcomed
Elizabeth into the cottage. "The kettle just boiled. Tea?"

"Oh, yes, please," Elizabeth said.

Which undoubtedly meant that the girl wasn't in any hurry, Bessie
thought as she got another teacup out of the cupboard. She put some
biscuits onto a plate and then made Elizabeth's tea. When they were
both sitting with their drinks at the table, she smiled encouragingly.

"What's wrong?" she asked.

"Nothing's wrong, exactly," Elizabeth sighed. "The thing is, Andy
still wants to buy the Looney mansion, but I'm not certain that I can
get past the murdered man in the main bedroom." She spoke quickly,
the words rushing out of her, before she sat back and took a sip of
her tea.

Bessie took a bite of biscuit and chewed it slowly while she tried to
decide how to reply. "Why does Andy want the house so much?" she
asked eventually.

"He loves the location. It is really nice, right in the centre of Laxey
and all that, I suppose. He also thinks it's a great house, on the outside,
anyway. Obviously, the interior needs to be completely redone, but he
reckons that that is just fine, since we'd probably want to remodel any

house we buy. He's spent a lot of time already sketching out his ideas for the ground floor. He wants a huge kitchen with restaurant-quality appliances and, well, just lots of other stuff."

"And what do you think of the plans?"

"I loved them when I first saw them, before Grant Robertson's body turned up in the bedroom."

Bessie nodded. The girl was clearly fixated on the body in the bedroom. Bessie didn't blame her, either. While she didn't believe in ghosts or negative energy or any of those things, there was something unsettling about buying a house where someone had been murdered. "If Grant hadn't been murdered there, would you be buying the house?"

"Probably. We were still working on agreeing on a price with the owner's estate, which has become a good deal more complicated now, by the way."

"Really?"

"You heard what Susan said about not wanting to inherit anything from her father if there was a chance that he'd killed Valerie. She wants a full police investigation into Valerie's death before she'll do anything."

"Oh, dear."

"Exactly. The police aren't especially interested in a death that happened so many years ago, especially since it was investigated at the time and deemed to have been an accident. That was before several other women in Gary Davison's life also met with unfortunate accidents, of course, but, even so, Susan has been having difficulty persuading the police to take her seriously."

"I'm not surprised. As you say, there was an investigation at the time."

"Susan also wants to have the will that Gary produced examined. She's afraid that it might have been forged, even though Harold believes that it's genuine."

"Harold's seen it?"

Elizabeth flushed. "I introduced Susan and Harold," she said. "Andy and I were at the house yesterday, just walking around the outside and talking. Susan was in the back garden again. I didn't really mean to do it, but I told her about Harold being on the island. She begged me to set up a chance for them to meet so that she could apologise to him."

"Apologise?"

"She's convinced that her father killed Valerie. She seems to think that he also killed her mother and several other women."

"Poor Susan."

"Yeah, it doesn't help that her brothers don't seem to care what their father did when he was alive. They're both more concerned with what they've inherited."

"I can see their point."

"Yes, I suppose I can as well, but I can't help but feel as if they could be supporting their sister more."

"Perhaps they're afraid that if the police do investigate, they might end up losing out on their inheritance. Susan did say that they both needed the money, after all."

"Yes, I suppose so. If their father did kill Valerie, he shouldn't have inherited anything from her, though? Isn't that correct?"

"I believe so. There's some sort of law about not profiting from a crime."

"So if police end up investigating and deciding that Gary murdered Valerie, the house will go to Valerie's children instead?"

Bessie shrugged. "I've no idea. You really need to talk to an advocate about all of this if you're really concerned."

"I am concerned, because we're having enough trouble dealing with Susan and her two brothers. If Harold and his siblings inherit, we'll have a lot more people to try to deal with if we do decide to buy the house."

"I will be very surprised if the police will be able to find any evidence of murder after all this time."

"There is that. As I understand it, the inspector who did the initial investigation passed away many years ago. They're working from decades-old records that probably aren't even complete."

"I don't think Susan is going to get the answers she's hoping to get."

"No, but that may just leave everything unresolved forever," Elizabeth sighed.

As you aren't certain you want to buy the house, that might be a good thing, Bessie thought. Rather than point that out, she changed the subject. "What did Susan say to Harold, then?"

"She told him that she was sorry for anything that her father may have done. Harold seemed confused more than anything, but then Susan explained that she thought maybe Gary had murdered Valerie. Harold acted as if the idea had never occurred to him."

"I suppose that's possible. The idea was widely debated on the island at the time, but he was only a child. I doubt his grandparents ever suggested any such thing to the children."

"Anyway, Susan made her apologies and then told him that she was thinking of signing her share of her father's estate over to the Looney children. Harold was even more surprised by that."

"I'm sure."

"He just kept shaking his head and telling her not to be silly. He told her that he and his siblings were doing just fine and that she should take the money. It was all very odd."

"I'm surprised he didn't want a share of the house, especially since he came back to see it again."

"Maybe if it were in better condition, he'd have been more interested, but as it is, it needs a huge investment just to make it habitable again. Anyway, as he said, someone was murdered in the house. It won't ever feel as if it's home to him again now."

Bessie sighed. No doubt the man's dramatic words had had an effect on Elizabeth. "Whatever the house's condition, it has some value. Surely he'd like a share of the money."

"He said he didn't need it and neither did his siblings. I think the idea of it being split into seven shares made it all less appealing."

"I thought two of his siblings had passed away."

"They have, but the estate would still have to be split into seven shares, as I understand it. His oldest brother left children who would be entitled to their father's share, surely. And his youngest sister left a partner behind. He should get her share."

185

Bessie nodded. "Of course, Harold can't make any decisions on behalf of all of the siblings. Susan can't decide anything for her siblings, either. It does seem to be something of a mess."

"Andy suggested that the house be sold and then the money be put into an account with an advocate until the details are all sorted."

"That seems a sensible solution, but I'm not sure it's a legal one."

Elizabeth nodded. "It seems as if there are going to be a lot of advocates and solicitors involved before this is all finished. Susan doesn't see it, but I think the only ones who are going to be happy in the end are the lawyers."

"You may be right," Bessie sighed.

"After a long debate about the property and whether Valerie was murdered or not, Susan asked Harold about her father."

"What about him?"

"She wondered what he could remember about the man. It was interesting, watching Harold try to word things to paint a positive picture of Gary, when you could tell he didn't have very fond memories of the man."

"It was nice of him to try, though."

"It was, especially after Susan accused Gary of killing Valerie. I wouldn't have blamed Harold for saying horrible things about his former stepfather, but he was actually very nice about him."

"What did he say?"

"He said that he was pretty certain that Gary had found himself in over his head once he was stepfather to seven children. He questioned the wisdom of both Gary and Valerie when it came to adding a new baby to the family, too. Of course, things were very different in terms of preventing pregnancy in those days."

"They were indeed," Bessie agreed.

"Anyway, Harold said that Gary tried hard, but he didn't know anything about being a parent. He admitted that he and his siblings did their best to make Gary miserable, too. They were all still upset about their father's death, of course, and they weren't ready for a stepfather, even if Valerie was ready to remarry."

AUNT BESSIE ZEROES IN

"I never did understand why they got married so quickly after Sam's death."

"How long after the wedding did Heather arrive?" Elizabeth asked.

Bessie smiled. "That's the obvious answer, of course, but they'd been married for just over a year when Heather arrived."

Elizabeth shrugged. "They talked about Gary for a long time, actually. From what Susan said, he didn't take to parenting any better when the children were his own. He sent all three children to boarding school when they were still pretty young and, from what Susan said, he didn't encourage them to come home during breaks, either. Susan said she spent nearly every Christmas and summer with her closest friend from school at her friend's home in Dorset."

"That poor child."

"If Gary really did kill anyone, Susan was probably better off as far away from him as possible."

"Yes, but she couldn't possibly have known that when she was young. I'm sure she felt as if her father didn't care about her."

"She did. She told Harold as much. He actually said that he felt really bad for her. In spite of everything that he and his siblings went through, he said they never stopped feeling loved. He knew that both of his parents had loved him and that his grandparents and his aunt and uncle cared, too. While he isn't close to his siblings now, he said they all looked out for one another when they were growing up, as well. Susan said she's always felt as if she barely knew her brothers. They were away at school by the time she was old enough to truly get to know them, she reckons."

"Both situations seem very sad."

"I agree. Andy and I talked about it a lot. Some of it reminded him of his own upbringing, of course, with a stepfather who didn't truly care for him. Of course, Andy didn't know that his stepfather wasn't his real father, which complicated things."

Bessie nodded. "It was a difficult situation."

"Yes, and Andy and his mother have talked it all through now. He understands why she made the choices that she made, even if he feels that she should have done things differently."

"He needs to understand the context of the times, though, which is also true for Susan and Harold. They need to realise that their parents made the choices that they made in a world that was very different to the one in which we now live."

"Harold said something about that. They were talking about why Valerie and Gary had married so quickly. Harold said something about his mother being alone in the world. Her parents had already passed away, apparently. When Sam died, she found herself truly on her own with seven children."

"Sam's family did their best to help, but I believe there had been some issues between them and Valerie over the years."

"Really? Harold told us that his grandparents never said a bad word about Valerie, not even when the children were older and questioned why she'd remarried and how she'd died. They always insisted that she'd met with an unfortunate accident. They wouldn't even say anything bad about Gary, he said."

"They never believed that he'd had anything to do with Valerie's death, but they did question the will," Bessie told her. "I don't know if they truly doubted its legitimacy or whether they were simply desperate, though."

Elizabeth shrugged. "As fascinating as all of this is, it doesn't solve my problem. Do I let Andy buy the house or not?"

"It sounds as buying the house won't be that easy."

"I don't know. In spite of what Susan is saying, the estate agent seems to think that the sale can go ahead, assuming Andy still wants to buy the house and that a price can be agreed."

"I assume the price will be lower now, all things considered."

"We're going to offer less, certainly," Elizabeth said. "I mean, assuming we make an offer at all." She sighed. "I just don't know what to do. Andy reckons we were going to redo the entire house anyway, so the finished bedroom won't be anything like the one where we found the body. He thinks that will excise any ghosts that might be hanging around the place."

"Do you believe in ghosts?" Bessie asked.

"I don't know," Elizabeth said, sounding close to tears. "What if we buy the house and redo the whole thing and then find out that Grant Robertson is haunting our bedroom?"

Bessie shivered. "What a horrible thought."

"Exactly. We'd have to sell the house, and I'm sure we'd lose money because no one is going to want to buy a haunted house."

"Maybe you would be better off not buying it, then."

"Says you and everyone else," Elizabeth sighed. "I know that's the advice I want, but there's something about hearing it that makes me want to ignore it."

Bessie grinned. "You hate being told you shouldn't do anything."

"I do. Carolyn said we were crazy to even consider buying the house after the murder. I've never really cared for her."

"What did she say before the murder?" Bessie asked.

Elizabeth blinked in surprise. "Before the murder? What do you mean?"

"What did Carolyn say about the Looney mansion when you first started looking at it?"

"I don't remember discussing it with her before the murder," Elizabeth said. "I don't know that she knew that we were considering it, actually, not until after we'd found the body."

Bessie frowned. She was sure that Carolyn had said something about talking to Elizabeth about the property, but she couldn't remember exactly what had been said.

"Does it matter?" Elizabeth asked.

"I'm sure it doesn't," Bessie replied, not entirely truthfully. "Who else has been advising you not to buy the house, then?"

"My father has always thought it was a bad idea, but I think that's mostly because he wants me to stay right where I am, at Thie yn Traie."

"Really?"

"I think he likes knowing that I'm there for Mum, mostly, but I've always been his baby girl. He's never cared for any of the men I've been involved with, either. To be fair, most of them were idiots, but there were one or two who had good qualities. Daddy could never see them, though. He does seem to appreciate Andy, anyway, but then Andy feeds him."

Bessie laughed. "I'm not sure that anyone could eat Andy's cooking and not approve of him."

"Anyway, Daddy had been threatening to go and take a look at the Looney house himself before he'd agree to help with the purchase, but now he doesn't want to go anywhere near it. He doesn't want to see where his friend died, even if Grant wasn't much of a friend to him."

"Whatever happened between them, they had many years of shared history. I'm sure seeing the place where Grant died would be hard for George."

"Yes, well, that doesn't mean that Andy and I shouldn't buy the house, though. It isn't as if we're going to be inviting Daddy up to our bedroom once we finish everything."

"What does your mother think?"

Elizabeth chuckled. "She's struggling. She's always encouraging me to live my own life. I think it annoys her that Daddy wants me home to keep her company. She had her reservations about the Looney house because of the amount of work it needs, but she was being cautiously supportive. I get the feeling now that she'd prefer it if we didn't buy the house, but she can't bring herself to come right out and say that. After everything that's happened at Thie yn Traie, she can't really say that no one should buy a house where someone was murdered, anyway."

Bessie nodded, trying not to think about the murders that had taken place in and around Thie yn Traie. "Hugh and Grace seem happy with their choice."

"I know. I keep thinking about them and how lovely their little house is and what a cosy home they've made for themselves there. Maybe they have the right idea. Buy the house and turn it into a family home."

Was the girl thinking of starting a family with Andy, then, Bessie wondered. "What does Richard think?" she asked.

"Richard? You mean Richard Hart? I haven't the foggiest idea. I haven't discussed the matter with him."

"I simply assumed that he'd be acting as your advocate. He's been working for your father for years."

"He's Daddy's advocate, not mine. Andy uses Doncan Quayle, and I know you do, too. I think he's a better choice."

"I'm not going to disagree. What does Doncan think, then?"

Elizabeth laughed. "You know him well enough to know the answer to that. He doesn't have an opinion on anything, ever. He's offered us a great deal of advice for whatever we decide and he's leaving the decision to us, of course."

"That's Doncan, of course," Bessie agreed.

"His son, young Doncan, told us to be very careful about buying an old home that needs a lot of work."

"Because he bought the Teare mansion from Andy after Andy inherited it. I wonder if he's done anything to it since he bought it."

"Apparently he's working on it very slowly. He wants to do a lot of the work himself and he spent nearly every penny he had buying the place, so he can't afford to do much at any one time."

"Is Andy sorry he didn't keep that house?"

Elizabeth shook her head. "Not at all. The house has some negative associations for him after all the years when Moirrey lived there and made his mother's life so difficult. He was happy to sell the place and put the money in the bank. Thanks to Doncan's hard work, the money has grown more than Andy ever expected it would."

"Doncan's very clever with investments."

"Yes, I've been having him invest all of the profits from my little business. That's how I'm able to afford to buy something with Andy, although I will need some help from Daddy, regardless. Well, unless the murder at the Looney house drives the price down even more than we think it will."

"Has anyone else offered any opinions about you buying the house, then?"

"Oh, everyone," Elizabeth laughed. "I actually bumped into Maggie Shimmin the other day at the shops and she spent half an hour talking about what a horrible idea buying that house was. By the time she was done, I almost wanted to buy it just to spite her."

"She and Thomas are thinking of making an offer on the house," Bessie told her. "They want to tear it down and build a small block of flats on the site."

"Tear it down?" Elizabeth repeated. "They can't tear it down. The exterior is in good condition, aside from a few sections of the roof and one or two of the walls. It just needs a little bit of love. No wonder she was so adamant that the house had to be haunted now. She was hoping Andy and I would withdraw our offer and leave her and Thomas to get the house at a ridiculously low price."

"For what it's worth, she may well believe that the house is haunted. She hates going inside the last holiday cottage now, after two murders there."

"Still, imagine telling someone not to buy a house when you're considering buying it yourself. I'm so glad that you told me. I won't take anything that woman says seriously again."

"If anyone else offers you advice, you might consider what their motives might be," Bessie cautioned.

Elizabeth nodded. "I never think of such things. Andy tells me that I'm very naïve. I just believe the best about everyone."

"Doncan will keep you from making too many mistakes," Bessie told her. "I was incredibly naïve when I first asked him to act on my behalf. He saved me from making a great many mistakes over the years."

"Yes, I like him a good deal more than Richard already, and he hasn't actually done anything for us yet."

"Your father may be a bit too trusting," Bessie said cautiously.

"He is, for sure. I keep hinting that Richard isn't the best advocate on the island, but Daddy won't hear a bad word about him. Then again, he actually seems to have believed Grant when he rang and said that Scott was behind everything illegal that had happened. I suppose I simply trust John Rockwell and the island police more than I'd ever trust Grant."

"John's very good at his job. If Scott had truly been behind everything, John would have found evidence to support that."

"Exactly. That's what I told Daddy when he told me that he'd known that Grant was on the island. Daddy never could believe that Grant was responsible for all of the things that he was accused of, though."

"If there was someone else involved, he or she was very careful not to leave any evidence behind."

"And if someone else was involved, he or she must still be on the island," Elizabeth said thoughtfully. "No one else disappeared when Grant did, did they?"

Bessie shook her head. "If anyone was involved, it must have been Scott, though, surely."

Elizabeth sighed and then shook her head. "We're wandering all over the place, aren't we? I came to find out what you thought about Andy and me buying the Looney house, though. What do you think?"

"I think you and Andy have to decide that for yourselves and that this is a conversation you should be having with Andy. What does he think about ghosts?"

"He doesn't believe in them. He thinks that once we've redone the house, it will feel warm and cosy and that I'll forget all about the murder."

"So you have to decide whether you can do that or not. If you truly don't think you'll ever be able to forget what happened in the house, then you shouldn't buy it. Maybe you should visit Grace and have a chat with her. I know she was very concerned about buying their house."

"Why did they buy that house?" Elizabeth asked. "I mean, there are lots of nice new houses on the island that they might have chosen. Why deliberately buy a house where someone had been murdered?"

"Because they got that house for nearly half of its original sale price," Bessie told her. "They'd have never been able to afford a house that new and large any other way."

Elizabeth flushed. "Of course. I should have realised."

"Your situation is very different, of course."

"It is and it isn't. While Andy and I could afford to buy a house just about anywhere on the island, we've been looking for months and haven't been able to find anything at all suitable. Andy wants something with some history. If anything, the Looney mansion is more modern than he'd like. He'd prefer something even older. The thing is, though, he remembers growing up in Laxey and walking past that house nearly every day. To him it represented an attainable dream. The Teare mansion was huge and strictly off limits to the son of the hired help, but the Looney mansion was still a mansion, at least in Andy's eyes. He told me that he often used to dream that one day he'd earn enough money to buy the Looney mansion for himself and his mother."

"Except his mother doesn't want to live anywhere other than her cottage," Bessie said.

Elizabeth laughed. "Andy keeps trying, though. He's offered to buy her everything from a large modern house to a small flat in an older building, and she's turned every single one down. She's finally agreed to let him make some improvements to the cottage, at least, but Andy wants to do so much more for her."

"And she doesn't want him spending his money on her."

"Exactly that. Anyway, she thinks we should go ahead and buy the house. She doesn't believe in ghosts or any such nonsense, as she put it. She knows all about Andy's dreams, of course, and she'd love to see him getting to fulfill them."

"I can see her point."

"I can, too, and I was totally on board before, well, before."

Before the murder, Bessie silently finished the thought for her. "By when do you have to make a decision?"

"Andy wants to make a new offer soon, at a lower price to reflect recent events. He's talking about early next week, hoping that if we move quickly enough Susan won't have time to stop things from proceeding."

"That doesn't seem fair to Susan."

"Andy is hoping that if we have an accepted offer, she'll agree to let the sale go through and then settle things with the Looney children later."

"What do the other Looney children think?"

"Harold was actually going to ring his siblings and talk to them.

He's pretty sure that none of them have any interest in coming back to the island ever again, at least."

"Which means none of them are interested in the house."

"Not as far as Harold knows, anyway."

"And Susan's brothers don't want it."

"They just want the money from the sale."

"Which makes sense, as neither of them have ever been to the island and they were totally unaware of their father's connection to the place before Susan arrived here."

"I find that whole situation very odd," Elizabeth said. "Imagine finding out that your father had been married before he'd met your mother, that he'd had seven stepchildren and a child of his own, and that he may have murdered his first wife. It's a lot for Susan and her brothers to take in, I'm sure."

Bessie nodded. "I'm sure they're still working through it all, as well."

Elizabeth looked up at the clock and sighed. "I promised Andy that I'd take another walk around the Looney mansion this afternoon. We have a party to plan later, so we can't take too long at it, but I'm sure he thinks he'll be able to wear me down by having me visit the house regularly."

"Is it working?"

Elizabeth giggled. "It probably is, actually. I'm not dreading it nearly as much today as I did yesterday. We aren't allowed inside anyway, and the gardens are lovely, even though they're really over-grown. I'm sure the Thie yn Traie gardener would love to get his hands on that garden. He's always complaining that everything at Thie yn Traie is already done."

"Is he the same man who did the gardens at the Douglas house?" Bessie asked, remembering gorgeous flowerbeds in rainbows of colours.

"No, our Douglas gardener is still there, tending those gardens, at least until the house is sold. I think Mum expects that the new owners, if we ever find any, will want to keep him on, too. He came with the house, if you see what I mean."

Bessie nodded. "When are you meeting Andy?"

"In half an hour," Elizabeth sighed. "I really need to go. Thank you for your time. I wish you'd tell me what you really think, but I'd probably just do whatever you told me and then regret it later. I know I have to make my own decisions. Mum said the same thing. Being an adult is more difficult than I'd been expecting."

Bessie laughed. "It has its rewards, though."

Elizabeth nodded. "Andy is one of them. I may end up agreeing to the house simply because I know how much he wants it and I truly do love him a lot."

"I'm sure, if you told him that you truly couldn't stand the idea of living in that house, he'd drop the idea."

"He would. That's one of the reasons why I love him and why I feel as if I'd be letting him down if I said that."

Bessie nodded and then followed the girl to the door. Elizabeth gave her a hug.

"Thank you so much. I think I'm closer to a decision, anyway."

"I'm glad I could help," Bessie replied, feeling as if she'd done very little.

She watched as Elizabeth walked back to her expensive sports car and drove away. As the car disappeared up the road, Bessie remembered her book. Locking the door, she grabbed the book and settled into her favourite chair in the sitting room, determined not to move again until she'd finished the story.

CHAPTER 14

It was time for lunch when Bessie finally shut the book and set it down with a happy sigh. She'd guessed the killer in chapter six and she'd been correct. Most of the characters had been enjoyable to read about and she'd already developed a real fondness for the protagonist. It was a shame that the next book in the series wasn't due to be released for nearly a year, according to the information in the back of the book. In the kitchen, Bessie made herself a note to add the next book to the list of titles she wanted at the bookshop in Ramsey. They were good enough to send her boxes of books regularly, based on her list.

After heating some soup and slicing some bread, Bessie sat down to eat, with her mind still full of the story she'd just finished. It was only as she washed her lunch down with a cup of tea that her thoughts turned back to Elizabeth and their earlier conversation. But what had Carolyn said about the Looney mansion? She'd said something about Grant dying in a dark bedroom and something about being shown the house when she was searching for homes for George and Mary.

"The thing is," she told John when she reached him, "she told me that she was too polite to object when the estate agent took her to the Looney house, even though it was clearly not suitable."

"And that's odd because?"

"Because I can't see her being polite, not when it was business, anyway. Do you remember when we went around the Looney house? I refused to go past the sitting room because it clearly would have been a waste of our time. I can't imagine Carolyn going through the entire house, not if she were truly looking at properties for George and Mary."

"So you think she told you that as an excuse for why she knew anything about where Grant died?"

"That's the most obvious conclusion, I suppose, although I'm not sure what motive she might have had for murdering him. I'm assuming you didn't find anything to tie her to what Grant was doing when you investigated his crimes."

"We didn't find anything to suggest that she was involved in any criminal activity," John confirmed. "There were rumours, though, that she and Grant might have had a personal relationship."

"Really? I'm sure Mary told me that Carolyn had sworn off men years ago after a relationship went badly wrong."

"When I said rumours, they were more hints or speculation than anything else. I had one of my best investigators try to pin things down, but he couldn't find any hard evidence that they were more than business associates."

"What did Carolyn say about the subject?"

"You know I can't repeat what people say in interviews."

Bessie sighed. "I'm sure she will have denied everything. If you couldn't find any evidence, then they either weren't having a relationship or they went to great lengths to hide it."

"I'd lean towards no relationship. This is a small island. Such things are difficult to hide, especially in the relatively small social and business circles in which they moved."

"So if she did kill Grant, we don't know why."

"I'm going to talk to her later today. Maybe, if I question her about the Looney house, she'll let something important slip."

And maybe she already has, Bessie thought to herself as she put the phone down. After spending most of her morning lost in a fictional world, Bessie was surprised to look outside and see the sun shining. Her early morning walk had been wet and uncomfortable, so now seemed the perfect time to take a second one.

What about Onnee, a voice in her head whispered as she got ready to go out. Andrew was arriving the next day. She'd probably have little time for Onnee while he was on the island. Pushing the thought out of her mind, she slipped on a jacket and headed out the door.

The stairs to Thie yn Traie seemed closer than normal as Bessie crossed the sand. Perhaps it was the sun that was giving Bessie extra energy. It did feel as if it had been a long time since she'd seen it, really. As she pressed on, she wondered if she should walk to the new houses or not. Then she thought about the building site beyond them. Maybe it was a good day to truly push herself.

The last time she'd walked that far, she'd walked back with Harold. She could only hope that whatever Susan decided, it wouldn't interfere with Elizabeth and Andy's attempt to purchase the house. From everything that Elizabeth had said, it seemed as if they were likely to buy it, if things could be agreed.

When she reached the new houses, Bessie stopped for a minute. After several minutes of having had the beach to herself, there suddenly seemed to be a crowd in front of her. A quick head count made her laugh at herself, as there were actually only six people on the beach. They were all spread out, though, which was probably what made it seem busier.

"Hello, Aunt Bessie," a familiar voice called as Bessie began to walk again.

Grace was sitting on a blanket on the sand, with baby Aalish lying beside her.

"Hello," Bessie said when she reached the pair. "It's a lovely day to be outside, enjoying the sunshine."

"I'm doing my best to keep Aalish in the shade so her skin doesn't burn, but she seems to be enjoying being outside."

"It's her first spring, of course. I'm sure she'll be even more excited when summer gets here."

Grace laughed. "I don't know that she'll really notice any of it this year, but I'm excited for summer to get here. I can't wait to take her in the sea and let her splash around. It's far too cold at the moment, of course."

"It never gets all that warm, really."

"No, but if the air is warm enough, I should be able to put her feet in the water, at least."

Aalish had been looking back and forth as the women had been talking. Now she scrunched up her face and began to cry softly.

"That isn't even a real cry," Grace laughed. "You're just upset because you aren't the centre of attention at the moment."

She picked the baby up and cuddled her. "There, is that better? Mummy loves you loads and loads and loads."

Aalish gave Bessie a self-satisfied smile as she snuggled into her mother's arms.

"She knows how to get what she wants," Bessie said.

"Yes, especially from her daddy. He melts whenever she looks at him. I'm a bit worried about her being spoiled rotten, actually."

"I'm sure Hugh is far too sensible to spoil her too much."

"I'm not," Grace said. She laughed. "I don't think you can spoil them at this age, though. All Aalish wants is my full attention at all times. That doesn't seem too much to ask, really. Mum keeps telling me that I shouldn't pick her up every time she fusses, but I love holding her and I know one day, probably too soon, she won't want to cuddle with me all the time. She'll be crawling and then walking and then running and then starting school and..."

Bessie was surprised when a tear slid down Grace's cheek. "Are you all right?"

Grace shook her head and then laughed again. "I spent yesterday with two of my teacher friends. They both have older children and they couldn't get enough of Aalish. They kept passing her back and forth and telling me to enjoy every second because it goes by incredibly quickly. Then, when I got home last night, Aalish cut her first tooth. It just makes her look so much older."

Bessie stared at the baby, who looked exactly the same to her as she had the last time she'd seen her. "If you say so."

"Oh, I know it's just me," Grace sighed. "And there are days when I wonder if she'll ever stop just crying and shouting all the time. I am looking forward to her actually speaking, even though I don't want to rush." She sighed again. "You're probably better off just ignoring me, really. I'm something of a mess today."

Bessie patted the girl's back. "It's quite all right. I'm sure it all goes with having just had a baby."

Grace nodded. "I'm starting to think that my hormones will be going crazy until Aalish is my age. Every time I talk to my mother or my midwife about how I feel, they tell me that it's all perfectly normal."

"As long as you aren't feeling depressed or unhappy."

"Oh, no, not really. My mother suffered from some postnatal depression after she had my brother, so she's watching me very closely. My emotions are just all over the place, which is apparently normal. Some of it probably stems from not getting enough sleep, but we're working on that."

"That's good to hear. Hugh said something about taking turns getting up with the baby."

"Yes, except I'm not very good at letting him take his turn. Oh, I let him get up, but then, if the baby doesn't stop crying immediately or if she makes any odd noise, I rush down to see what's wrong. I know Hugh is perfectly capable of giving her a bottle and changing her nappy, but I can't seem to stop myself."

"I hope you can learn to trust him to do the job so that you can get more sleep. I'm sure you'll feel better with more sleep."

"I will, although Aalish actually slept through the night last night. I feel as if I should whisper that, in case she hears and decides to never do it again."

Bessie laughed. "Did you get some extra sleep, then?"

Grace flushed. "I woke up at three, worried that something was wrong, and then sat by her bed until morning just in case."

The pair chatted for a while longer before Bessie turned for home, feeling grateful that she'd never had children herself. It all sounded as if it was incredibly hard work. As she approached the steps to Thie yn Traie again, she began to regret not walking further. It hadn't taken any time at all to get back home. Movement from the cliff face startled her. She stopped and then watched as Carolyn made her way down the steep wooden steps.

"Bessie, hello," Carolyn said. "I've always wanted to try those stairs, but now I'm sorry that I have. I can't imagine climbing back up them. They're awful."

Bessie nodded. "They're very steep and incredibly slippery when it rains."

Carolyn glanced up at the sky. "At least I don't have to worry about that today."

"No, and doesn't the sun feel wonderful?"

"I suppose so," Carolyn shrugged.

A dozen questions sprang into Bessie's mind, but she was suddenly aware that the pair were alone on an empty stretch of beach. Now was not the time to confront Carolyn about the things she'd said about the Looney house.

"I was thinking of coming to see you, actually," Carolyn said as Bessie took a step away from her.

"Oh, really? Why?" Bessie asked, trying to find her mobile phone in her pocket without Carolyn noticing.

"I said too much last night," Carolyn sighed. "I was worried about speaking with you. Everyone on the island knows that you've solved dozens of murders over the past two years. I was worried that I would say the wrong thing and then I did."

"Did you?"

Carolyn looked at her and then shrugged. "I've an appointment with Inspector Rockwell later this afternoon. I've decided that I may as well confess to everything. I've nothing left to live for, really, not anymore."

Bessie found her phone. Could she dial 999 without taking it out of her pocket, though? No matter how hard she tried, she couldn't even remember if the device was switched on or not.

"Confess?" she repeated after an awkward pause.

"I'm sure you caught my slip last night. I know Elizabeth came to see you this morning. There's no doubt in my mind that you asked her what I'd told her about the Looney mansion. I never discussed it with her, though. I never got taken around it when I was looking at houses for George and Mary. The only time I was ever in that house was the night that I met Grant there."

"You need to have this conversation with John Rockwell, not me," Bessie said, taking a step away from the woman.

"I will, I promise," Carolyn told her. "You look worried, but you don't need to be. I won't hurt you. I just came down here to get some fresh air and some sunshine before I speak to the police. I'm assuming that I won't get much sunshine in prison, but I don't know. As I said before, it doesn't really matter."

"I'm going to ring John and have him come here now," Bessie said.

"If you really want to, please do. The sooner this is all over, the better. I thought about ending it all. If you hadn't been here, maybe I would have just walked into the sea. I doubt it. I'm not really that brave."

Bessie pulled out her phone and found John's mobile number. "It's Bessie. I'm on the beach behind Thie yn Traie, having a chat with Carolyn," she said.

"I'll have the first available constable there as soon as possible," he replied. "I'm on my way. Don't end the call. I'll have someone listening on this end."

"Perfect," Bessie said. She turned back to face Carolyn. "John's on his way," she said, trying to hold the phone casually, as if she'd forgotten it was in her hand.

"Have you ever been in love?"

"Many years ago, I thought I was," Bessie replied.

"We've a lot in common, then. I fell in love with Chester when I was nineteen. He was twenty-six, and I thought he was the perfect man. I was in my first year at university, but Chester convinced me that I was wasting my time studying when I could be living. I quit school and ran away with him."

"That was brave of you."

"It was stupid of me," Carolyn replied harshly. "I thought he truly cared about me, but he didn't. After a few months, he got bored and disappeared. I should have gone home and gone back to school, but I became obsessed by the idea that he'd been kidnapped or that he'd fallen ill and forgotten his identity or some such thing. I spent three months trying to find him."

"And did you?" Bessie asked when Carolyn fell silent for a moment.

"Oh, yes, I found him. He was living with another woman and, when I turned up, he laughed at me. He told me that he'd had a bit of fun with me, but that that was all that it had been and that I should go back to my boring life because that was all that I was ever going to have."

"I'm sorry," Bessie said as she spotted Hugh walking towards them. She held up her hand, getting him to stop some distance behind Carolyn.

The movement made Carolyn look around. When she saw Hugh, she sighed. "I still want to tell you the rest of the story," she said. "I need to tell you. I feel as if you'll understand."

"Go ahead," Bessie told her.

"I went home, of course. There was nothing else that I could do. I was four months pregnant and alone in the world. My parents didn't want to let me return, but they did what they felt was their duty and let me stay with them until the baby arrived. I gave it up for adoption and then moved to London with twenty pounds in my pocket."

"My goodness."

"I was done with men, of course. I focussed on my career. It wasn't impossible, in those days, to do well even without a university degree. I pushed myself harder than anyone else, working seventy or eighty hours a week. Eventually, I went back to school and got the degree that I should have earned when I was younger. I worked with a succession of very wealthy businessmen, acting as a personal assistant but often doing a good deal more in terms of helping them run their businesses. In reality, I'm a good deal smarter than most of the men with whom I've worked."

"That doesn't surprise me."

Carolyn gave her a tiny smile. "I could talk endlessly about the sorts of men I've worked with and how idiotic most of them have been, but I won't. We don't have time. I was working for a banker in London, doing everything for him except tying his shoes, only because he wore shoes without laces, when I met George. He was impressed by how hard I worked and he offered me a job at twice my current salary. I'd have been crazy to turn it down. Besides the money, though, George has been the best employer for whom I've ever worked. He's kind and he's fair and he truly values what I do for him. I'm going to miss him, and Mary as well."

"I'm sure he'll miss you."

"He's ready to retire. Michael will miss me, but Michael is quite clever. I'm sure he'll be fine on his own." Carolyn fell silent, staring out at the sea.

John appeared on the beach some distance from Bessie. He began to walk slowly towards them, his eyes focussed on Carolyn. After a moment, she looked around and then shrugged.

"I'd better talk faster, hadn't I? George hired me, and I was happy working for him. Then he started talking about moving back to the Isle of Man. I wish now, more than anything, that I'd quit when the subject was first raised. I've been wishing that for years, though. At the time, it seemed almost too good to be true. George was going to mostly retire. He'd only need me to handle a few little projects and he was prepared to keep me on the same salary. I didn't have any reason to turn him down."

"Of course not," Bessie said encouragingly.

"And then I arrived on the island. It's beautiful, but I'm sure you know that. I fell in love with the island within days, maybe even hours. Everything would have been perfect, I think, if I hadn't taken a call a few days after George and Mary finally arrived. A man called

Grant Robertson wanted a meeting with George. I tried to put him off, explaining that George had just moved back and needed time to get settled, but he insisted, explaining that he and George were old friends."

"George had never mentioned him?"

"No, and he wasn't terribly pleased when I told him about the meeting, either, but he didn't object. I met Grant a few days later."

"Ms. White, perhaps we should continue this conversation at the station," John interrupted in a gentle voice.

"Can Bessie come along?"

John frowned. "I'm afraid not."

"Then I need to finish. I need her to understand. I need her to explain everything to George, too."

"You may have five minutes," John said, looking at his watch.

Carolyn nodded. "Grant immediately reminded me of Chester. He had the same overconfidence and arrogance, but he was also attractive and he could be charming when he wanted to be. The day we met I felt a flood of emotions that I'd thought I'd buried. He barely spoke to me, of course. I was simply George's assistant and, therefore, inconsequential."

"That sounds like Grant."

"I wasn't included in the meeting, which was unusual for George. He generally included me in everything to do with his business concerns. When Grant left, George told me that he'd agreed to work on a few projects with the man. Then he told me that he was going to have me work with Grant on some things, too. He'd pay me double for the hours when I was working with Grant. I didn't want to do it, not even for double pay, but George wouldn't take no for an answer. I didn't want to lose my job, so a few days later, I started working for Grant a few mornings each week."

"Doing what?" Bessie asked.

John frowned at her.

"Helping him with some new business ventures he was starting. He was providing the funds for several small businesses on the island, but they all needed careful monitoring. The very first day I went

AUNT BESSIE ZEROES IN

through all of the files for every business that he'd agreed to fund. At the end of that day, I gave him lists of which ones were going to succeed and which were going to fail. He laughed, but he kept the lists and six months later he had to admit that I'd been exactly right on every one."

"You were smarter than Grant."

"Maybe. At business, anyway. I never realised what he was really doing, though. I should have been smart enough to question where all of his money was coming from and how he was funding all of the investments he was making, but I never thought to question any of that. I also should have been smart enough to see how he was using me, but I didn't see that until very recently."

"Using you?"

"As I said, he'd kept those lists. Exactly six months after I'd made them, when I'd been proven right about every business, he took me out for dinner to celebrate my success. We shared a bottle of wine. He insisted and I didn't take much persuading. I'd already fallen in love with him, even though I didn't want to admit that to anyone, not even myself."

"Are you certain you want to tell me all of this?"

Carolyn laughed. "I won't bore you with all of the details. We ended up back at his house, in his bed, that night. When I woke up the next morning, I was horrified. Grant was amused. He suggested that we keep seeing one another, but very discreetly. I refused. He didn't argue. We spent nights together fairly regularly from that day onwards. After every time, I'd swear it wasn't going to happen again, but I simply couldn't resist the man. And I truly believed that he was in love with me, as well. I thought we were both fighting against a growing obsession. After what had happened with Chester, I should have known better, of course, but, well, I was madly in love."

"No one knew."

"We were incredibly discreet. It became part of the relationship, really, sneaking around, hiding our true feelings. Sometimes, in a meeting, he'd look at me a certain way and I'd be sure that everyone would realise, but no one ever suspected. Grant saw other women, of

207

course. He often needed an escort for charity events and that sort of thing. I was dumb enough to believe that they were all simply for show. Now I don't know what to believe."

"Does it matter?"

Carolyn looked surprised and then shrugged. "Probably not, really."

"Ms. White?" John said.

She sighed. "I'm sorry. This is proving more difficult to talk about than I thought it would be. I'll talk faster. You know the next part of the story, anyway. One day Grant disappeared. He simply left the island."

"He didn't tell you he was leaving?"

"Of course not. If he'd told me, he would have had to explain why he was going, and he couldn't have done that. I'd like to believe that, if I'd known about his criminal activities, I would have rung the police, but I'm probably lying to myself. I didn't ring them when he contacted me several weeks ago, after all."

"He contacted you?"

"He rang me at home. It was a conversation that I'd imagined us having at least a million times since he'd gone. I shouted at him for going without telling me. I cursed him for lying and stealing. I threatened him with the police and more. Then he turned on the charm. He told me that Scott had been behind everything illegal and that he'd not told me he was leaving so that he could protect me. According to him, Scott knew all about our relationship and had been threatening to ruin me if Grant didn't do exactly as he was told. Of course, I wanted to believe him."

"Of course," Bessie murmured.

"He told me that he'd never stopped loving me and that he was coming back to the island just to get me. I told him it was too dangerous and that I could meet him somewhere, anywhere," Carolyn said, her face red as she blinked back tears. "I was such an idiot."

"He knew exactly what to say to you."

"He did. I collected him from the ferry, determined to take him straight to the police, but he begged me to let him prove that he'd been set up. I let him stay in my flat, even took him back into my bed," she said bitterly. "He stayed with me for a week, promising every day that he'd get everything sorted the next day. Finally, he arranged a meeting between himself and Scott. He rang Scott and set it up for the last holiday cottage here on Laxey Beach. It seemed like the perfect spot for a meeting."

Bessie shivered. Two people had already been murdered in that cottage. "What happened at the meeting, then?"

"The two men talked. Grant had me drop him off early so that Scott wouldn't know that I was involved. After I dropped him off, I parked some distance away and then walked back and stood outside the cottage where I could listen. Grant told Scott that he needed money. Scott laughed at him and said he was out of luck. Apparently, Grant had left a few bank accounts on the island under different names, but, from what I heard, Scott had found them and emptied them into his own accounts. The men fought, and then Grant stormed out. He was furious when he rejoined me where we'd agreed to meet. I drove around for a while until he'd calmed down. When he was finally calm, I suggested that we simply leave the island together. I have plenty of money myself. I've never been one for spending, and George pays very well. When I told Grant how much I had in the bank, though, he just laughed. He told me that he wouldn't be able to live for more than a year or two on my savings and that coming back to the island had been a huge waste of his time."

"That must have hurt."

"I was devastated. I reminded him that he'd told me that he'd come back to get me, but he just laughed again. He said I'd been useful in giving him a place to stay, but that was all that I'd given him. Then he started talking about killing Scott and getting his hands on Scott's money before he left the island again. I was very tempted to take him to the police, but I couldn't do it."

"Why not?"

"I was too angry. Prison seemed too easy. Instead, I told him that he couldn't stay with me any longer. I remembered that the Looney house was empty. Elizabeth had been talking about it, although I didn't realise that she and Andy were seriously considering buying it or I would have chosen somewhere else. Anyway, I drove over and Grant broke in through the back door. I suggested that we take a quick look around to make certain the house was actually empty. When we got to the last bedroom, I, well, I suggested that we spend some time together for one last time. Grant wasn't going to say no. As soon as he lay down on the bed, I stabbed him with a knife I'd found in the kitchen. He looked shocked, as if he couldn't believe what I'd done. I tried to apologise. I've never wanted to take back a moment of my life as much as I want to take back that moment. If I could do it over again, I'd drive Grant straight from the ferry to the nearest police station. He lied to me and I was too dumb to see it for too many years."

Carolyn stopped, tears streaming down her face. Bessie looked at John, who slowly shook his head.

"Ms. White, you need to come with me," he said.

"Please tell George that I'm sorry," Carolyn told Bessie. "He truly cared about Grant, even though I'm certain that Grant didn't care about him. I'm sorry I won't be there to help with the retail park and all of his other projects. I'm sorry, well, I'm just sorry."

Bessie nodded. "I'll make sure that George understands."

"Thank you. And thank you, Inspector, for letting me tell Bessie the whole story. I feel much better for it."

John and Hugh walked up the beach together with Carolyn between them. Bessie took a step towards home and then stopped, feeling badly shaken. Hugh was at her side a moment later.

"John had backup in the car park," he told Bessie. "He sent me back to make sure that you're okay."

"I'm not okay," Bessie replied. "That was horrible."

"It was," Hugh agreed. "Let's get you home."

In her cottage, Bessie sank down at her kitchen table. Hugh rushed around, making tea and putting biscuits onto a plate.

"Eat something. You need the sugar," he told her as he dropped the plate onto the table.

Bessie nibbled listlessly on a biscuit while she waited for her tea. After a few sips, she began to feel slightly better. "That was awful."

"Grant broke her heart. I felt really sorry for her by the end."

"Nothing excuses murder, of course, but I did feel sorry for her as well."

Hugh's mobile buzzed. He glanced at it and sighed. "I need to get your statement," he said. "John's going to be busy with Ms. White for a while. Apparently, she won't stop talking, and you only got the short version."

CHAPTER 15

*W*hen Bessie opened her door the following afternoon, Andrew Cheatham was quick to pull her into a hug. As she stepped back from him, she could feel his eyes studying her.

"You look tired," he said after a moment.

She nodded. "I didn't sleep well. Yesterday was a difficult day."

"Let me take you somewhere for tea and conversation," he suggested.

Bessie smiled. "We can do that here and we won't have to worry about anyone overhearing what I tell you. The police haven't released any information about the arrest yet."

"Arrest?" Andrew repeated. "Oh, dear."

Bessie made tea. When she offered Andrew biscuits, he shook his head. "I'm hoping you'll agree to let me buy you dinner somewhere in a few hours," he countered.

"That would be nice," Bessie replied, not giving herself time to think about refusing. She'd have to buy him dinner another night during his stay.

"Tell me about yesterday, then," he suggested when she was sitting across from him at the table.

"I'll have to start the story considerably earlier than yesterday, actually," Bessie told him. "It goes back a great many years, really."

An hour later, she was finally finished telling him everything that Carolyn had said on the beach the previous day. Andrew sat back in his chair and shook his head.

"I do believe you've heard more confessions in the past two years than I've heard in my entire police career," he told her.

Bessie sighed. "I don't want to hear them."

"But I'm sure John Rockwell appreciates your help with his cases."

"Carolyn was going to confess anyway. If she hadn't seen me, she would have simply told John everything."

"That's what she said to you, anyway. In my experience, people often believe they are going to confess to the police right up until they're sitting across from an inspector, answering questions. I'm sure she felt that you were a considerably more sympathetic audience."

"I did feel sorry for her. I still do. John said that she spent three hours telling him her entire life story, seemingly unable to stop herself from talking."

"That happens sometimes. I'm sure John was very good with her."

"Apparently, she isn't talking today. George sent Richard Hart, his advocate, to try to help, but she refused to see him. Richard gave a statement to the press, which means Dan Ross was there when Richard came out of the police station. According to that statement, George is going to do everything he can to help her."

"I'm not sure there's much he can do. She's confessed to murder, after all."

Bessie shrugged. "That's for the advocates and the courts to work out. I'm just glad that Grant's killer is behind bars. Not that I think she was a danger to anyone else, except maybe herself."

Andrew nodded and then patted her hand. "After all of that, I'm sure you're tired of being involved in murder investigations."

"I am, indeed. It's all been rather awful. I can't help but hope that maybe that was the last one for a while. I'd be quite happy to never be caught up in another, actually."

"That's a shame."

Bessie frowned. "You have another cold case you wanted to discuss with me," she guessed.

"Something along those lines, anyway."

Bessie took a sip of her tea. Was she truly tired of murder investigations or was it more to do with finding dead bodies? The idea of another cold case intrigued her, even though she hated to admit it.

"Cold cases are rather different, aren't they?" Andrew asked after a moment.

"That's exactly what I was thinking. I won't know any of the people involved, for a start. I enjoyed helping with the case we talked about last time."

"You solved the case we talked about last time," he laughed. "Which is why I have a proposition for you."

"A proposition?"

"It isn't just for you, actually, it's for you, John, Doona, and Hugh. The four of you make a good team, bouncing ideas off one another and finding unexplored avenues."

Bessie nodded. "We enjoy talking about cases together, and eating too much good food while we're doing so."

"I've been talking with some of the men I used to work with at Scotland Yard about setting up a sort of semi-informal cold case unit," Andrew told her.

"Semi-informal?" Bessie echoed.

He laughed. "We're still working out the details, actually. I envision it as a group that meets fairly regularly to talk about cold cases, probably just one at a time. The hope would be that the group would spot things that had been missed, or think completely outside the box and offer new ideas about areas to investigate. We'd work with constabularies all over the world, tackling the cases that they think are lost causes. I would hope that we'd be able to help in perhaps one in ten of the cases, but that might be optimistic."

"Ten per cent? That seems awfully pessimistic to me."

"We're talking about cases that have already been investigated thoroughly, but I hope you're right. I just don't want anyone to expect us to solve every case we consider."

"And you want John, Doona, and Hugh in the unit?"

"And you. There are three of us who are working together on getting things arranged. Charles Morris has his own little group of associates whom he thinks will be helpful. Harry Blake is more of a loner, but he may consult an acquaintance or two along the way. And I want to bring in the four of you from here. It will be a larger group than I'd initially planned, but I think we need everyone I've selected."

Bessie took another sip of tea while she tried to think. "If I decide later that I'd rather not do it, I can quit?"

"Of course. It's a cold case unit, not a hostage situation," Andrew laughed. "You'll be paid for your time, of course."

"Paid?"

"Yes, paid."

"I've never had a paying job before."

"Well, there's a first time for everything, right?"

Bessie nodded slowly. "I'm not sure what to say."

"I'm really hoping you'll at least agree to give it a try. I have to talk to the others, of course, but I'm fairly certain they'll all be eager to take part."

"You're probably right about that," Bessie said, as she thought about her friends. It was perfect for John and Hugh, and Doona would probably be eager to be a part of it, if only because John was doing so.

"There is one more thing to consider," Andrew added. "The whole thing needs to be kept quiet. I'd rather you didn't tell anyone what you were doing, although I do understand that might be difficult. What really matters is that it doesn't get into the papers. Some of the cases we might investigate could be ones that generated a lot of interest in their day. We'd rather not deal with dozens of eager reporters badgering everyone in the group."

"I'd have to tell my advocate, if only to explain why I'm suddenly getting paid for something."

"I'm sure he can be discreet."

"Oh, yes, he won't tell anyone anything. It can be quite annoying."

Andrew chuckled. "Annoying about other people, but useful when he's acting on your behalf."

215

"Yes, of course. I think I'm going to have to give the whole thing some thought."

"I suspected that you might. That's why I'm telling you now, before I discuss it with the others. If you aren't interested, I'll talk to them somewhere other than here."

"Would we have our meetings on the island or elsewhere?"

"I would hope to have them all here. Not only does it give me an excuse to visit the island regularly, but the island is far enough away from the UK to give us privacy and space. Charles and Harry will probably come over for the first meeting, but I might meet with them separately in London after that."

"So you don't think we'll be able to solve anything in a single meeting."

Andrew shook his head. "My plans, at the moment, are to focus on one case a month. I would send the details to Charles and Harry and then come over and present them to you and the others here. You'd be given copies of everything in the official records. The hope would be that someone might spot a new angle or a missed detail, that's all. After a month, we'd move on to another case."

"Even if we haven't solved the first one yet?"

"As I said earlier, I don't think we'll solve very many cases. I've been with the police for a long time. There are probably a dozen cases over all of those years that have really stuck with me for one reason or another. Three or four of those cases are unsolved cases. The thought of getting fresh eyes to look those cases over is what's driving this entire project. Every inspector I know has a handful of the same sort of cases and I know they would all love to have someone new look at the notes, review the files, and see what he or she might have missed. Many times, we may have to conclude that nothing was missed. That will be frustrating, but it's going to come with the job."

Bessie nodded. "Give me some time to think," she said.

"Take as much time as you need. I'm here for a week, during which I want to talk to the others, but I haven't actually brought a case with me this visit, well, not an official one."

"What does that mean?"

Andrew chuckled. "Something happened the other day that was unusual. I'll tell you about it over dinner."

The pair took a long walk on the beach, talking about anything and everything other than Andrew's proposition. As Bessie combed her hair and changed for dinner, her mind was racing. Was she actually going to agree to join Andrew's cold case unit? While she kept telling herself not to rush into a decision, in her heart she already knew that she wasn't going to be able to resist saying yes.

GLOSSARY OF TERMS

House Names – Manx to English

- **Thie yn Traie** — Beach House
- **Treoghe Bwaane** — Widow's Cottage

English to American Terms

- **advocate** —Manx title for a lawyer (solicitor)
- **aye** — yes
- **bin** — garbage can
- **biscuits** — cookies
- **bonnet (car)** — hood
- **boot (car)** — trunk
- **brewing something** — catching something (a cold or flu)
- **car park** — parking lot
- **charity shop** — shop run by a non-profit that sells donated goods
- **chemist** — pharmacist
- **chips** — french fries
- **crisps** — potato chips

- **cuppa** — cup of tea (informally)
- **dear** — expensive
- **estate agent** — real estate agent (realtor)
- **fairy cakes** — cupcakes
- **fancy dress** — costume
- **fizzy drink** — soda (pop)
- **flat** — apartment
- **hire car** — rental car
- **holiday** — vacation
- **jumper** — sweater
- **lie in** — sleep late
- **lift** — elevator
- **midday** — noon
- **pavement** — sidewalk
- **plait (hair)** — braid
- **poorly** — unwell
- **primary school** — elementary school
- **pudding** — dessert
- **puds** — pudding (informal)
- **skeet** — gossip
- **skirting boards** — baseboards
- **starters** — appetizers
- **supply teacher** — substitute teacher
- **telly** — television
- **thick** — stupid
- **torch** — flashlight
- **trolley** — shopping cart
- **windscreen** — windshield

OTHER NOTES

The emergency number in the UK and the Isle of Man is 999, not 911.

CID is the Criminal Investigation Department of the Isle of Man Constabulary (Police Force).

When talking about time, the English say, for example, "half seven" to mean "seven-thirty."

In the UK, when describing property with more than one level, the lowest level (assuming there is no basement; very few UK houses have basements) is the "ground floor," and the next floor up is the "first floor" and so on. In the US, the lowest floor is usually the "first floor" and up from there.

With regard to Bessie's age: UK (and IOM) residents get a free bus pass at the age of 60. Bessie is somewhere between that age and the age at which she will get a birthday card from the Queen. British citizens used to receive telegrams from the ruling monarch on the occasion of their one-hundredth birthday. Cards replaced the telegrams in 1982, but the special greeting is still widely referred to as a telegram.

When island residents talk about someone being from "across," they mean that the person is from somewhere in the United Kingdom (across the water).

ACKNOWLEDGMENTS

And that's the end...the end of the Isle of Man Cozy Mystery series. There are so many people to thank, but the most important people that I need to acknowledge are the readers. You have supported me through twenty-six titles and I'm deeply appreciative of each and every one of you. Thank you for embracing Aunt Bessie and her friends and following her story from beginning to end. (Not that this is the end, of course...)

Thank you to my editor, Denise, who has worked her way through twenty-six titles and must have now concluded that I'm never going to learn where to put my commas.

Thank you to Kevin, whose beautiful photographs grace my covers. I'm going to miss getting new collections of photos that let me revisit the island that I love.

And thank you to my family who have been hugely supportive throughout this journey.

On to the next adventure...turn the page to read more...

The Adams File
An Aunt Bessie Cold Case Mystery
Release Date: January 15, 2021
Turn the page for a sneak peek.

Bessie is both excited and apprehensive about her new role in Andrew Cheatham's cold case unit. When the first case involves a missing five-year-old who may well have been murdered by her own father, Bessie has even more second thoughts.

As if Andrew's cold case weren't enough to keep her busy, Sandra, the young girl who works at the shop near Bessie's house, has just been accused of stealing from her employer. Sandra is desperate to clear her name, and adamant that Bessie not involve the police.

Can Bessie work with her friends and the two Scotland Yard detectives on the cold case unit to work out what really happened to little Rachel Adams? Can she help Sandra clear her name and find out who has really been stealing from the shop? Or is she in over her head, working with police detectives who don't seem at all interested in her opinion?

A SNEAK PEEK AT THE ADAMS FILE

Author's Note

Please note: Final edits have not been completed on this book. Please excuse typos and misspellings.

Having written twenty-six cozy mysteries featuring Aunt Bessie, I couldn't imagine not writing about her, even though I'd reached the end of the alphabet. I'm hoping this new series will prove as popular with readers, even though the focus will be slightly different.

Instead of Bessie stumbling over dead bodies everywhere, she's now part of a cold case unit that was started by her friend, Andrew Cheatham, a former Scotland Yard detective. Bessie met Andrew in *Aunt Bessie's Holiday,* and he's been to visit the island on multiple occasions since.

While she won't be finding as many murder victims as she did in the first series, she's still going to find herself caught up in investigations, both with the cold case unit and elsewhere. You do not need to read that series in order to enjoy this one, but you'll learn a lot more about

Bessie and her friends if you start with those books. (There's a full list of the titles in back of this book.)

As with the original series, this book is set on the Isle of Man. I use British English terms and spelling as much as possible. I'm aware that some Americanisms are finding their way into my books. I do try to avoid them, and take them out whenever they are pointed out to me. I'm no longer including the glossary in the back of my books. If you miss it, please let me know and I'll consider including it again.

This is a work of fiction and all of the characters are fictional creations by the author. Any resemblance they may have to any real persons, living or dead, is entirely coincidental. The businesses named throughout the book are also fictional and, again, if they resemble any real businesses, on the island or elsewhere, that is also coincidental. The historical sites mentioned within the book are all real, but the events that happen within them in the story are fictional.

Please let me know what you think of the new series. I'd really love to hear from you. All of my contact information is available in the back of the book. I hope you enjoy spending more time with Bessie and her friends, both old and new.

* * *

Chapter One

"Good afternoon, everyone," Andrew Cheatham said from his seat at the head of the large rectangular table. "Just to make certain that I have your attention, I'll start by telling you about our first case. Just a few details, though. We'll talk about the rest after introductions."

Bessie Cubbon shifted in her seat. Andrew had already told her a few things about the case they were going to be discussing. Surely introductions could wait until the end?

"Our first case is a missing person case," Andrew continued.

"So this one is for Charles," one of the men that Bessie didn't know said.

Andrew shook his head. "I should have said that officially this is a missing person case. The inspector in charge of the investigation was convinced that it was murder, but could never find enough evidence to charge anyone."

"Hard to charge someone with murder without a body," the same man muttered.

"Exactly," Andrew agreed. "The inspector who conducted the original investigation passed away a few years ago. A young man who has just been promoted to inspector has replaced him. He's incredibly eager to make a name for himself, so he's been going through every cold case he can find. He's had some luck with a few of the old missing person cases, but he's become rather fixated with this case. He happens to know one of my daughters, which is how I came to hear about it."

"And you think something was missed, or else we wouldn't be considering it," John Rockwell suggested.

"I think there are people out there who know exactly what happened to Rachel Adams. Inspector Davison has conducted recent interviews with everyone involved in the case, those people who are still alive, anyway. He's read through the original file and his own interviews dozens of times and he's certain the answer is there somewhere," Andrew replied.

"The first inspector thought it was murder, though?" Hugh Watterson asked.

"He did, and Inspector Davison agrees," Andrew told him. "But before we go into any more detail on the case, I need to say a few words about the unit and then introduce everyone."

"Or we could talk about the case first," someone suggested.

Andrew chuckled. "We could, but then you'd all want to go home and read through the case file right away, and no one would want to listen to me talk at all."

Bessie hid a grin. Andrew was right. She was incredibly eager to get her hands on the file about the case. It wasn't every day she was given access to police reports, after all.

"I'll start by thanking you all for being here, especially Harry and Charles, who had to make the trip from London. It seemed easier to bring you two here than to bring the other four members to London, but that's always an option for future meetings," Andrew said. "We don't necessarily have to all meet in person every month, although I would prefer it and that's how our meetings are currently planned for the foreseeable future. We'll see we progress as we work through the cases."

"I can't imagine coming across here every month," one of the men said. "I mean, the hotel is nice enough, but I'd rather be at home."

Bessie knew the men were staying at the same hotel where they were having today's meeting. The Seaview in Ramsey was the nicest hotel on the island, and Bessie thought it was much better than "nice enough," but she didn't want to argue with a man she didn't know.

"It was also easier to bring you here being that you and Harry are both retired," Andrew told the man. "Inspector Rockwell, Constable Watterson, and Mrs. Moore all have other jobs to work around. They can't necessarily take days off every month to fly back and forth to London for our meetings."

The man shrugged and then picked up his coffee cup and took a sip.

"I feel as if I should apologise for it being October," Andrew continued after a moment. "This unit is completely unique and it took some time to get permission to structure it the way that I wanted. I've been talking about this unit for months, but actually getting everything into place took a good deal longer than I'd expected."

As far as Bessie was concerned, that was a good thing. For over two years, she'd been involved in a murder investigation nearly every month, but ever since Andrew had first mentioned the cold case unit, six months earlier, no one on the island had been murdered. She'd been busy, as well travelling back and forth to the UK for a wedding, among other things. She could only hope that Andrew's cold cases would now be the closest she'd get to another murder investigation.

"Now that we're up and running, though, we'll be considering a different case each month. For this first case, we're meeting today for a preliminary discussion and then I'll give you each a copy of the complete police file from both the original and the more recent investigations. You can read through the file in your own time and we'll meet again tomorrow afternoon to discuss everything."

"As soon as that?" Bessie asked. She'd been hoping to have time to meet with her friends to discuss the case before the next group meeting. She was certain she'd have a great many questions about what she was going to read in the case file and she didn't want to look dumb in front of the two strangers or Andrew.

"I have the room here booked for tomorrow and then again on Friday," Andrew told her. "I'm expecting everyone to come back tomorrow with a list of questions for Inspector Davison. Hopefully we'll have the answers by Friday."

Bessie nodded. Andrew's plan made sense, even if it didn't give her much time to talk about the case with her friends before the next meeting. Maybe they were all available tonight, she thought as Andrew took a sip of tea. She glanced over at her dearest friend, Doona Moore, who was across the table from her. Doona was busy writing something in the notebook she'd brought along. Bessie had her own notebook, but she hadn't yet written anything in it.

"Cold case units can be very useful," Andrew said after he'd set his teacup down. "In many cases, a fresh set of eyes, someone thinking outside the box, maybe, can find that one little thing that was missed in the original investigation. Having said that, we're going to be working on very difficult cases. My expectation is that we'll be able to provide new ideas for investigating in about twenty to thirty per cent of the cases. If we manage to actually solve ten per cent of the cases we consider, we'll be successful in my eyes. I want you all to remember that number as the months go past. We'll be looking at one case each month, which means I hope to solve approximately one case each year. I don't want anyone getting discouraged as the months go past if we aren't solving cases."

Bessie frowned. Andrew's words already had her feeling discouraged. Surely, they'd do better than solve a single case in a year. Otherwise there seemed little point in bothering. Andrew had insisted that they get paid for their time. It wasn't much, more of a stipend, really, but it was the first paid employment Bessie had ever undertaken. It seemed wrong somehow, though, to be getting paid for a job where they weren't expected to be successful ninety per cent of the time.

"Let's begin with introductions," Andrew said. "I'll start on my right. This is Elizabeth Cubbon."

The two strangers nodded at her.

"Bessie, why don't you tell everyone a little bit about yourself," Andrew suggested.

"As Andrew said, I'm Elizabeth Cubbon, but everyone calls me Bessie," she said, wondering how much she was meant to say. Nearly everyone at the table knew her, and she didn't want to share too much with the two men she'd not met before. "I was born here on the island, but then my family moved to the US when I was two. My parents decided to return here when I was seventeen and I've been here ever since." That seemed enough information for now, she thought as she reached for her cup of tea.

"How old are you?" one of the men asked.

Bessie frowned. "It's been some time since I received my free bus pass, but I'm still a considerable number of years away from receiving a telegram from the Queen," she said stiffly. "I consider myself to be in the later years of middle age."

The man looked surprised and then shrugged. "Over sixty and under a hundred. I suppose that's all I need to know."

It had been some years since Bessie had bothered to work out exactly how old she was, so she was quite certain that was all the man needed to know.

"Have you ever been married?" the other man asked.

"No, I have not," Bessie replied, feeling uncomfortably as if she was being questioned by the police, which, of course, she was. Her relationship with Matthew Saunders was not something that she discussed with people very often, though. Once she had an opportunity to get to know the men, maybe she'd share the sad story with them, but she didn't feel it was necessary to do so today.

When her parents had decided to return to the Isle of Man, they'd insisted that Bessie accompany them, even though she'd wanted to remain behind with Matthew, the man whom she'd been seeing for a few months. When Matthew had attempted to follow Bessie, he'd failed to survive the ocean crossing. That had been a great many years ago, of course, but Bessie still found it difficult to talk about Matthew's untimely death.

"What did you do for a living before you retired?" was the next question that was fired at her.

"I never worked," she replied. "I received an inheritance when I was eighteen that allowed me to live comfortably, if frugally, in my small cottage in Laxey."

Before Matthew had set sail, he'd written his will, leaving everything he had to Bessie. Smart investments by her advocate had allowed Bessie to survive without ever having to find paid employment. She'd spent her time doing volunteer work, reading, and working as an amateur historian in the local museum archives.

"But you are getting paid for being a part of this unit, aren't you?" one of the men asked.

Bessie nodded. The stipend she was receiving for her work on the cold case unit was not large, but it was an unexpected windfall and she was already planning to spend some of the money on several new bookcases for her ever-growing book collection.

The taller of the two men frowned. "How did you meet Andrew?"

"We met at Lakeview Holiday Park in the UK," Bessie explained. "He was on holiday with his family and I was on holiday with my friend, Doona."

She nodded at Doona, who gave the two strangers a small, somewhat awkward wave. Some months earlier, Doona had had her brown bob cut into a shorter style. Bessie hadn't really liked the change, and Doona had hated it, but it seemed as if her hair was taking its time to grow back. It was now at an odd length, and Bessie wasn't sure what she'd call the style if she'd had to give it a name. Doona wore brightly coloured contacts that gave her stunning green eyes, although they were somewhat lost behind uneven fringe at the moment.

"What was a Scotland Yard detective doing at Lakeview Holiday Park?" one of the men asked.

Andrew chuckled. "As Bessie said, I was on holiday with my family. Unfortunately, while we were there, we all became caught up in a murder investigation. That's how Bessie and I became acquainted."

"Interesting," one of the men muttered.

"Charles and Harry, you may think that Bessie is an odd choice for a cold case unit. She's never worked for the police or as an investigator in any capacity," Andrew said. "She is, though, very clever. I don't know if it's because she's spent a lifetime reading murder mysteries or because she's been involved in more than her fair share of real-life cases in the past few years, but Bessie has a real knack for spotting what's truly important in a case."

"Just what we need, then," one of the men said lightly.

Andrew nodded. "She's exactly what we need. She was the inspiration for setting up the unit, actually. When I came to visit Bessie and the island last year, I was planning for a holiday and a chance to visit a friend. I mentioned a cold case to Bessie as a topic of conversation, not because I thought she'd be able to solve the murder. She did solve it, though, and I started to really appreciate the value of new perspectives on old cases. That's what this unit is all about. Bringing together a select group of people, all of whom can bring unique perspectives to the cases we're going to discuss."

"I hope I don't let you down," Bessie said softly, feeling somewhat overwhelmed by the introduction. She was already nervous about her role in the unit, and now Andrew had increased that feeling by a factor of ten.

"Next to Bessie is Inspector John Rockwell. John, tell everyone a bit about yourself."

John was a handsome man in his mid-forties. His dark brown hair contrasted nicely with his stunning green eyes. He was fit, and Bessie thought he looked healthier than he had in a while, as he emerged from a very stressful time in his life.

He nodded. "I've been with the police for my entire career, but I only moved over to the island about four years ago. I'm currently the inspector responsible for the constabulary in Laxey and Lonan, two villages near here. Before I moved to the island, I was with the CID in Manchester."

"He's intelligent, and a solid inspector who is going to bring a lot to the team," Andrew told everyone.

John flushed. "Now *I* hope I don't let you down," he told Andrew.

"Are you married?" one of the men asked.

John took a deep breath. "I was married when I first came across, but my wife wasn't happy here. After a year, she moved back to Manchester with our children. We got divorced and she remarried. Sadly, she passed away on her honeymoon, so I'm now raising our children on my own."

Bessie thought that was a tremendous oversimplification of everything that had happened in John's life over the past four years. Sue had hated the island and had done everything she could to persuade the children, Thomas and Amy, that they hated it as well. As soon as she and John had separated, she'd started seeing a former boyfriend, a man she'd told John that she'd never stopped loving. Harvey was a doctor, and after they'd married, they'd travelled to Africa so that Harvey could fulfill a lifelong ambition to save lives in a developing country. A few months later, John had been told that Sue had fallen ill with a fever and some months after that, she'd passed away. As far as Bessie knew, John was still trying to find out exactly what had happened to the woman he'd once loved.

"Raising children on your own must be difficult," one of the men said.

"They're teenagers, so they really only need me to drive them places and feed them," John replied. "And Doona helps a great deal with both jobs." He nodded at Doona, who flushed and looked down at the table.

"Next to John is Harry Blake," Andrew continued. "Harry, tell everyone about yourself."

"I worked at Scotland Yard in the homicide division for years. I took early retirement about ten years ago and I've been travelling around the UK ever since, looking into cold cases for various constabularies. I've never been married. I'm sixty-three years old, and I think that's all anyone needs to know," the man replied.

Andrew smiled. "He's being modest. I can tell you that most constabularies around the UK are more than happy to let him go through their old files to see what he can find. The last I'd heard, he'd solved about half a dozen murders and opened up new lines of inquiry in dozens more. I wasn't sure he'd agree to join the unit, because he tends to prefer to work alone."

Bessie studied the man in question. Harry had been the last to arrive, strolling into the room just one minute before the meeting had been due to begin. He had dark hair that Bessie doubted could be natural, although she could see some grey scattered through his tousled mop. When he'd arrived, he'd stood just inside the door, slowly looking around the room. At the time, Bessie had been certain that he hadn't missed a single thing as he'd studied the room's occupants. When their eyes had met, she'd felt as if she were looking into the eyes of a much older man, one who had seen a great deal of tragedy during his lifetime. He'd taken a chair with his back to the wall, refusing the offer of refreshments.

"Nice to meet you all," Harry said now before he sat back in his chair, his eyes moving around the room, seemingly studying everyone yet again.

"On my left is Doona Moore," Andrew continued after a moment. "Doona works as a receptionist at the Laxey station. Those of you with a police background will know that that means she knows as much, if not more, about policing than most senior inspectors."

Harry chuckled. "There's a lot of truth in that," he said.

"I'm not actually working at the station any longer," Doona told Andrew. "I've, um, taken early retirement."

Bessie grinned. That was one way to describe things, she thought.

Doona and Bessie had become friends nearly five years earlier when they'd met in a Manx language class. Doona had been nearly forty, and her second marriage had been falling apart at the time. In the years since she and Bessie had become friends, Doona's life had changed dramatically.

"You're very young to be retired," Harry said.

Doona shrugged. "I inherited some money, along with half of a holiday park, when my second husband died. I spent several weeks this summer in the UK, trying to help manage the park, and now I seem to spend hours on the phone every day talking to the park's manager and to the man who owns the other half of the park. It isn't exactly a job, but it certainly takes up a great deal of my time."

"Was your second husband much older than you?" Harry asked.

"Not at all," Doona replied. She stared at the man for a moment and then shrugged. "We were separated when he was murdered. His murder investigation was the case to which Andrew was referring earlier."

"So you now own half of Lakeview Holiday Park?" the other man asked. "That has to be worth a fortune."

"It's probably worth a good deal less than you think," Doona replied dryly. "But it was nice to spend some time there this summer, and John's children came and spent a week with me there, as well. I think they really enjoyed themselves."

"They had a wonderful time and they didn't want to come back and go back to school," John said with a laugh.

John and Doona had a complicated relationship. From what Bessie knew, they were in love with one another, but they'd both been hurt before, so they were taking things very slowly. The children were also a factor. Both John and Doona wanted to do what they could to protect the children from any more upset, so they were being very cautious. The children's week at Lakeview seemed to have brought the children and Doona closer together, even if it hadn't done anything to advance Doona's relationship with John. Bessie was doing her best to mind her own business, but she was starting to think she was going to have to give one or the other of the pair a good hard push if the two were ever going to do the right thing and get married.

"Next to Doona is Constable Hugh Watterson," Andrew said. "Hugh works for John and is one of the finest young constables on the island. He and his wife, Grace, have a beautiful baby girl who is going to be a year old in December."

Hugh flushed. "I can't believe how big she's getting."

"Enjoy it while you can. I'm told once they hit their teens, girls are impossible," Harry told him.

"Tell us a little bit about yourself," Andrew urged Hugh.

He flushed. "I'm twenty-five and, as Andrew said, I'm married and we have a baby girl named Aalish. My parents didn't want me to become a police constable, but Aunt Bessie always encouraged me to chase my dreams. She was something of an honorary auntie to me and it's because of her that I'm here today. I've just recently started working towards a university degree so that one day I can become an inspector."

Bessie smiled. To her, Hugh looked no more than fifteen, the age he'd been when he'd been a frequent guest at her cottage. His brown hair nearly always seemed to need cutting and he was perpetually hungry, though he never seemed to gain weight, no matter how much he ate. As she'd never had children of her own, Bessie had acted as something of an honorary aunt to all of the children of Laxey who'd come every summer to play on the beach outside of her cottage. Over the years, many of those children had come to see Bessie's cottage as the perfect place to stay when they weren't getting along with their parents. Nearly every teen in the village had spent at least one night at Bessie's before he or she had finished school, and some of them, including Hugh, had stayed far more frequently.

"And last, but not least, is Charles Morris," Andrew said. "Charles, tell the others about yourself."

The man was probably close to six feet tall, and he looked to be of average weight. His grey hair was thinning, and he was casually dressed in black trousers and a grey jumper.

"I worked with Andrew in London for many years, specialising in missing person cases. I've never married. I'm sixty-five. I think that's everything," he said.

"Charles is responsible for what are now the standard procedures for dealing with a missing person scenario. He's been retired for a few years now, but he still does some consulting work on high-profile cases," Andrew added.

Charles shrugged. "I do my best."

Andrew mentioned a few names, all of which Bessie recognised as people who'd gone missing in the past few years. She knew some of them had been found, but others hadn't.

When he'd first come into the room, Bessie had thought that Charles looked shrewd, and she was pretty sure she hadn't imagined the frown that had flashed across his face when he'd seen her. Now Charles nodded and then picked up his coffee mug and took a drink.

"And you all know me, of course," Andrew said with a grin. "Let's get started on the case, shall we?"

ALSO BY DIANA XARISSA

The Isle of Man Cozy Mysteries

Aunt Bessie Assumes

Aunt Bessie Believes

Aunt Bessie Considers

Aunt Bessie Decides

Aunt Bessie Enjoys

Aunt Bessie Finds

Aunt Bessie Goes

Aunt Bessie's Holiday

Aunt Bessie Invites

Aunt Bessie Joins

Aunt Bessie Knows

Aunt Bessie Likes

Aunt Bessie Meets

Aunt Bessie Needs

Aunt Bessie Observes

Aunt Bessie Provides

Aunt Bessie Questions

Aunt Bessie Remembers

Aunt Bessie Solves

Aunt Bessie Tries

Aunt Bessie Understands

Aunt Bessie Volunteers

Aunt Bessie Wonders

Aunt Bessie's X-Ray

Aunt Bessie Yearns

Aunt Bessie Zeroes In

The Aunt Bessie Cold Case Mysteries

The Adams File

The Isle of Man Ghostly Cozy Mysteries

Arrivals and Arrests

Boats and Bad Guys

Cars and Cold Cases

Dogs and Danger

Encounters and Enemies

Friends and Frauds

Guests and Guilt

Hop-tu-Naa and Homicide

Invitations and Investigations

Joy and Jealousy

Kittens and Killers

Letters and Lawsuits

Marsupials and Murder

Neighbors and Nightmares

Orchestras and Obsessions

Proposals and Poison

The Markham Sisters Cozy Mystery Novellas

The Appleton Case

The Bennett Case

The Chalmers Case

The Donaldson Case

The Ellsworth Case

The Fenton Case

The Green Case

The Hampton Case

The Irwin Case

The Jackson Case

The Kingston Case

The Lawley Case

The Moody Case

The Norman Case

The Osborne Case

The Patrone Case

The Quinton Case

The Rhodes Case

The Somerset Case

The Tanner Case

The Underwood Case

The Vernon Case

The Walters Case

The Xanders Case

The Young Case

The Isle of Man Romance Series

Island Escape

Island Inheritance

Island Heritage

Island Christmas

The Later in Life Love Stories

Second Chances
Second Act
Second Thoughts
Second Degree

ABOUT THE AUTHOR

Diana Xarissa lived on the Isle of Man for more than ten years before returning to the United States with her family. Now living near Buffalo, New York, she enjoys having the opportunity to write about the island that she loves so much. It truly is a special place.

Diana also writes mystery/thrillers set in the not-too-distant future under the pen name "Diana X. Dunn" and fantasy/adventure books for middle grade readers under the pen name "D.X. Dunn."

She would be delighted to know what you think of her work and can be contacted through snail mail at:

Diana Xarissa Dunn
PO Box 72
Clarence, NY 14031.

You can sign up for her monthly newsletter on the website and be among the first to know about new releases, as well as find out about contests and giveaways and see the answers to the questions she gets asked the most.

Find Diana at:
www.dianaxarissa.com
diana@dianaxarissa.com

Made in the USA
Monee, IL
24 October 2020